This Side of the Divide

New Lore of the American West

This Side of the Divide

New Lore of the American West

Introduction by Vanessa Hua

Edited by Danilo John Thomas and the editors of Baobab Press

with the University of Nevada, Reno
MFA Program in Creative Writing

BAOBAB PRESS

RENO, NV

First Printing

ISBN-13: 978-1-936097-46-3
ISBN-10: 1-93609-46-x

Library of Congress Control Number: 2022945506

Baobab Press
121 California Avenue
Reno, Nevada 89509
www.baobabpress.com

waters parting . . .

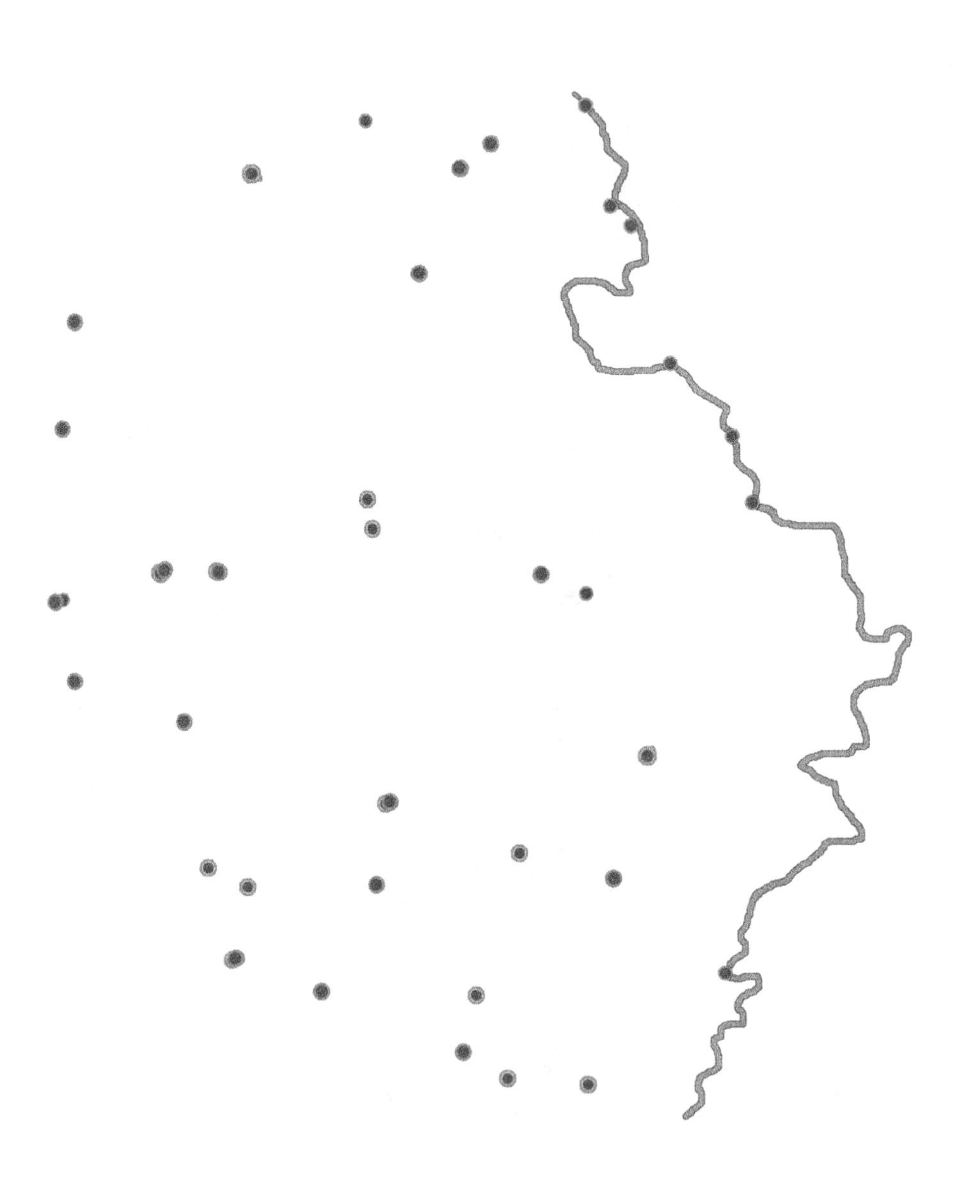

Contents

This Side of the Divide

New Lore of the American West

Introduction

Vanessa Hua

As my family tromped through the hills east of Berkeley, green with abundance, I spotted the disk of a leaf, perched on a slender stem, delicate as a lady's parasol: miner's lettuce?

I texted a photo to a naturalist friend to confirm my find. The excitement I felt at the confirmation might have rivaled James Marshall's when he discovered gold at Sutter's Mill on the American River in 1849. Eureka! "Lore has it that gold rush prospectors dined on the greens, high in vitamin C, to prevent scurvy," I told my twins, then eight years old.

It was early April 2020, a couple weeks after the world went into retreat. I'd been foggy-headed, sleepless with worry about the coronavirus, but giving this impromptu science and history lesson fired my synapses.

"Scurvy causes your gums to bleed, and your teeth to fall out," I told my sons, a ghoulish bit of lore that had fascinated me when I was their age.

Just as intrigued, they vowed to try the greens to ward off the disease. Decades ago, someone taught me this knowledge, and in turn, I had passed it down to my sons.

I'd always wanted to try foraging, which had an aura of pioneer independence, so different than my 1980s upbringing in the suburbs east of San Francisco, in which my working parents called upon the convenience of every canned and frozen meal to keep us fed.

Back at home, I nibbled it raw, the leaf tender but a bit grassy for my taste. I stir-fried the rest with garlic and sesame oil, the sort of recipe a Chinese fortune seeker might have conjured for himself in the gold fields, or later on, while toiling on the Transcontinental Railroad.

The tender sprig was a gateway to other finds that spring: chickweed, tri-cornered leeks, and mustard greens. When so much in the world felt fraught, complicated and uncertain, foraging felt imperative.

And so too, lore. At a time when our understanding of Covid-19, of the world itself, is rapidly developing, rapidly shifting, I have craved a deeper kind of narrative: the legends, myths, and folktales that went beyond the official record, and spoke to the truths that can only be conveyed through the fantastic. When fact is seemingly impossible to distinguish from fiction, the nearly two dozen stories curated by the editors of Baobab Press are at once timely and timeless, ancient and futuristic—reimagining and remaking a region long potent in the imagination.

It's the second installment of *This Side of the Divide* series, in which Baobab Press—in conjunction with the University of Nevada, Reno's MFA program in creative writing—sought out stories, legends, tales, hearsay, myths, set west of the Continental Divide.

In *Western Lore and Language: A Dictionary for Enthusiasts of the American West*, published in 1996, Thomas L. Clark writes, "The West can represent wide-open spaces, freedom of mind, freedom of expression, freedom of action, even the Marlboro Man image—all reflected in the language of the West. Westerners seem to relish the notion they are less restricted than people from other parts of the country."

That openness, that freedom is under threat. In September 2020, Octavia E. Butler's novel, *Parable of the Sower* reached the New York Times bestseller list—14 years after her death—with its eerily prescient narrative of California in 2024, beset by climate change and vast economic inequality. "I didn't make up the problems. All I did was look around at the problems we're neglecting now and give them about 30 years to grow into full-fledged disasters," Butler wrote.

In *This Side of the Divide: New Lore of the American West*, we rocket forward into the post-apocalyptic future of Las Vegas and Los Angeles. "It's easy to find cities built on myths: they're the ones that aren't cities anymore . . . they only endure as examples or as warnings," writes Phoebe Barton, in the haunting "A Billion Miles from What Was Home."

Global warming is but one kind of environmental damage wrought by humans, relentless in their desire to reshape the West into their vision of paradise. In Jac Jemc's "What We Tell Ourselves," she skillfully interweaves a retelling of Cahuilla legend of the Tahquitz—a spirit who causes death and destruction—with the modern birth and death of the

Salton Sea. "Developers advertised the Salton Sea as a desert riviera, a blue-collar getaway for veterans who remembered their good times off-base as young men. Land was sold, houses built, but the speed of the municipal infrastructure never caught up. The location was remote, the low desert an inhospitable climate, too expensive and complicated to properly establish and maintain."

In hearkening to the past, the stories serve as an elegy. Kathleen McNamara's touching "Pyrosome" begins: "I never saw an otter in Otter Creek. Dad said there used to be thousands of them, a hundred years ago, or maybe earlier: before Arizona was a state . . . 'Imagine big giggling packs echoing through the canyon. Then the pioneers killed them all for meat and pelts.'"

But the lessons of loss—which should serve as a warning for the changes still unfolding in the Anthropocene—go unheeded.

As I write, it's the start of summer and already, the first wildfires are flaring up across the West, parched by years of extensive drought. I'm dreading the inevitable gutting of entire neighborhoods, families and communities torn apart. Forests set afire, the choking smoke and black ash sifting through the air for hundreds of miles.

We see the economic precarity is another menace in these stories, late-stage capitalism crushing the characters. That's compounded with the trauma of war, and toxic masculinity in Benjamin Percy's engrossing "Someone is Going to Have to Pay for This."

David and Stephen come achingly close to connection but only through violence; Stephen, a war veteran, takes revenge against a wealthy customer who has disrespected David, who has a large birthmark on his face. "With a roar, the backhoe comes alive. It crushes a path across the sidewalk, the driveway, the lawn, eating up with its tread the grass and mud. When the man tries to intervene, waving his arms in a fury, the backhoe swings around like a scorpion, its shovel knocking him down. An accident, everyone agrees."

The span of this volume, capacious in time and geography, includes Ken Liu's gripping "What I Assume You Shall Assume" set in 1890 in Idaho territory. The chilling hunt for "vermin" reflects how anti-Asian attacks have deep roots in this country. But the resistance to xenophobia is just as deeply rooted, embodied by the courageous Liew Yun, who introduces herself as "formerly a general of the Heavenly State of Taiping, and now placer gold miner of Idaho" and Amos, a lone rider, who joins forces with her.

Yun traffics in magic from her homeland, creating mazes out of "the dark, dense woods, the twisty trails, the thick mist."

That is also the story of the American West: that of the pioneer, the immigrant, the newcomer bringing their stories, their powers, and their traumas. Their ghost stories, as in Day Al-Mohamed's "The Ghost in the Desert" in which Majid, a guide from the Nejd region of Saudi Arabia, recounts to his rapt clients how Arizona once had herds of camels. By story's end, he's discovered the body of an immigrant who attempted to cross. By story's end, he's riding the Red Ghost, a demon camel. "How could this be? Was it real? Did it matter?"

Magic is a common thread in numerous narratives. The curse is both inheritance and a source of strength for the daughter in Tessa Fontaine's evocative "Crepuscular," an exquisite coming of age story about a mother and daughter who live in the between, in the liminal, at the edge of the redwoods, "so big they made their own damp world where the fog they drank and light they blocked cast perfect shadows for the sword fern below, azalea and salamander, for the shy deer and elusive fox and all manner of other creatures for whom the wide, open world was just too much."

Deeply moving narratives throughout this volume reveal the kinship between people and animals, and the relationship that can heal and renew. In Alyson Hagy's surreal, darkly hilarious "Broken Crow," a sardonic corvid urges the unemployed narrator to look after Darren, the "sad man" next door. "My parents had taught me to be neighborly, to lend a hand, to be compromising when it came to property lines or snow on sidewalks or party noises after dark. They'd both grown up in shrinking towns, one in Wyoming, the other in eastern Oregon. In their minds, a neighbor was someone you couldn't afford to waste." In helping each other, they begin to heal.

In Willy Vlautin's poignant "The Run," Bill Casey, the hardscrabble protagonist, has a streak of good luck—winning enough to rent a decent duplex and picking up free furnishings. Moving back from the brink returns his dignity, at least momentarily. After he tips a waitress twenty dollars, "He was walking through the casino and didn't feel like he was disappearing. He didn't feel like he was drowning at all." Then he buys a puppy, Winnie, who turns out to be harboring illness that will be expensive to treat, and he injures himself on the job.

Will bad luck prevail, and return him to a desperate existence? Is doom imminent or inevitable, for Bill, and for the planet? Ultimately, the stories in this anthology lead us to hope that the streak might continue—a flicker, a flame of resilience that burns on and on in the West, past, present and future, despite it all.

Broken Crow

Alyson Hagy

It was August. I was walking my dog down a private alley when the birds just tore into us, two of them cawing from the limb of a leafy poplar, another on the powerline right above our heads. Screeching bloody murder. This was unusual, mostly because my dog is a better citizen than I am. She has a good relationship with other creatures, human and animal. The local crows don't harass her like they do the bull terrier that lives around the corner. She's not a threat to anything.

But this was different. The birds were furious, all three of them. I could see their black throats pulsing with outrage. My dog juked left, then right. She wanted out of the alley. She considered our transgression rude from the start.

The crow on the powerline, the largest, swooped past my ear to the top of an unpainted fence and pivoted toward us, its right eye a spark of menace. Then I got it. They were protecting something all right, but it wasn't a smashed squirrel or a pizza box—it was another crow. They wanted us out of there. We obliged, my dog pulling like it was the Iditarod. When we reached the mouth of the alley, right behind the house that now displays patriotic Christmas lights all year round, the ruckus had settled. I glanced over my shoulder—my dog wouldn't dare—and witnessed the Kabuki dance of an injured crow trying to flap onto the fence where its mate waited. Not happening. The bird's right wing was as limp as a Baptist church fan. I reminded myself of one of our Western rules: Let nature take its course. If the crow was lucky, the cat—or coyote—that inflicted the damage would finish the job next time.

I was wrong, of course. Less than a week later I left the house to take a run. My dog doesn't like long routes on hard pavement, but such things are the perfect torment for me, especially on mornings when the wildfire smoke thins out. The crow was waiting. I recognized it right away. How could I not?

You know me? it asked.

I said I did. I wasn't arrogant about it. I didn't know its family or its clan, but I knew it was the bird from the alley. The feathers of its busted wing sprawled like an abandoned hand of cards. I'm stupid about a lot of things in this world. I've been trying to be less stupid when it comes to animals.

Water, it said.

Sure, I said, thinking of the extra dog dish I had in the garage. *What about food? Shelter?*

Got friends, it said, giving one of those Charlie Chaplin hops they favor. There was nothing wrong with its legs. Or its confidence. I followed the angle of its beak into the trees. Two crows in the cottonwood on the corner. Two more shitting on the roof of my 4Runner. All of them silent as morticians.

The gray cat that lives there—I pointed with my own beak—*is usually out at night,* I said. *You might want to be careful.*

A coward, the crow said. *You worry about the sad man in the nest next to yours. The cat is ours.*

I KNEW WHAT the crow meant. My parents had taught me to be neighborly, to lend a hand, to be compromising when it came to property lines or snow on sidewalks or party noises after dark. They'd both grown up in shrinking towns, one in Wyoming, the other in eastern Oregon. In their minds, a neighbor was someone you couldn't afford to waste. But this was no longer the season of neighbors. I hadn't seen the man who lived in the blue house for a couple of weeks. I heard he'd been laid off from the Union Pacific. Not enough demand for coal in California or anywhere else, so the railroad was cutting back on its crews. The man's truck was in his driveway, a waxed Dodge Ram 2500 with the premier wheel package I coveted. It hadn't been moved for a while. I thought about that during my run to the river and back. Then I thought about what it meant that I was considering advice from a talking crow.

I'D LOST MY job too, but it was my fault. One too many social media posts about how the town was wasting ground water to keep the golf course alive. That's not a smooth move when the mayor owns the golf course and you work for the mayor. I was making ends meet by keeping the books for a bike shop that was doing well despite the owner's obsession with brewing kombucha in the basement. I also pulled shifts at Tina's Toy House, a knick-knack shop owned by a friend of mine. It was tourist season. Tina had declared she was going to be open every god-damned hour there was a tourist in sight. She hoped they never stopped coming, no matter how crowded the roads got. We sold a lot of national park t-shirts and plastic mountain lion claws. Also, skeletons on toilets which I never understood.

The crow was waiting for me after I closed Tina's the next day. Right on top of my wood pile. *Talk to the sad man*, it said. It wasn't a question.

I don't know the sad man, who I think likes to be called Darren, I said. *He keeps to himself, which is how we do it out here, which you ought to know since you spend most of your time spying.* I paused to check the cottonwood. Yep, the praetorian guard was there, glossy as Kardashians. I wondered what it would be like to have the unstinting support of an extended family. It wasn't something I'd experienced. *Also*, I continued, *I don't eat with anyone except Netflix.*

Liar, the crow said, flaring its chest feathers. Then it began to list the places I frequented for meals. Brick house with long worms under the petunias—that was Glenda's. Food truck with fat beetles on the roof. Taqueria patrolled by yapping rats that claimed to be dogs.

Jesus, I said, *whatever happened to the right to privacy? Besides, shouldn't you be begging for peanuts or something?*

No need to beg, the crow said. *New people in the stone nest, those who dress for cows they have never met, leave seed. So much seed we share with pigeons, the lazy fucks*. The crow spun on its talons, so I had the benefit of its profile. *I become fat.*

THE CROW HAD its own way of getting me face to face with Darren Stubbs. Its family, and about a zillion cousins, gathered on Darren's roof and pretended they were mobbing an owl. They did it during a Raiders game, when they knew Darren would be coherent unless he really *was* dead. This was territory Darren and I had covered before and not in a calm way. You can't shoot birds in town—not owls, not crows—even if they are being a nuisance during the fourth quarter.

Darren had a wife once. I recalled her as nice enough. She frequently went to Utah to visit family, and one day she didn't come back. I had a partner too, for a while. She did what she could, but there just weren't enough projects for her to tackle around here, especially with the locals being suspicious of a lawyer whose family hadn't starved for four generations on a dry land ranch. She tried. I tried. But the siren song of the city was too much. She's in Santa Fe now, happy as a clam. There are plenty of lawsuits in Santa Fe.

Anyhow, Darren came busting out the back door of his house with a shotgun, and I came busting out the back door of mine with my opinions. He looked terrible. Bloated, unshaven, dark patches under his eyes like he'd been punched. He racked his gun and cussed at the crows, but he didn't pull the trigger. He didn't need to. The damn birds melted away as soon as they saw him, like shadows in the sun.

There was no way I was going to tell Darren there wasn't an owl in his spruce tree. I wasn't going to launch into explanations of any kind. *I think you scared them*, I said, scanning his yard for my conniving one-winged friend. *Not sure what the fuss was, but it seems to be over*.

He grunted in my direction. I could see how it was going to be. He was going to circle his yard for a while, marching with his gun hot in his hands, then he'd go back inside his airless home and watch the Raiders try to generate some offense. He'd forget he'd laid eyes on me. And I could feel good knowing my neighbor was alive even if he was neither safe nor sound. It turned out, however, that neither of us was quite in charge of the situation. I'm still not sure how it happened, but my dog—never assertive—slipped past me and through a gap in the fence to hurl herself with joy at Darren's steel-toed boots until he had no choice but to lower his shotgun and pat her on her silly head.

Then a second weird thing happened: I asked Darren if I could borrow his stepladder. I'd never done a thing like that before, even when his wife was around. I mean the guy seemed decent enough. He kept his lawn mowed. But we didn't have that kind of relationship.

He paused at my request. His eyes were slits. The layoff had been hard on him, a union man without enough seniority to retire or be reassigned. I remember when he and his wife moved in, how happy they were to have a place with a backyard and a finished basement. Darren pulled a lot of overtime, and he was pretty vocal in the union for a young guy. I knew that from my friend Marcos. All Darren cared about was the work. And then the work was gone.

I repeated my question.

Sure, he said, hesitating. He probably hadn't spoken to anyone in days. *I need to—*

No hurry, I said, the words coming to me from nowhere. *After the game is fine. And just so you know, Raiders win 20-17. Promise.*

HAVING MY GUTTERS cleaned for the first time in years wasn't enough to keep me from quarreling with the crow. I didn't care for the owl stunt. And I definitely didn't like the hocus pocus about a football score which turned out, incidentally, to be correct. I said so when I saw the bird soaking what looked like a frosted donut hole in my dog's extra water dish.

Typical scavenger, I said, leaning into my sarcasm.

Who's a scavenger? You got your gutters cleaned for free.

I don't need you to take care of me, I said.

Not taking care of anyone, it replied, lifting the soggy donut with its beak and dashing it on the concrete of my driveway. *Thinking about family. Do you know how much it sucks ass not being able to fly? Of course not. You have no sense of glory.*

No sense of what? I really wasn't in the mood for insults. *You have no idea what I'm capable of. You hardly know me.*

The bird cocked its fine head to one side, then the other. Even I couldn't miss the implied smirk in its eyes. *I've watched humans and their selfish dramas every day of my life. No glory.*

What do you expect? I sputtered, taking the bait. *The planet's dying. Housing costs are crazy. This town can't even support a decent grocery store. What would you do?*

The crow was silent as it pecked at the donut. I had to admire its plan. The crumbs and smears of pink frosting would soon attract ants, lots of ants. The bird's stomach would be filled for another day. But it refused to speak again until it had taken a gooey dump at the foot of my mailbox. *You'd be happier if you were more honest,* it said, bluntly. *I come from thieves and tricksters, many nests of them, and I admit it. You should be so lucky.*

Leave me out of whatever you're planning next, I said, feeling righteous. *I'll keep the water dish full. That's it.*

But that's not what happened. As the crow had said: I should be so lucky.

WHEN I WAS a kid, my dad tried to get me interested in orienteering. I refused. He loved everything about it—the problem solving, the maps, plotting points with a compass. He'd grown up in a mining town and thought only fools went somewhere without memorizing the landmarks that surrounded them. He also kept emergency supplies in every car or truck he ever drove. *The world is bigger than we are,* he told me. *Big and disinterested. You can't afford to forget that.*

I thought of my dad when I woke one night to find it snowing. Snow in September—that wasn't climate change. That was an answer to our prayers. The drought had been a sucker punch all summer long. Still, I found myself worrying about the crow, clever as it was. I made a plan to get up early, shovel, then leave some raisins near the dog bowl. But I got distracted. First, Darren had already shoveled everyone's sidewalk for four blocks in each direction. Then, Tina texted and asked if I could be at the store early. A truck loaded with merchandise had been delayed by the weather. She'd made a side deal to grab some bear spray. It didn't matter that we were 300 miles from the nearest grizzly. Tourists bought the spray canisters by the armful when we had them.

So, I forgot about the crow.

When I got home, my boots soaked and wet, I found it shivering against the side of my house, wedged behind the gas grill for safety. Its companions were huddled on the eavestroughs. I counted six of them, bedraggled and worried. My first inclination was to offer my arm. I'd take the bird in the house.

But it refused my help. *Tik-tik-tlik-tlik*, it said, a sound that seemed designed to shame me. *Stick to what you believe. Let nature take its course.*

Would you say that to the rich people in the stone nest? I asked, more than a little stung.

For a moment, it seemed like I might have stumped my sparring partner. One of the birds on the eavestrough made a noise that sounded like a strangled fart. Then the crow righted itself and worked to shake itself dry, an effort that clearly caused pain in its damaged wing. *No,* it said. *I would live like an emperor in the stone nest while I plotted mischief morning, noon, and night.*

Then consider me rich for the moment, I said, trying to remember if I had any hamburger left in the fridge. I knew crows liked hamburger.

Need a favor, the bird said, stopping me in my tracks.

A favor? Or a chance at mischief? I asked.

The birds above us produced a string of very human chuckles, then flew into the sturdy cottonwood tree, one by one.

Serious favor, it said. *Your father's compass. You need to give it to me.*

My mouth hung open longer than I meant for it to. My crow *did* know me well. The compass, which had also been my grandfather's when he logged in the Cascades, was the rare family talisman I'd held onto. I knew refusal would be a dark mark against my character. This was the kind of test you weren't allowed to fail. But man, the critter had balls. *Uh . . . sure*, I replied. *Right now?*

Now, it said. *Call it a down payment on glory*.

Or a big joke on me, I thought, remembering the pride these birds took in larceny. *Give me two minutes*, I said. It didn't take me that long. I knew exactly where the compass was, safe and polished on a bookshelf next to a photograph of me with my parents on the south rim of the Grand Canyon. I kissed it once, then carried it outside in my bare hands and lay it face up in the fresh snow. One of the crows from the cottonwood glided down and filched it with a sharp and efficient motion. I couldn't read the expression in its gelid eye.

The world is large, my crow said to me, lurching from behind the gas grill. I could see that some feathers were missing in its good wing and the scales on its talons looked flaky and dull. *Is it disinterested? I leave you to ponder. You must also borrow sad Darren's truck. Tomorrow morning. We will be waiting.*

Dismissed, I stood in my driveway watching snow slide off my boots in patches. What a bunch of assholes, I said to myself. All that and not even a pretend thank you. I couldn't believe I'd handed over my dad's precious compass. What had gotten into me? Taking a deep breath, I grasped for my better angel and left the door to my garage ajar as I trudged inside. When I went out to lock the door for the night, I found . . . nothing. I had no idea whether the crow had come in out of the cold or not.

TINA WAS IN the middle of one of her meltdowns about shoplifting. She'd learned the hard way that Girl Scout troops were the worst, and there was a jamboree coming up, but I still managed to get the next morning off. Then I built up the momentum to knock on Darren Stubbs' door.

He answered quickly. He still hadn't shaved, but his red plaid shirt gave off the smell of laundry soap and his eyes were more or less clear. *Hey*, he said.

Hey back, I said. *I'm wondering if . . . I mean is it appropriate for me to ask if I could maybe borrow your truck tomorrow? Just for a minute? In the morning?*

Sure, he said. *Your boss moving a load of bicycles, something like that? I could help.*

No, no, I said, waving my hands. I was trying to think quickly. I wasn't ready for Darren, or anyone else, to see me chauffeuring crows. *It's . . . it's my dad's grave site. I want to plant a tree out there. Tomorrow's an anniversary, so if it's all right with you, I'd rather be alone.* The lie unfurled as smoothly as a cheap sleeping bag. Somewhere high in Darren's spruce tree I was sure I heard a corvid guffaw.

Whatever works for you, Darren said. *I'm not going anywhere. I have an appointment at Job Corps after lunch. Your friend Alanna was real friendly on the phone. Thanks for that.*

You're welcome, I said, remembering I'd promised to check out an ad he'd seen in the online edition of the newspaper for a business manager. *So . . . ?*

I'll leave the keys in your mailbox. After my beer with the shop guys, he said.

And that was that, easier than expected, except for Darren's sweet inquiries about my very sweet dog.

THE ONLY PERSON outside before me the next morning was the owner of the gray cat who was stapling fresh MISSING posters on telephone poles up and down the street. The crow was perched on my wood pile again, looking thoughtful. When I showed it Darren's key fob, it launched into a set of loud and bossy caws. In less than a minute, we were surrounded by crows. I stopped counting at fifteen.

They're in back, my crow said, directing me to open the tailgate. *I got shotgun.*

That's how I found myself driving a feathered frat party across the river. The birds in back, underneath Darren's custom-made bed cover, screeched and squawked the whole way. At one point, it sounded like an actual fight had broken out. *Youngsters these days*, my companion sighed. *No manners*.

When I asked where we were going, the crow was direct. *You're taking me to fly*, it said. Then it gave me clear directions to a tall communications tower located past the riverside park. I made a couple of wrong turns, but we got there. When I opened the back of Darren's pristine truck, I was met with the stink of bird poop and a black tornado of feathers. I figured it would take me half the day to clean up the mess.

So, the crow said, hopping to the ground and tucking its undamaged wing into place with military precision. *You lie with skill, as I have noted. You also follow directions. I should not be surprised.*

I was too confused to be offended. *I don't get it*, I said, staring at the bristly lattice of the tower. It was camouflaged to look like a sick pine tree.

I could have done this close to your nest, the bird replied. *But I was hatched on the river. I am happy to find my fate here.*

You're going to live in the tower?

Not quite, it answered, pinning me with the white gleam of its left eye. *I fly here, one last time. After I climb that fucking ugly thing. Which my cousins have assured me is possible because of its idiot false branches. It is a necessary ladder to my sky. You are not to stay for that part. You have done what I asked.*

I'll admit it. I didn't like what I heard. I wasn't ready for nature to take its course. I waited a moment before I spoke again because it's not easy to feel honored and manipulated all at once. *Okay*, I said, gulping in some fresh morning air. *Okay. I get it. I respect what you want to do.*

Thank you, it said, not paying attention to me at all. It was looking upwards into the fathomless purple sky.

Squeezed by unexpected grief, I made my way back to the driver's side of Darren's truck. Yesterday's snow had begun to melt, forming trickles that would flow into our river and the river beyond that and the river beyond that until their cold promise reached the thirsty sea. There were crows everywhere, soaring and diving, barrel rolling and gliding, but for once they were absolutely silent.

The compass? I asked my stoic bird. *What do you need it for? If you knew where we were going all along?*

Oh, that, it said, giving one last comedic hop. *We took that to fuck with you.* And it began a steady, lopsided waddle toward the base of the tower, never looking back and expecting me not to either.

Thank You, Little Queens

Laura Arciniega

A gray-haired woman in a red robe turns on the dining room light. She sings a milk song as she washes the table, a black wood, harder than any on Earth. When the table is dry, she begins to sing a years song and a tall young woman in a green robe brings in a huge lapis lazuli canvas drop cloth. She rolls it out on the table. It spills over the edges and onto the floor, but that does not signify. The young woman in green laughs. It is time to make the mobile of golden spheres.

"How are you?" asks the woman in red.

"Living the dream!" shouts the young woman in green. Now they're both laughing.

A short woman in a yellow robe runs in, her feet pounding the floor. Taking a brush and a jar of paint from her pocket, she makes a golden sphere on the drop cloth—a moon. It is soft and pliable like an orange. She could call the youth in the indigo robe to reach in and deliver it right now, but that is not their way. Next she makes the quarters. The new moon is always tricky, but she masters it. Then she paints all the intermediate phases in between the new and the next.

The woman in yellow slips the brush and paint back into her pocket. She exhales heavily. An older woman in a blue robe enters the dining room with scissors. She hugs the women in red, green, and yellow, then, leaning in close to the dropcloth, she silently cuts two centimeters around the golden phases.

The cutting takes a while. About halfway through, a very small white-haired woman in an orange robe enters the dining room with lapis lazuli cord and thread. The woman in blue squeezes her shoulder and hands her the golden phases. Everybody leaves to rest, and the woman in orange remains.

The woman in orange sits and sews and sews for hours, for days, until each phase is hemmed and each phase has a length of lapis lazuli cord. The woman in yellow sometimes brings her water cake and manzanilla while she works, and sometimes paints a round wooden frame to match the dropcloth.

"What is the Morning?" asks the woman in yellow.

The woman in orange is silent for three days. Finally, she says, "It is the freshwater oceans at the beginning of Earth. It is the sky opening its eye. It is the love at breakfast. It is lovers on opposite sides of the planet dropping something at the same time. It is Sister Death."

Three more days pass. To the woman in orange, the woman in yellow says, "Thank you, Grandmother." Tears stream from her eyes, but she smiles.

When the woman in orange finishes, she calls the youth in the indigo robe. The woman in orange embraces the woman in yellow and says, "All fairest beauty finds a voice," before going to lay down.

While the youth builds the whole, uniting the cord to the lapis lazuli frame that will bring together the lunar mobile, the rest of the women sit together at the black table. The woman in red combs the hair of a mature woman in a violet robe. The young woman in green jokes, "Comb mine next!" They all laugh. The young woman in green is bald. The woman in yellow begins to dance.

"Will you sing a sugar song?" she asks the woman in red.

"For you? Of course." And she does.

The woman in yellow smiles and holds her hand out to the woman in blue.

"Oh . . ." the woman in blue groans, but she rises and they dance.

"See?" says the youth in indigo without looking up from her work. "You're the best dancer of us all."

"I don't know about that," the woman in blue says slyly. She is now sweaty from dancing.

When the woman in red finishes combing, the woman in violet disappears from under her hands.

"Oh!" cries the woman in blue. "I hate when she does that!" But she's laughing.

The woman in orange, finished with her nap, appears where the woman in violet was sitting, but she's wearing violet and laughing hysterically. The woman in violet, wearing orange, walks into the dining room with an innocent face. "I don't know anything about it," she says.

By now the whole room is roaring. The youth in indigo puts down the mobile. She can't work because she's crying with laughter.

When they start to calm down, the woman in violet snaps her fingers and she's wearing blue. The woman in orange is wearing violet, and the woman in blue is wearing violet.

"Hey!" cries the woman in blue. They collapse into laughter again.

"Sorry!" The woman in violet snaps and everybody is wearing the right robes again. The youth in indigo resumes her work.

"Grandmother, did you rest well?" asks the young woman in green.

"Yes, I had comfort." The woman in orange is not as small and her hair is not as white as it was before her nap.

"Why?"

"I will tell that at the end."

"What about joy? Did you have joy?"

"I will have joy at the end." Her face is bright like her needle as it hems and her face is dark like the lapis lazuli dropcloth.

"You are younger now."

"So are all of you. You only notice me because I went away."

The young woman in green looks around. It's true.

The youth in indigo hands the mobile to the woman in violet. The woman in red goes to get the ladder, and all of them follow the woman in violet to the nursery. The woman in violet climbs the ladder. She hangs the mobile from the ceiling, above the children.

The children celebrate. They process in circles around the room, jumping and singing sugar songs in their white robes. One of the children tosses golden sand in the air. It sprinkles down onto their heads and crystallizes into golden *diademas*. Now the children are all little queens.

"*This* is my joy," says the woman in orange.

"Mine, too," the other women agree. The youth in indigo and the young woman in green cry; this is their first time beholding the translation.

The woman in yellow puts her arms around them. "And imagine, it only gets better," she says quietly. "It gets harder, but it gets better."

The women join the procession, which continues until everybody is exhausted.

Finally, the woman in yellow rises. She pulls a sphere of fire from her pocket. "Let's walk to the kingdom of yawns." The children hold hands with the women as the woman in yellow leads the way across the nursery.

Holding the fire up before her, she leads them into the kingdom downstairs, the library where the silver Pacific laps the sand near the shelves.

"Choose a book, children," says the woman in yellow.

The children disperse and browse. They all choose different books, but the story is the same. The reading goes on for hours, for days, until each book is hemmed and each child has a length of lapis lazuli cord around her wrist. Lapis lazuli *diademas* emerge from the silver ocean and join the children on the sand.

"What is the Morning?" the *diademas* ask.

The children are silent for three days. Finally, they say, "It is the birthday of the Chaotian fires. It is one year of sleep in the Field of Stars. It is the lighting of candles on Earth. It is the greatness of the baby. It is Child Winter and Woman Summer."

Three more days pass. "Thank you, Little Queens," say the lapis lazuli *diademas*. They return to the silver ocean.

When the reading is done, the women sit down with the children at the black table to eat water cake and drink manzanilla. The woman in orange whispers to the young woman in green, "*This* is my comfort."

The children's robes have begun to change from white to red, green, yellow, blue, orange, indigo, and violet. The child in the green robe speaks. "Now we are beginning to know. What is the Answer? It is the Question. The Answer and the Question are one. What is the Morning? It is the Night. The Morning and the Night are one."

"Yes," says the woman in blue quietly. The joy in the room is almost too much to bear.

One day, the children will be the Measure Men, sent out into the worlds to help people. But for now, they are babies—only five years old. With the mobile of golden spheres floating above them as they sleep, one day they'll be moon-years-old and as beautiful as their mothers. One day, they'll slice the *mazapán* with a knife and eat it together, the nutty creaminess dissolving into a sugar song without words, the *mazapán* that is the sphere of fire in the woman in yellow's pocket. One day, they'll show themselves.

What I Assume You Shall Assume

Ken Liu

Idaho Territory, circa 1890

AMOS:

The ray of light came over the eastern horizon like a sunrise, like the door to a dank jail-cell cracking open, like the sweeping fiery sword before an angel of judgment. It elongated into a thin, bright, yellow wedge that washed out the stars and revealed the shining parallel tracks before it, dividing the vast, dark continent into halves, leaving behind the endless vegetal sea of the Great Plains and plunging heedlessly towards the craggy, ancient, impassive peaks of the Rockies.

Only then did the piercing cry of the steam whistle finally reach Amos Turner on the hill a half-mile away. His mass of untrimmed white beard and shaggy hair was momentarily illuminated, making his face—full of deep lines carved by the winds of many winters and summers spent in a saddle in the open—seem like a snow-capped mountain in the wilderness.

"Whoa," Amos said, and patted Mustard's neck as the mare snorted and skittered back a few steps. The ground trembled as the locomotive rushed by, pulling behind it cars laden with the goods and people of the East, contentedly dreaming of free land and fresh starts.

But to Amos, the train seemed a malignant serpent, a belching, unfeeling monster, a long and heavy chain that ended in shackles.

"Time to go on."

Gently, he turned Mustard west and began the long journey into the unknown. Soon, the sound and light of the locomotive faded away, and he was again alone with his thoughts under a sky studded with brilliant stars, the way he preferred.

THE PONDEROSA PINES and Douglas firs grew denser as the days passed. This used to be gold-mining country, and from time to time the horse and rider came upon abandoned mining camps next to streams, now full of the late spring meltwater. Some nights, Amos chose to camp in one of them, sitting alone amidst the abandoned shacks while he fed Mustard a handful of oats; chewed a rabbit leg or sipped venison stew; and puffed on his pipe long into the night as he sat by his lone fire, the light dancing against the shadowy cliffs of his face, the crackling of logs the only sound in the darkness.

This particular morning, the fog had rolled in, and Amos felt as though he and Mustard were floating in a sea. The deer trail that they had been following also seemed to dip and twist more than usual. Since he had no particular destination in mind, he allowed Mustard to go wherever she pleased.

"Slow down, girl," Amos advised. "Don't rush and hurt yourself." He felt uneasy, being unable to see more than a few yards into the fog.

But Mustard liked the taste of the grasses and shoots along the trail, many of which were new to her, and she picked her way slowly through the mist and carefully sniffed each plant to be sure it wasn't poisonous.

"Smart," Amos said, leaning forward and lightly scratching her withers.

He looked up at the sky, trying to see the sun, but the fog refracted the light so that it came from every direction at once, and he could not tell east from west.

A passing breeze momentarily revealed a ghostly figure in the mist, like a fish seen through murky water.

"Who goes there?"

There was no response. Amos straightened in the saddle and reached for his Winchester. *Is it a mule deer, a bear, or a Shoshoni hunter?*

A stronger breeze tore away more of the mist, and a man appeared, standing between two trees. He was tall and lean, and there was a long white scar dividing his face diagonally. He politely tipped his hat to Amos, but Amos noted the gleaming handles of the pistols at his belt, ready to be drawn.

Amos drew back on Mustard's reins, signaling her to back up. He kept the rifle pointed at the sky.

"Just passing through," Amos said. "Fog here always this thick?"

The man between the trees chuckled. "It's especially bad today." But his voice held no mirth. "Not the best day for hunting," he muttered in a lower voice.

The man's tense posture hinted at something darker. Amos didn't want to linger. "I'll be on my way then. Anyone else down the trail I should know of? Don't want to be shooting at shadows in the fog."

"There are a few more of us if you go down that way," the man said. "We're hunting vermin. You don't want to be hurt accidentally. Best you go back the way you came."

Amos sat still on his saddle. "I reckon it's best I keep going where I'm headed. You see, I've already been where I came from."

"Suit yourself," the man said. "But don't get involved in business which ain't yours."

AS AMOS WENT on, the trees grew denser, the trail turned more twisty and the fog thicker. Mustard moved forward gingerly.

He noticed bits of paper fluttering in the branches lining the trail. Reaching out, he took hold of a few. They were full of dense, tiny print, and appeared to be pages from law pamphlets of some kind.

Whereas, in the opinion of the Government of the United States the coming of Chinese laborers to this country endangers the good order of certain localities within the territory thereof . . .

. . . the coming of Chinese laborers to the United States be, and the same is hereby, suspended; and during such suspension it shall not be lawful for any Chinese laborer to come, or, having so come after the expiration of said ninety days, to remain within the United States . . .

Like most matters pertaining to the law, the crooked, impenetrable sentences seemed to Amos to pile one upon another, twisting and turning, writhy and snakish, growing foggier and foggier the more he read. He threw the papers away.

Mustard splashed across a small stream. Amos gazed at the water, looking for fish. Maybe this would be a good place to camp for the evening. It was getting late, and Idaho spring nights were chilly.

A clump of bushes rustled somewhere up the hill.

Amos was just about to shout out a warning not to shoot, that he was no vermin, when the bushes parted, and a human figure stumbled out and rushed at him.

He almost shot at the figure before realizing that it was a woman, who wasn't dressed like the Indians and not like the settlers either. She had on a loose, grey dress, cut in a manner Amos had never seen, long strips of cloth that wrapped around her legs like large bandages, and black cloth shoes.

A few steps from him, she collapsed to the ground, and a knife fell from her hand.

The woman thrashed and struggled to sit up.

They stared into each other's eyes.

Amos saw that she was probably in her fifties, short and lean. Her clothes were drenched in mud and her left shoulder was a bloody mess.

Some kind of Oriental, Amos thought.

"Damn it," the woman croaked. "Thought the words would hold you longer." Then she collapsed and stopped moving.

YUN:

Yun dreamed.

In her dream she was again fifteen, a Hakka girl lying—dying really—under the hot sun.

But she did not sweat. The field she was in was as dry as her body. It hadn't rained for three years, but the governor still refused to release the grain from the Imperial warehouses.

All around her, the lifeless land was stripped bare, as though a swarm of locusts had passed over it. Every shred of tree bark, every blade of grass had been eaten, and the bodies of men and women were strewn about, their bellies filled with dirt, the last meal of desperation to assuage the demons of hunger.

Could it be? A line of ants appeared in the distance. She licked her lips, her tongue dry and heavy as a stone. She would wait until the ants got closer, and then she would eat them.

The ants came closer, grew, and became a line of marching men, their banners flapping and shimmering in the heat. She watched them approach, thinking they were like soldiers descended from heaven, like wandering *hsiake* that the traveling storytellers always spoke of, who toured the land to right wrongs.

"Drink, Sister," one of the men said, and held a cup to her lips. She drank and tasted rice, as cool and nourishing as *ganlu* dripped by Guanyin, the Goddess of Mercy. She felt every pore in her body scream with the almost-forgotten pleasure of food and water.

"We're soldiers of the Heavenly State of Taiping," the man said. "We worship the Heavenly Father and Jesus, His Son. *Tienwang*, Jesus's Brother, has been sent to deliver us from the Manchus."

Yun remembered the tax collectors who had come the fall before, warning the villagers about the Taiping Rebels and their dangerous leader Hung Hsiu-ch'üan, who called himself *Tienwang*, the Heavenly King. Anyone who dared to oppose the Manchu Emperor and support the rebels—really just brazen bandits—would be put to death by being sliced a thousand times by a knife. And oh, of course the Emperor's taxes still had to be paid, even if it meant taking away the last cup of rice left in the family's grain jar.

"Thank you, Master," she tried to imitate the unfamiliar words of the man. "If you give me another drink, I will join the Heavenly State of Taiping and become your servant forever."

The man laughed. "Call me Brother, and you shall be my Sister. In the Heavenly State of Taiping, there are no masters and servants. All of us are equal before the Heavenly Father."

"All of us?" This made no sense to her. The world was made up of chains, hierarchies, rules that ranked superiors and inferiors. At the top was the Emperor, his Throne held up by the noble Manchus; below them came the servile Han Chinese, with the Hakka lowest of all among them, their lot to till the rockiest fields. And a Hakka woman? She was like a worm, a nothing, barely worth the air she breathed.

"All of us," the man affirmed. "Men and women, Han and Chuang,

Cantonese and Hakka, we're all equals. *Tienwang* even has armies made up of women soldiers, who can rise to become generals and dukes just like men. Now drink to your heart's fill, and let us pray of toppling the Manchu Emperor and opening his storehouses so that all of us can eat white rice!"

And she drank, and drank, and the cold rice porridge tasted like heaven.

STILL DRINKING FROM the cup held to her lips, Yun opened her eyes.

A face, framed by unkempt hair and a bushy beard, hovered a foot or so from hers. In the flickering firelight, it looked like the face of one of the men who had attacked the camp, killed Ah San and Gan and the others, and then chased her all the way here.

She shuddered and tried to push herself away, but she was too weak and only managed to spill the water all over herself.

"Easy now," the man said. "I won't hurt you."

It was his voice, more than the words, that calmed her. She could hear in it a gentle weariness, like an old mountain that had been worn down by eons of ice and water. She saw now that, though the man was white, he was much older than the five who had come to her camp.

"You a lawyer?" Yun asked.

"No," he said, and chuckled. "Though I tried studying to be one, a long time ago."

"Then how did you get through my maze so quickly?" she asked, gesturing at the dark, dense woods, the twisty trails, the thick mist that made the fire crackle and turned the sparks into glowing fireflies. She spoke slowly, so that he could understand her accent.

He looked around at the foggy forest again, like a man who suddenly found himself in an unfamiliar place. "This fog, the trees, the trails—*you* did all this?"

She nodded.

"How?"

"With these," she said, and reached inside a fold in her dress to pull out a few sheets of paper, full of tiny, dense print.

Of course the man wouldn't understand.

She sighed. So much had happened. So much to explain. Words, she needed words to help her, words in this beautiful, foreign tongue that she loved but would always wield like an unfamiliar sword.

"Excuse me," she said, and struggled to sit up straight. Slowly, carefully, she bowed to Amos. She tried to put grace and deliberateness into her movements, as though she were sitting at a formal banquet, dressed in ceremonial armor draped with silk. "We haven't met properly. I am Liew Yun, formerly a general of the Heavenly State of Taiping, and now placer gold miner of Idaho."

THE FIVE MEN had come to her camp in the evening.

Hey, Chinamen, said the one with the scar across his face. His name was Pike, and he had been threatening the Chinese miners in the valley all spring. *Didn't we tell you to get out of here last week? This is my mine.*

The mine's ours, Ah San explained. *I told you, you can go to the courthouse and check our claim.*

Well lookee here! We got ourselves a law-abiding Chinaman! Pike exclaimed. *You want to talk about the law? The law?*

Then Pike explained to the Chinese miners that Congress had already decided that all Chinamen needed to be gone from these mountains and go back to where they came from. Indeed, all law-abiding citizens had a right and duty to *deport*—he savored the word—the Chinamen into the sea.

One of Pike's men took out a sheaf of papers and shook them in the miners' faces. *These are laws,* he said. *Some old, some new. You Chinamen are scared of laws, aren't you? Then you better pack and run.*

Yun grabbed the sheaf of papers out of his hand and started to read from them aloud:

. . . and may be arrested, by any United States customs official, collector of internal revenue or his deputies, United States marshal or his deputies, and taken before a United States judge, whose duty it shall be to order that he be deported from the United States as hereinbefore provided . . .

I don't understand, she said. *I can't make any sense of these words. Do any of you really understand them?*

Pike's gang gaped at her, amazed that she could read.

One of the men recovered. *The law says that you have to pick up and leave before we make you.*

Before we shoot you like vermin, Pike added.

Gan was the first to take a swing at him, and the first to be shot. Then chaos was all around Yun as deafening gunshots and flowing blood seemed to put her in another time, another place.

Run! Ah San screamed, and pushed her.

She saw Ah San's head explode into a bloody flower before her eyes as she turned to run into the woods. Something hit her left shoulder hard and made her stumble, and she knew that she had been shot. But she kept on running along the deer trail, as fast as she could.

She heard more shots fired after her, more cries that suddenly became silent, and then, the sounds of pursuit.

She said a prayer to God and Guanyin each. *I'm hurt. But I can't die. Not yet. I still have a mission.*

And she saw that she still clutched the pamphlets that the men had brought to the camp with them, pamphlets full of words that none of them could understand, words that made up laws they claimed said she was unwelcome in this land.

They were her last chance.

She ripped the papers into strips and scattered them behind her. As she passed, trees gathered behind her, the mist rose, and the path bent, forked, and curled around itself.

The sounds of pursuit scattered and grew fainter.

AMOS:

"You can do magic with words?" Amos asked.

"Words hold magic for the desperate and the hopeful," Yun said.

Amos looked at her, certain that the woman was mad. *A general of the Heavenly State of Taiping*. He shook his head.

When she had been asleep, her face had been relaxed and peaceful, almost smiling. He had thought she looked a bit like one of the taciturn but friendly Shoshoni women on the plains of Wyoming sitting around the fire on those cold nights he had sought shelter with them.

But now her eyes, feverish, intense, bore into his face like a pair of locomotive headlights.

A wolf howled in the distance, soon echoed by others.

Then followed the sound of a gunshot, and the howling ceased.

"They're getting close," Yun said, gazing into the dark mist. "It's this fire. You've led them straight to me."

Amos picked up the kettle and poured water on the hissing fire to put it out. Soon they were wrapped in darkness, lit only by the light of the moon through the fog.

"I can carry you on Mustard," Amos said.

Yun shook her head. "I'm not leaving."

"Why?"

Yun's glance flickered to a small mound some distance away. Amos squinted and made out a conical shelter made out of chopped tree branches leaning against each other.

"It's the gold, isn't it?" Amos asked. "That's why you ran here."

After a second, Yun nodded. "We moved it out here when Pike's gang started to harass us this spring. All the gold we've mined and saved for two years is here."

Amos's heart grew heavy. "You can always get more gold."

She shook her head.

"This is not my fight," Amos said.

"Then leave."

Amos felt a wave of disappointment that turned into anger. He strode over to Mustard and mounted. Gently, he nudged the mare with his calves, and rode away from the hill, away from the howling wolves and the pursuing men.

AMOS HELD MUSTARD'S reins loosely, lost in his thoughts.

She can't let go of that gold, he thought. *A fool.* He had seen far too many die from greed out here.

In the years he had been wandering, he had grown more and more mistrustful of the hearts of women and men. Having more than a few of them together always seemed to lead to schemes, plots, robbery disguised as something more respectable. He would sometimes go warily to the towns to trade for goods that he could not do without, but he far preferred to be alone under an open sky, accompanied only by the howls of coyotes and wolves, dangers that he understood better and feared less than the dangers hidden behind the smiling faces of settled men.

In Kansas, he had seen the light of hope go out in the eyes of Black families as they realized that they were free in name only. In New Mexico, he had seen the sorrow on the faces of the Indians forced to swallow their pride and anger as they learned of yet another betrayal. And now, it was the Chinamen's turn.

He tried to push Yun out of his thoughts, but the grief and terror of her tale refused to let go. He shook his head angrily.

Every year, as the railroads expanded and ramified like the roots of some tenacious weed, they brought along with them the homesteaders, and farms turned into villages turned into towns turned into cities.

In his mind, Amos saw the railroads as chains yoking the land around him to an East that was full of noise and stale air and invisible bonds that weighed down a man's spirit until nothing was left of it except the capacity for brutality in masses. Even the Chinamen were once welcomed out here, when the land was open and empty. But now that it was filling up and fewer mines were panning out, they became vermin.

Was it really greed? he thought. The look on her face when she had refused to leave wasn't one of lust for the luster and weight of gold, but one of determination to live like a free woman, not hounded prey.

*A Chinaman's chance was bad enough. But a lone, crazy China*woman*?*

An image from long ago came unbidden to his mind. *Help me*, a young man's voice croaked. Amos closed his eyes, trying to make the voice go away. Then he shuddered as he heard the gunshot again.

He opened his eyes. Somehow Mustard, who knew him better than he knew himself, had already turned around and was heading back the way they came.

AMOS DISMOUNTED, GRABBED his rifle from the saddlebag, and walked over to Yun. The woman sat serenely and followed him with her eyes, not having moved since he left her.

"I knew you'd be back," she said.

"Why?"

"You're like a *hsiake* from back home in China."

"What's that?"

"A hero."

Amos laughed bitterly. "I'm no hero."

AMOS (1864):

The generals and politicians would eventually call it the Battle of Olustee, but for Amos Turner, it had been hell.

A young clerk struggling to learn the law in Boston, he had volunteered out of a sense of duty, a desire to end the sin that was slavery, the stain upon the honor of the Republic that the abolitionists denounced in the streets.

But in those Florida pine woods on that day, there were no beautiful ideals, no duty and honor, no God and country, only confusion and slaughter. Too frightened to even think, he charged mindlessly into hailstorms of bullets and screaming artillery, even as his companions disintegrated on each side of him.

"Leave them!" He looked over and saw a white Union commander shouting at the remnants of some colored troops, who had barely been trained before entering the battle. The Black men were reluctant to leave their wounded comrades behind, but the officer wanted them to haul away the artillery instead, in the hasty retreat.

Then the ground exploded near him, and Amos was thrown into oblivion.

When he awoke, it was evening. All around him, he could hear the intermittent cries of the wounded. Union or Rebel, they sounded equally pitiful. After a while, he realized that he was crying out too, whether for rescue or the quick relief of a bullet to the head he knew not.

Then he saw the Rebels. In small groups, they scoured the field, methodically picking rings, watches, money from the wounded and stripping the clothes from the dead.

He saw some of the Rebels raise their bayonets and thrust down, and a cry would be silenced. The Rebels moved efficiently and mechanically, like marionettes.

They were murdering the wounded, Amos realized.

Desperately, he tried to crawl away, but his legs and elbows slipped in the mud.

"Help me," a soldier nearby said, his voice rasping.

He saw that the soldier—one of the Black men the Union commander had ordered abandoned—was very young, barely more than a boy.

"Quiet," Amos whispered to him harshly. "You'll draw them."

The soldier turned his head and focused his eyes on Amos. "Help me," he begged, louder.

A few Rebels turned in their direction.

Amos pushed the soldier down and crawled away as quickly as he could. He shifted a few corpses around and buried himself under them, praying that the ruse would work.

And then he forced himself to remain still as the men came closer. One of the Rebel officers stepped over the pile of bodies that Amos hid under and squatted next to the dying soldier.

"Help me," the soldier said. "Please."

"You dumb thing," the officer said. "The devil has you now." Amos willed himself to get up and say something, to stop what was happening, but his body refused to obey.

He heard the sound of a gunshot. And it echoed in his head for a long time.

Though many Union men were taken as prisoners on that day, very few were Black.

Amos crawled away from the field in the night. He did not know for how many days he lay in a feverish dream, licking the water from the leaves that draped about him and chewing the leaves sometimes for sustenance.

When he was coherent again, he was consumed with shame at his cowardice. He was no better than the commander who had given the order to abandon the wounded black soldiers.

There was also rage, and fear. He could not understand how men who joked and drank and collapsed into fits of laughter over some bawdy tale could suddenly become automata, like interchangeable gears in a machine that they did not comprehend, and become as will-less as the guns in their hands. When the right orders were given, all men could murder in cold blood like devils.

Amos got up and walked west, hiding from anything that looked like an army patrol, until he had left behind the world of cities and laws and the men who crafted them and submitted to their power.

Was it not the world of strictly construed laws and glittering money and elegant clothes and refined speeches that had decided one man could be the property of another? Amos remembered. *And it was that same world that had declared ritualized, anonymous slaughter sweet and fitting. It was that same world that would abandon the wounded, knowing what fate awaited them. What was the use of talk of freedom and ideals? Civilization was a lie, through and through.*

And so he moved ever westward, searching for and escaping into the trail-less, wordless wilderness beyond the frontier line.

"I DON'T CARE what you did or didn't do," Yun said. "What matters is you're here now."

An owl hooted not too far away, startled from its perch.

"They're coming," Amos said. "We better get ready."

He had already decided that the best spot for defense was between two fallen trees near the top of the hill. It would give them some cover and allow them to see the men approach.

"Get me there first," Yun said, pointing to the conical shelter made out of sticks.

"It's not gold you need right now."

"It's not gold I'm after," Yun said impatiently. "It's words. Magic."

Amos had no choice but to help her over. Her legs were unsteady and her breathing was labored as they walked. She leaned into him, as light as a foal.

"Open it up," she said. There was a natural authority to the way she spoke, as though she really was used to giving commands and having them obeyed.

Amos peeled back the branches to reveal a few wooden boxes underneath, on top of which lay a few bundles wrapped in oilcloth. Yun pointed at those. Amos handed them to her.

She unwrapped the bundles. They were filled with all kinds of printed material: pages torn from books, sheets of newsprint, picture cards with words on their backs.

Though worried about the approaching pursuers, Amos was intrigued. "What are they?"

She stroked the papers lovingly. "Another kind of treasure. Probably the better kind. Words I've read and liked."

She picked up a page from the top and handed it to him. "I'm tired. Read it to me."

By the faint light of the moon, Amos read:

The mass of men lead lives of quiet desperation. What is called resignation is confirmed desperation. From the desperate city you go into the desperate country, and have to console yourself with the bravery of minks and muskrats.

"Wise words," she said.

"Wise words are not enough," he said, thinking of all the ugliness in the world.

"Are they not?" And before he could stop her, she snatched the page out of his hand, tore it into tiny pieces, and began to eat some of them.

"What are you doing?" He stared at her, dumbfounded.

"I am in *desperate country*," she said, after swallowing, "and I need all the *bravery* I can get. But I will have nothing of *resignation*." She spat out a wad of wet pulp.

And he saw a hardened set to her jaw that was new, and heard a strength in her voice that had been absent before. She seemed literally to have grown bolder.

"You read but do not believe," she said.

"You do not know what I have seen," he said. He thought of that young man long ago who had believed himself to be brave and noble until the truth was revealed to him.

She laughed. "I have seen words free the minds of men who thought they were slaves."

YUN (1855):

The men who had rescued her brought her back to Tienching, the Heavenly City, capital of the Heavenly State, where she became a soldier just like all the other Taiping women. She was bright and worked hard, and soon she was selected to study how to read and write.

Her teacher, Sister Wen, was a former prostitute who had learned to read and write from her clients in Canton. She freely admitted that she did not know how to write like the scholars, only like a child. "But the magic of writing is strongest in the least skilled," she said, "just as in the Bible it is the last that shall be first, and the first last."

Sister Wen wrote the characters for the Heavenly State of Taiping on a slate.

"This is the character *tien*, which means 'heaven,'" she said, pointing to the third character. "It is like a man standing with a beam over his head, which he must keep balanced over him."

This made sense to Yun. It was her old life. A man was weighed down by the world of his superiors, and a woman's burden was even heavier. Looking at the character, she could almost see the person's back bend with the weight.

"It has been written this way for thousands of years, but no more." Sister Wen erased the line at the top and redrew it, so that it tilted like the man was throwing off his weight.

"*Tienwang* decided that we can write 'heaven' like this, and already you can hear the Emperor in Peking quaking with fear."

Yun looked at the character on the slate and felt her heart beat faster.

But still, she doubted.

"How can we just change it?" she asked. "Hadn't our ancestors always written *tien* the old way?"

"Our ancestors are dead," Sister Wen said. "But we are alive. If we want something, then we must take it and make it true. Have you ever known poor women like you and me to read and write, to fight with swords and arrows next to their brothers and fathers? Yet here we are."

Yun could almost see the invisible strands of power rise from the slate into the hearts of all the men and women around her.

"If we wish to express that which has never been thought, we must create new characters. There will be no more concubines, no more bound feet, no more rich and poor, and no more shaved foreheads and queues to show our submission to the Manchu Emperor. We will be free."

And Yun felt the ground tremble under her, and she was sure that the tremors could be felt in far away Peking.

YUN (1890):

No way of thinking or doing, however ancient, can be trusted without proof.

She chewed on the words and swallowed them.

"I saw a single character shake the foundation of an Empire," she said to Amos. "And you dare tell me that words are mere words. Now, eat."

She handed him a slip of paper.

What a man thinks of himself, that it is which determines, or rather indicates, his fate.

He ate it, masticating the bitter pulp slowly.

She looked at him. "You could have left me to those men. Yet you stayed. Doesn't matter if you want to be. You *are* a *hsiake*."

A wave of heat rose from his stomach and suffused his body, gradually seeping even into his limbs and extremities. He felt as though he had the strength of many men flowing through him.

"Now, you see," she said, her voice strong as a Douglas fir.

AMOS:

As the shadowy figures crossed the stream, Amos fired his first shot. It hit the water near the leader and made a big splash, the water glinting white in the moonlight.

"Go back!" Amos shouted.

The man in the lead—Pike—swore. "I told you to mind your own business, stranger!"

"There's been enough killing," Amos said.

"It's her hoard, isn't it? What did she promise you? Don't be foolish. We can take it all, together, and pay you your share."

The stream, reflecting the moon, gave him light to aim by. Amos shot again, closer to Pike's feet. The men scrambled back onto the bank of the stream, fell back among the trees, and returned fire. In the darkness, their shots thudded into the fallen trees Amos and Yun hid behind, and bits of bark and dirt rained down around them.

"Foolish," Yun said. "They're wasting bullets."

"They're wiser than you think," Amos said. He showed her a handful of brass cartridges. "These are all I've left. If they keep on drawing my fire, I'll run out before they do."

Yun shuffled through the papers in her bundles. "Here, I knew this would come in handy."

Amos saw that she was holding a small poster showing a colored drawing of a Fourth of July celebration. Someone was making a speech. In the background, fireworks filled the night sky.

Yun flipped the poster over: the words to the *Star Spangled Banner*.

She tore the paper into strips, wet the strips with her mouth, and wrapped a few of the words around the cartridges: *red glare, bombs, rocket*.

Silently, Amos loaded the cartridges. The added bulk of the paper seemed to not hinder the smooth slide of metal on metal, but he was afraid that the doctored cartridges would misfire.

Muttering a prayer, he aimed and fired.

The first shot exploded into a bright ball of red fire in the woods on the other side of the stream. Pike's men yelped and rolled on the ground to put out the flames on their clothes.

The next shot turned into a series of explosions that was so loud and bright that Amos was temporarily blind and deaf.

The return fire from the woods ceased.

"They're not dead," Yun said. "But this will stun them and make them think twice about shooting. Maybe they'll be more reasonable in the morning."

"I suppose we're safe for the time being," said Amos, still not quite believing what he had seen.

Satisfied, she sang in a low voice:

Then conquer we must, when our cause it is just,

And this be our motto: "In God is our trust."

Amos settled in for the standoff.

"Tell me," he said, "what happened to your rebellion?"

YUN (1860):

The Taiping armies were invincible. Wherever they went, the Emperor's forces fell back like sheep before wolves. Half of China now belonged to the rebels. *Tienwang* spoke of sending emissaries to France and Britain, fellow Christian nations that would come to the Heavenly State's aid.

But, gradually, rumors began to spread of how the commanders and generals had taken concubines and hoarded treasure for their own use, even *Tienwang* himself. While food was still plentiful in the capital, stories described men and women starving in far away provinces, just like they had under the Manchu Emperor. There was even talk of how the other Christian nations said *Tienwang* was a heretic, and they would support the heathen Manchus, who were amenable to European demands for concessions, and not the Taiping.

The Taiping armies began to lose battles.

Now a general herself, Yun steadfastly refused to believe those stories. She was always the first to lead a charge and the last to retreat. She kept none of the conquered goods but shared them all with her sisters and brothers. She prayed and preached, and taught everyone in her army how to write *tien* with a tilted roof.

Still, the convoys of supply wagons from the Heavenly City dwindled, and streams of refugees stole away from the Taiping territories at night like rats leaving a burning building. Yun noticed that the banners of the other commanders were becoming tattered, their character for 'heaven' drooping, falling back into the old ways.

One night, Sister Wen came to her tent in the middle of the night and woke Yun.

It had been a few years since Yun had last seen her teacher, who had stayed behind in the capital. She was startled to see how white the older woman's temples had grown and how stooped her once-straight back had become.

Sister Wen wore a thick coat meant for a long journey. Yun's heart sank. "You're leaving?" Yun could not keep the anger out of her voice. "You would abandon the Heavenly State in its hour of need?"

Instead of turning her face away in shame, Sister Wen looked at her calmly. "You visited the capital a year ago. Could you tell Tienwang's palace apart from the Forbidden City in Peking?"

Yun had no answer to that.

"It's not too late to leave," Sister Wen said. "You can still escape to the remote mountains and hide in the bamboo groves, where the Manchus will never find you and you can leave this world to its own ugliness."

Instead of answering, Yun took her sword and wrote the character *tien* on the ground, the bar at the top tilted like a ladder to the sky.

Sister Wen stared at the character. She was weary. "When the heart no longer believes, the magic of words is useless."

And that was the last time Yun saw her.

"WHEN TIENCHING FELL a few months later, the Manchu slaughter turned the streets into rivers of blood: men, women, children, the elderly, the wounded, none were spared.

"I and a few others escaped into islands scattered in the East Sea, and made our way to the Philippines. From there we got on a ship and came to America."

"So the magic of words failed," Amos said. He was disappointed. The story had seemed like a fairy tale, one that he wanted to believe in.

"No," Yun said. "We just picked the wrong words."

YUN AND HER companions had never seen so much empty land.

The wilderness of Idaho was pristine, absolute. In China, every *mu* of land had been worked on and shaped by the plow for generations, but here, there were no marks but those of God. It was an empty page waiting for old ideas to be thrown away and new ones to be written.

(Later, she would learn about the Indians who had once been here. Every story was more complicated than it appeared at first, yet hope sprang eternal.)

Refugees from every land, following every creed, had come with the dream of striking gold. In this place with no rules, they became violent, soulful, self-reliant. They fought with the land, with the Indians, with each other, and yet they also discarded old animosities, welcomed strangers, gave the newcomers aid and succor when they needed them.

Yun and the other Taiping survivors worked hard to carve a fresh life in their new home, and in the evenings, she studied the language of this new land, as hardy as her mountains, as pungent as her forests, as varied as her population, as rich as her mines.

Along with gold, she discovered words, bountiful and beauteous words that sang of a love of freedom that beat in sympathy with her rebellious heart. Nowhere else were men so ready to embrace new words—*pogonip, pai gow, cowboy*—immigrating from other tongues, arising from inventive minds, becoming respectable despite origins in error. Like fresh trails crossing virgin territory, new words allowed thoughts to travel to glimpse new vistas.

Yun read and savored and built up a treasure trove of words that struck her. She saw that no people believed more in equality, in the power of ideas, in the right to take up arms against tyranny, than the people of America.

And she saw where the Taiping had erred.

With a stick, she began to write on the ground.

"There are countless ways to write the last character in the name of the Taiping, *kuo*, which means 'state.' *Tienwang* could have chosen to write it like this—

"—composed of the character *min*—that means 'the people'—inside the four borders. But instead he chose to write it like this—

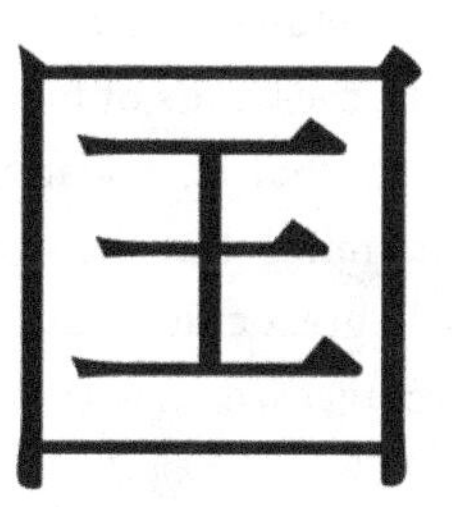

"—composed of the character *wang*—that means 'the king'—inside the four borders."

"So he created the Heavenly Kingdom instead of the Heavenly Republic," Amos said. It was an old story, and a familiar one. Those who sought freedom were tempted by power instead, and became indistinguishable from those they sought to overthrow.

"For years, decades now, we've mined gold and sent it back into China, where the money has kept the fire of rebellion alive. Right now, there's a young man back there, Sun Yat-sen, the greatest magician with words I've ever seen. His pamphlets have given the people faith again, and struck terror into the heart of the Emperor. The gold in those boxes isn't for me, but for him and his revolution."

"What if he fails? What if this rebellion, like yours, also turns dark? You said that the magic of words is fragile, subject to the corrupt hearts of mortal men. What good is a lovely name if you can't live up to it?"

"Then we'll just try again, and if that fails, yet another time. It's not so easy to shake off heavy chains. The Taiping Rebellion failed the same year that a war ended slavery here. Yet this country still feels the shadow of those shackles. China may not be free from the phantom of the Manchu yoke for a hundred years. But my time here has shown me what is possible when men believe."

"How can you say that?" Amos wanted to grab her and shake her. "Have you not seen how Congress has decided that you're to be deported, like rats for Pike and his men to slaughter?"

Yun looked him straight in the eye. "And yet here you are, defending a crazy Chinawoman against the likes of them."

"I am just one man," Amos said.

"Everything starts with one person, a man or a woman." She paused, chose her words carefully, and went on. "You doubt because you see only the ugly words, the words of hypocrisy and fear. Dark laws grow out of confused hearts that have lost faith, and I hope one day to see Congress change its mind. But the words I love I found not in the smoky halls of power in great cities, but in the wilderness out here, among lonesome rebels, refugees, men with nothing to their names but hope."

Amos closed his eyes. She seemed to say aloud what he had only thought. *The Western frontier, like a kite high in the sky, is where the ideals of the Republic take flight and soar, with the stagnant East pulled behind it like a reluctant boy.*

She caressed the papers in her lap lovingly. "Words do matter. Their magic comes from one mind reaching another across miles and years, and what one assumes the other shall also assume, what one believes the other shall also believe. Words take root and grow in the hearts of men, and from there faith springs eternal."

He looked at the pages, at the woman, and at the land bathed in starlight around him. And he seemed to see the land itself as a laid-open book, a record of the long and winding struggle towards freedom by one people—out of many, one.

Yes, it was true. Words did matter. A piece of paper from a court, a little novel, a proclamation, a few amendments to an old parchment—had these not torn a Republic apart and then sewn it back together?

AMOS:

For a while, there were occasional shots from the woods across the stream, as though Pike's men were trying to keep them awake. But even that had stopped an hour ago.

The eastern sky was growing brighter.

"I think they're gone," Amos said.

Yun let out a deep breath and almost fell over. Amos was quick with his arm and held her up.

"It's been a long night," Yun said. She sounded exhausted. "Well, if you think we're safe, maybe you can patch me up." She winced as she tried to move her left arm.

"I'm no doctor."

"Not that way," Yun said. She picked up another sheet of paper from her bundle, turned it over so that the blank side faced up, and handed it to him along with a pencil she found in the folds of her dress. "Write down how you want me to feel."

Amos stared at the paper, surprised and confused. "I don't know how. Why can't you just do the magic yourself?"

"It doesn't work that way. The magic of words comes from two people: one writes, one reads. I can't just write whatever I want and make it come true–that's just wishful thinking. I can pull out the magic of words others print in books, and it works just as well if they write it by hand. But the writer has to believe what he writes, which is why I had to wait till now with you."

Amos took the pencil and wrote:

ALRIGHT

"Sorry." He paused. "I always write it as one word though it's supposed to be two. Let me try again."

"Write it the way you like," Yun said. "Dictionaries and schoolmarms care only for binding words down with rules, fitting them into neat little grids where they can't move. If they had their way, there'd be no new words and no new magic. Who knows, maybe your shorter word will heal me quicker."

Amos laughed. And he wrote some more.

O.K.

"Now that's an American word, a real word of power."

She took the paper from him, chewed it, and swallowed. Amos was pleased to see she had that contented, happy look again. A healthy glow returned to her face, and when she moved her arm again, there was no wince.

"See if you're recovered enough to get on Mustard. When the sun's up we can get out of here."

WHILE YUN SHORTENED the stirrups and talked to Mustard to get acquainted, Amos sat by the fallen trees and flipped through the other papers in Yun's bundle.

The runaway slave came to my house and stopt outside,

I heard his motions crackling the twigs of the woodpile,

Through the swung half-door of the kitchen I saw him limpsy and weak,

And went where he sat on a log and led him in and assured him...

Limpsy, he thought. *Yun is right. This is a land of new words and new ideas, always renewed by the endless wilderness in which man can find solitude and faith in himself—*

A loud shot shattered the peaceful air like thunder. Mustard whinnied and reared up on her hind legs. Yun barely hung on.

Amos looked down and saw the wound in his stomach from which blood flowed freely, then the pain doubled him over and he dropped his rifle.

Pike and his men stood in a semi-circle about twenty feet away.

"You didn't think we'd try crossing the stream upriver and come up behind you?" he sneered.

"You're right," Amos said. He felt waves of dizziness and struggled to stay sitting up. "You got us."

"Now you can die with your Chinawoman."

From the ground, Amos looked over at Yun, still sitting on Mustard.

She made no attempt to get away. Indeed, he could tell that she was thinking of coming over to his aid, even if they would both die.

He locked eyes with her, and then quickly glanced over at the boxes of gold, making sure she remembered.

He dragged his left arm listlessly in the ground, through the leaves, the bits of bark, and the dark soil, as though he was in too much pain to control himself. As Yun stared at him, her eyes full of fire, he traced out the strokes of the character *tien*: one, two, three, and then the last stroke, a defiant diagonal, like a ladder to the sky, like lifting off the weight from a limpsy heart.

Her eyes grew wet. But she nodded, almost imperceptibly.

What I assume you shall assume.

"Now, run!" Amos shouted.

Yun dug her heels into Mustard's sides, and the mare leaped down from the hill, galloping away towards the woods.

Pike's men scrambled to aim their guns at her fleeing figure. No one was paying any attention to the dying old man.

With every bit of his remaining strength, Amos snatched up his rifle.

Yun had wrapped three cartridges in the words of the *Star Spangled Banner*: *red glare*, *bombs*, and *rocket*.

He had shot two, and now the last one was levered into place.

He pulled the trigger, and Pike and his gang—along with the smiling Amos—disappeared in a great ball of fire.

YUN:

When Yun came back, she saw a little charred crater where the fallen trees had been.

She jumped off Mustard, who sniffed the ground, whinnied, and then kept her head low. Yun knelt next to the crater and bowed her head to the ground three times.

"Today, I have seen a true *hsiake*," she whispered.

The wind carried a few pieces of paper, their edges burnt, to her feet. She picked one up:

They are alive and well somewhere,

The smallest sprout shows there is really no death.

Author's Note: *The Heavenly Kingdom of Great Peace (1850-64), or Taiping Tianguo, did indeed modify the way the character tien is written in its name; however, the particular modification presented in this story was used only on coins minted in a particular province for a brief period.*

In general, Wade-Giles is used instead of pinyin to romanize Chinese names in this story for historical reasons.

In Fresno, One Last Bath in Dust

Matt Carney

The coyote lay basking in the dust and fire-filtered moonlight, still waiting to die, but with enough life to daydream, again, of canned fruit. The hunger had long become mouth-froth around can-worn teeth and skin with muscles burning like rolling needle pricks for days and days.

There is a sense in many animals to nuzzle into threadbare acceptance. That when the food is gone, when the air is too heavy, when the water and skin dry and fur falls in clumps—it's the handshake with the void again—the other animals feel entropy like echoes rushing into deafness and sleep.

Behind this tableau in the dirt stood moonlit towers tinged in orange from the ash in the sky. Coyote, like the departed others, had learned from birth to avoid LED and hollering, guzzling walkers that used to live in the city. The humans. All kinds of animals killed with exploding lungs in moments of thunderclaps, torn bodies from the metal beasts hurtling through them, dying in the era of humanity.

The humans either abandoned this place or died in it. One-by-one their lights faded out. They released millions of cattle to wander, or killed them sometimes with efficient mercy, but always the sun desiccated the animal hulks faster than coyote could eat them.

The humans left in many ways. Some of them tore others to pieces on their way, or tore themselves to pieces with blown minds, or turned themselves inside out. Some succumbed to the despair of their generation. Some of them dried up, some of them swallowed enough of their favorite food and pills, but never enough to hydrate. There really was no water. The towers went dark and succumbed to gravity, and the heap they called Fresno became a ruin.

That's when coyote, this coyote and the others, stopped being afraid of the city. Tuna, yams, apricot, pineapple, craft apple beer—coyote had no names for these things, nor for the humans' abandoned city, but knew that with grit they could chew through the millions of cans and bottles, and feast. Cats, dogs, snakes, ferrets—likewise, they had no names for the human pets alone to fend for themselves, but coyote grew fat devouring them all anyway, ripping them to pieces in revelry. The coyote never had so many siblings in those years, the baby booms tearing to bits the manicured world after humanity, caloric celebration, liberated, picking apart leftovers.

Years later, with cans empty, with pets devoured, with the feast on civilized remains over, what remained to eat but one another? Nothing more of the feast; everything left of time to turn, to devour friends and family and loved ones—cannibalism—until a sole survivor. And eventually the moment of this sole survivor starving to death.

Other animals accept death howling, then in silence. Somewhere in between, the howl cradled genetic memory of the billions of generations who rose and slept in ecstasy and agony before them. But finally, the ring of unconsciousness became louder than howling, and then *the end*, the sinking to sleep, the nuzzle into dirt, and the silence of the lines of memory.

This was the state of the coyote's demise until finally the ruby-eyed cobra arrived.

There was no more strength for coyote to be shocked anymore or feel fear or outrage. The coyote lay basking in the dust and the red-ash moon, still waiting to die, as this abomination slithered around, over and past, rising up on rock and flaring its hood.

The cobra was truly an abomination. It was not a pet of the humans, but it was *of humans*. No snake existed like it in the world. A Philippine Samar cobra, but so very large. It reared comfortably at nine-foot-one. It wore some other snake's sunbeam skin, smooth, milky scales that cast rainbow glints. In sunlight, one could imagine color cast in blinding radiance. But even in moonlight, its prismatic skin shone bright in all directions so that, were coyote not burdened by thirst and starvation, its eyes could never focus on the cobra's true shape or place in space, almost incorporeal, an unseen body. Except its eyes. Its eyes glinted. Red stones, actual rubies, glinted between the surgical scars at the edges of its emptied orifices. Someone had replaced the cobra's eyes.

I am stronger than you, the cobra hissed to coyote.

Of course you are, coyote retorted. I am dying. I will be dead in hours, or hours and hours.

The cobra's hood retracted. It coiled, tightening for warmth before the coyote. No, but that's not why I am stronger than you. I've always been stronger than you ever were.

Flashing through coyote's mind, then, were the years of howling, marauding nights and days scavenging and picking. And then years of more savage times: the needing to fight in the mud, skin-from-skin tearing with other coyotes, killing kin over the last cans, the last scraps, to eat each other in the ruins of some other generation's decadence. Cannibalizing family in the absence of any other prey or predator. Starving, scraping by in the ruin of the city. How many of its own kind had it bested? One hundred? A thousand? All that were left? Maybe. Now all that was left was coyote, this coyote, here, in Fresno, one last bath in dust.

It's not true, the coyote insisted. I was strong. Until the end. I was a survivor. Until the end. We always were and always had been. I survived everything.

The cobra only flexed its hood. This is exactly your weakness, it hissed. You rose from that unending lineage of scavenged survival; I rose from imagination. You are trapped in biologic history; I have no past; I have no future. You evolved; I was created. You embraced entropy; I was created beyond it from a people who denied it. I am the blank slate. I have no responsibility to the natural world; I am a creation and a fantasy of the human world. It made me a slave while they roamed the earth. But it makes me a god now that they are extinct.

Cobra was born in a sterile room as fiber distilled in glassware, entertainment for rich people until its hosts turned, and it wandered away from the compound after consuming them. Cobra could survive forty years without a meal. It fed anyway in moments of fancy. For joy. To quench something distant and innate, but not essential. Cobra never fed to survive.

Coyote could hardly bring itself to growl, but did, its last breaths stirred the dust with a final pang of anger, recognizing the cobra was no hallucination. A last breath, and anger became its contrition. I was strong, it insisted. I was a survivor. I survived it all. It *matters*. I survived. *I survived.*

The cobra uncoiled, stretched, opened its mouth as if to purge. It readied itself to devour coyote.

I am not death. But I am your death. You can fight as much as you want. Now I am going to swallow you whole.

The hours passed, the sun rose, and the natural being used its final breath to protest in mutinous growls its demise to the insides of the imagined being, that ruby-eyed sunbeam cobra, who finished its meal with steady diligence in the ashen noontime sun, daydreaming of creation.

There Are Ghosts Here

Dominique Dickey

The day Leo Johnson disappeared, his sister Louisa waited for him next to his hand-me-down minivan. She texted him, to no avail. She called him and left voicemails accusing him of abandoning her at school, even though the old Honda was still in the student lot where he'd parked it that morning. She was annoyed at first—he'd probably gone off with his friends and forgotten about Louisa—then angry, then worried, then terrified.

When the winter sun started to set, Louisa realized that Leo was likely in worse trouble now than she could bring upon him by telling their parents. She sat on the curb and called her father, who then called her mother, who reported her eldest son missing.

By the end of the night, all the police knew was that he had vanished.

A FEW DAYS after Leo went missing, Maisie and her family had flown to Los Angeles and camped out in the Johnsons' guesthouse. Maisie was a distant cousin, related in ways that Lucas, the younger of Leo's two siblings, didn't quite care to understand.

Maisie and Lucas were the same age, and minutes after her arrival the two of them were banished to the backyard with vague instructions to "go play" as their parents sat at the kitchen table in solemn silence. Maisie immediately began to explore the Johnsons' neglected flower-beds, lacing her fingers through the spiderwebs that had formed between the rosebushes. Lucas stood on the back porch, arms slack at his sides, and watched the adults through the kitchen window. His parents sat across from Maisie's, all eight of their hands touching in the centre of the table. He thought he heard a humming—the kind that comes in through your bones rather than your ears—from somewhere inside the house. The grown-ups were all still, eyes closed, silent except for that hum.

Maisie tugged on his hand. "Play with me," she said, and ran off across the yard, leaving Lucas to follow. He glanced back through the window once more and saw Maisie's mother open her eyes and shake her head. He couldn't hear what she said, but from the movements of her mouth it looked like "I can't."

Lucas turned away and chased his cousin across the crisp, dead grass. It was deep winter then, but his cousin didn't care—she ran barefoot over the hard ground, looking for beautiful things like bugs and bones, and it was all Lucas could do to keep up. Maisie had been raised with an acceptance of death that Lucas strived for—perhaps if he thought of things as simply as she did, his brother's disappearance wouldn't hurt as much.

Maisie stopped suddenly, her head lolling back to stare up at the hazy sky. "Point to a star," she said, though few shone bright enough to cut through the city's pollution. "I know them all."

Lucas lifted his arm toward the twilit horizon. The gesture was languid, lazy, his body exhausted from their play.

"Jupiter," she said, and hummed a single, droning note.

Across the city, Leo was dying, although Lucas could not have known it.

In the kitchen, Maisie's mother sat with her hands folded on the table in front of her and explained that it was too late, that a death had already been traded for a life.

In the house next door, a newborn baby cried.

MAISIE MOVED IN a few months later, a few weeks before the LAPD started speaking of Leo in the past tense, a few days after her parents' car was hit head-on by a semi-truck. Lucas was shocked that, even as a new orphan, she was just as untroubled as ever. On her first day in the Johnson house, she strung hollow bird bones from her bedroom ceiling as if they were streamers.

"She's weird," declared Louisa, who was now the oldest Johnson child in Leo's absence. Louisa had spent the past months always looking over her shoulder, waiting for Leo to slip back into their family like a key into the right lock. "She's weird, and I don't like her."

LEO WAS DEAD and summer fell heavy on the Johnson house. Maisie rescued roadkill from the rushing thoroughfare at the end of their cul-de-sac. Raccoons, opossums, the occasional coyote. Mangled bodies came back together when she pressed her small hands to their crushed and bloody paws. Sometimes she vomited into the gutter afterwards, black sludge that Lucas thought smelled like weeks-old compost—like death made fertile. He held her hair back and rubbed her shoulders until it passed, every time.

The animals Maisie couldn't save—the ones that had been left to rot too long in the sun—she stripped down to bone with her bare hands. The bodies seemed to obey her, to yield, to unravel into their constituent parts neatly and with very little urging. The collection of skeletons hanging in her bedroom grew.

Maisie taught Lucas more constellations than he could remember. They forsook perfectly good beds to pitch tents in the yard and sleep on the ground, adorning each other with flowers and leaves.

In August, she sang that sad note to the sky, and readied herself for her long march to elementary school.

TWO SUMMERS BECAME three. Three became four. They were in middle school now, and Lucas fought Maisie's bullies with his bare fists. Louisa went to college on the East Coast and only came home for the month of July.

"There are ghosts here," she said. "And I've never liked those bird bones."

This puzzled Lucas almost as much as it puzzled Maisie. Of course there were ghosts here—there were ghosts everywhere. Dying was as natural as breathing, and that didn't scare him the way it used to. He was twelve years old and invincible.

Maisie and Lucas babysat Bodhi, the little boy next door, while his parents went to work. He was a smart kid, raised on organic produce, Mozart, and Dr. Seuss. His little mouth dropped open when he looked at the stars. "Jupiter," said Maisie, while Bodhi pointed and babbled. She'd tried giving him coyote teeth and snake bones to play with, but he didn't want them. At four years old, he was a clever boy, but never quite clever enough to see the beauty in dead things.

"He's just like Leo," said Maisie, although she had never known Leo at all. Lucas took her at her word, forgetting that Leo had already gone missing by the time Maisie's family first came to visit—something in the way Maisie spoke erased the need to ask questions.

"I miss him," Lucas told her.

"I know."

"Every single day."

"I know. He'll come back for you."

"You can't just say things like that," said Lucas. He didn't want to be like Louisa, always waiting, always wondering. He believed that his brother was dead, and that his brother's death was final.

But here Maisie was, holding out her hands for Lucas to inspect. They were small, brown, ordinary. He had seen them do incredible things, zip up wounds and unravel intact flesh. He had never once felt afraid of her.

"You can't just say things like that," Lucas repeated. He turned Maisie's hands over in his to look at her palms. "Do you . . . Do you miss your parents?"

Her mouth quirked. "You can't just ask things like that, Lucas."

"Do you?" In their years of being inseparable, they'd never talked about Maisie's family.

She looked up at his face, then back down at her hands. "Yes, but I wouldn't bring them back. Do you understand?"

"I don't."

She flexed her fingers back, then clenched her hands into fists. "When they died, they left me this."

IT WAS MAISIE'S fifth Los Angeles July, and Bodhi's fifth July at all. Maisie, Lucas, and Bodhi pitched tents outside, ran barefoot to catch the ice cream truck, and played in the grass while the sprinklers sprayed.

While Bodhi and Lucas lay on the lawn, Maisie hollowed out a curved length of bone, perhaps a rib, to make a pipe.

The pipe only played one note. Though Lucas was a terrible pianist, he knew that it was middle C.

"Bodhi," said Maisie. "Ice cream."

Bodhi looked up.

Down the street, a familiar tune played.

"I'll race you," Maisie said, and Bodhi was up in an instant, sprinting to the edge of the cul-de-sac. Maisie jogged alongside him; Lucas walked half a block behind.

Bodhi reached the corner and kept running, down to the pavement. "Leo!" Maisie called. He looked back at her, and then the truck hit him.

When Maisie hauled him out of the road he was life in the process of being unmade, beautiful and terrible all at once. "Leo," she whispered. She fluttered her hands over Bodhi's throat, barely touching him, and his eyes fell open. They were glassy and cold. Lucas could hear sirens approaching, paramedics coming too late. In a distant sort of way, he knew that Maisie could have saved Bodhi; in an even more distant way, he knew that she could have killed him far sooner. Why wait for a cataclysm, when she herself was cataclysmic?

Maisie gripped Lucas's hand so hard that he saw stars. He heard her breath come in a harsh and wet rasp through her open mouth. Lucas thought he felt a shift in the great big cogs of the universe.

"A reversal," Maisie said, chest rising unevenly as she inhaled. "A death for a life." Lucas tried to adjust his hand in hers, but she only gripped him tighter. "Please—I can't hold him alone. We'll lose him if you let go."

Lucas thought he understood. Leo's spirit—or soul—or whatever it was called—was nestled in Bodhi's broken body, and now Maisie and Lucas held it between them. Leo was in the space between their palms, twining around their arms, and Lucas had never known anything as certainly as he knew that he would not let his brother go.

"What do we do now?" Lucas asked.

"We find Leo's body, and then we wake him up."

WHEN BODHI'S PARENTS arrived, Lucas thought they had too many questions, and didn't understand why they insisted on complicating the simplest thing in the world. Their son was dead, and that was it. Why couldn't that be all?

In his impatience, Lucas thought he might have become too much like Maisie. Or maybe he had grown toward her just enough to survive, like a plant curling toward the sun.

"I waited," Maisie said to Lucas as they walked home from the scene of the accident. Their block had never felt so long. "You wanted your brother back, and I wanted to give him to you, but I waited."

"What?"

"You were going to ask why I didn't do this sooner, weren't you?"

"I'd never," Lucas said, and it was true. He'd gotten used to living with unanswered questions. He still hadn't found the edges of Maisie's abilities, still didn't quite understand the myriad ways she traded death and life, but he didn't need to.

"You wondered," Maisie said, and that was true as well. "Why didn't I do this sooner? Because you didn't want me to. You wanted Leo back, but you didn't want me to kill for him, so I waited." She paused, as if waiting for Lucas to speak. "It really was an accident, Lucas. And he was hurting. Before I touched him, he was really, really hurting. I would have waited—I know you would have wanted me to wait, right? I would have let his heart stop on its own, but I couldn't let him hurt like that."

"You could have *saved* him." It was confusing to watch her bend the lines between life and death, to watch her make these choices—why save some creatures and not others? Why let some die their own deaths, and why kill others? Coming from someone who had the power to save lives, putting someone out of their misery felt an awful lot like murder.

"Of course I could have saved Bodhi," Maisie said, "but wouldn't you rather have Leo?"

"But he was a *kid*."

"He was Leo," she said. Something in her voice made Lucas feel stupid for not understanding. "It doesn't always happen like this—the trade isn't always so direct—but when it is, we make the trade regardless. I do what I have to. A death for a life, Lucas. You know that by now."

"I DON'T CARE if you're my brother," said Louisa. "Hell, I don't care if it could save the world. I am *not* driving you across town in this traffic."

It took Lucas nearly an hour to convince Louisa. In that time, he never once loosened his grip on Maisie's hand.

"So what's this about?" Louisa asked as she backed Leo's old blue minivan out of the driveway.

"Magic and science," said Maisie.

"Leo," said Lucas.

"Magic. And science. And Leo?" She formed her mouth around his name as if worried that the vowels could cut her gums.

They were leaving the cul-de-sac, the silent summer suburbs. Without saying a thing, the four of them remembered tricycles and rapidly melting popsicles, running barefoot on freshly trimmed lawns, splashing around in kiddie pools.

"It's complicated," said Lucas.

"We have a long drive," said Louisa.

"IT'S A MANMADE lake," said Louisa, as the gang tumbled out of the car and marched into Echo Park. "There's no magic in a manmade lake."

She'd spent the entire drive demanding to know why they needed to go to the park, threatening to turn the car around in response to the kids' careful non-answers. She hadn't questioned the cluster of emergency vehicles at the end of the cul-de-sac or the drying smears of blood on Maisie's shirt.

"There's still science," Lucas said.

And then his sister's hands were on his shoulders, holding him in place, even as Maisie kept tugging him towards the lake. "Lucas, none of this is real. You know that, right? You have to know that."

"But . . . you already drove us all this way."

"Because, whatever this is, I think I'm going to have to let it disappoint you."

When Lucas didn't answer, Louisa settled for scowling and scuffing her feet against the ground. She followed Maisie and Lucas down to the lake.

Mosquitoes floated in the stagnant water and nipped at their bare legs as they walked laps around the lake, first clockwise, then counterclockwise. Every few steps, Maisie breathed through the bone pipe, tuned so unwaveringly that it made Lucas's head hurt.

The sun was beginning to set when they stopped. "Jupiter," Maisie said, and Lucas had never heard her voice so hesitant. She played that note again on her pipe. The sound was long and low, with a sort of mournfulness that Louisa associated with late August. It was the whole universe contained in a single tone.

"He's underneath us," Maisie whispered. They shuffled a few feet away from the lakeshore and looked up at the sky again, leaning slightly toward each other.

"Point to a star," she said. "I know them all."

Lucas understood then the exact moment that they were trying to recreate. Five years ago, winter, dead grass hard and cold under his bare feet, hours of hunting through the yard for pill bugs and bird bones, chasing Maisie until he could barely breathe. He felt it all, perhaps even more strongly than he felt it then. He felt the moment Leo died, the moment Bodhi was born, the way something shifted and clicked between them. He was awed by his cousin all over again, the arrogant way she claimed to know every star in the night sky. He pointed toward the twilit horizon.

"Jupiter," said Maisie. She played that note again.

The damp ground began to shift. Layers of mud retreated: a ribcage, a skeleton, Leo's tattered blue jeans.

Flies gathered around them and covered the skeleton. When they departed, the greying flesh had returned to his body, tattered in places, wounds not clear enough for Lucas to piece together what got his brother into this predicament. Worms appeared, looping through the spaces in Leo's skull, then slid back into to the ground. His eyes were swollen and bulging until they settled back into place, eyelids closing over them. His finely stubbled jaw shifted and creaked, healing from some invisible fracture.

In the wind, the leaves whispered "Galileo, Galileo, Galileo."

Maisie took up the chant. Lucas joined her, gripping her hand so tightly that his whole arm went stiff.

After the years had undone themselves, the three of them stood there, staring at Leo's pale corpse. He looked the same as he had when Lucas last saw him, save for the beating he'd taken.

"Galileo," Lucas whispered, and let go of Maisie's hand.

Leo's eyes opened.

The Drone Pilot

Andrew Colarusso

14 OCTOBER XX01
EGLIN AIR FORCE BASE
OUTSIDE VALPARAISO, FLORIDA

The hula girl dancing on the dash of his Ram pulled him apart, made him wonder, bouncing on her spring, about the arc of his life. Plastic banana leaves at her brown waist worn away from kelly green to weathered white. And his reflection in the rearview. Clean shaven. Showing signs of age. Son of Susan Sussilleaux and Orestes Huit. His mother, a creole from the bayous of Louisiana. His father, a guitarist from Guayanilla. Wanderers who met in the late seventies and settled in Miami. Both now in their late sixties. And his reflection in the rearview. Major T.P. Huit, son of Susan Sussilleuax and Orestes Huit, parted momentarily from his own body to see everything unspeakably from the verso. The emblem of the 53rd. A winged saber upward bound along a white stripe parting air and space, breaking at its foible two bolts of red lightning. Sprites in the upper atmosphere. The same prescription he wore since fourth grade. The numbers and tags. The boots—still covered in dust from Creech. The hula girl dancing on the dash of his Ram. In the front seat where he lost his virginity. The Clash on the radio.

He could've been a surfer.

California was a kind of heaven or hades to which his young loves let go were lost and sometimes from which reappeared, always and only before receding again to the red light of the west. But, as Susan Sussilleaux often reminded her boy, this was an unchristian sentiment—which merited no further thought—which could therefore be transcended.

There was Maia, first among his loves possessed by California, from Salinas, whom he'd mistaken for Persian. She was Mexican-American, in fact. They were young and eager students together at MIT, sharpening their teeth on the mechanics of the universe, Terry Gilliam, shrooms and orange juice. She was as tender as she was intelligent. Sensible. Bicurious or bisexual or just splintered and sensual. How quickly the veneer of freshman year faded into sophomoric disillusionment, weeded and spinning on the finer sounds of *Stadium Arcadium*, favoring the emotional vulnerability of Mars to the tender bravado of Jupiter. Tracks like "Tell Me Baby," synthetic and angular, which came to him in blocks of primary color. And "Hard to Concentrate." The fantasy of family in California.

Maia couldn't afford to stay in school. Her scholarship was paltry, barely enough to cover the cost of room and board. She had realized, after a year of listless study, that what she sought was conceptually simpler than four years of required courses toward ceremonious institutional discharge. Love and a life well lived. The only two things still cheaper than water and cleaner than air.

She had encouraged him, before dropping out, to hop on a cross-country train and be with her in California. There she would teach him how to surf. How to really surf. How to be a real surfer. And up until that point they had agreed, in eyes and smiles, that they were both in the gentle throes of what could have been worth a lifetime of shared exploration. So they made love and found it appropriately dull. Then she was gone.

He stayed in school designing cascading style sheets for more enterprising classmates, accruing academic language and debt, farming experience for two rogue night elves (Drizzt and Cattie) on his World of Warcraft account, illegally downloading albums, and frequenting porn sites—the full history of which, he would find out much later, was documented in his classified dossiers. He wondered if a posthumous biography could be based on one's porn history. He wondered what one's erotic tastes, one's fetishes, could illustrate about one's dark side.

To his (and everyone's) surprise, in his senior year before graduating from MIT he was tapped on the shoulder and asked by Uncle Sam to attend the most exclusive house party in the world. His country needed him. So began his military journey.

He was transferred from 53rd Test and Evaluation Group, stationed on Creech AFB in Nevada, to 53rd Electronic Warfare Group at Eglin AFB in Florida. Rather quickly he became one of the Air Force's foremost experts on MQ-9 long-range operations. His was a particular brand of nerdiness the military deemed too dangerous to dismiss.

The staff psychologist noted in his dossiers that this dangerous nerdiness may have been piqued by an early obsession with Nintendo's Game Boy. Miguel, his best friend growing up, owned an original Game Boy—a gray plastic brick of a machine with a black directional pad [+] and operational buttons, A and B, which looked like shiny raspberry colored candies. There was also start and select which looked like gray Tic Tacs arranged beside each other at a bias on the face of the machine. Miguel had on his Game Boy a sticker of the Kool-Aid Man between the directional pad and candy-coated buttons. For several months the young Major thought all Game Boys came with a Kool Aid Man totem, and was disappointed to find out that this wasn't the case.

He feigned a curiosity in the contents of Miguel's games—Tetris, Super Mario Land—but his actual interest was in how Miguel played the games, how he could assimilate the hardware of the machine to the functions of his own body. In short, he was interested in the Game Boy as an instrument. He liked to read the secret language his friend's thumbs made while playing. To watch Miguel play was something like watching a nervous portrait or a score to the music of his friend's mind. His tempo and interpolations. Improvisations.

A year later, when the young Major was gifted by his mother and father a Game Boy of his own—one with a neat transparent shell, but no Kool-Aid Man totem—he absconded with the machine and took it apart. He wanted what was inside.

Decades later he still found himself ogling people as they played with their smartphones, sliding and sweeping and arranging dream stuff across their retina-display multi-touch screen LCDs—gleaning their reflections from a mosaic of downloadable applications. Inputting magic into little black boxes. Their thumbs like prone asps spitting back and forth across the glass. He checked the lock screen on his phone. Twenty minutes until briefing.

The MQ-9 is a Remotely Piloted Aircraft—an unmanned aerial

vehicle popularly referred to as a drone, designated the Reaper, operated by a two-person crew consisting of a pilot and sensor operator with an additional intelligence analyst. The Reaper is classified by the Air Force as a Tier II MALE (medium altitude, long endurance) hunter-killer. Effective use of the Reaper is contingent upon their corporate performance. From ergonomic leather chairs in a ground control station no larger than a shipping container, not unlike a dorm room, they were given seraphic power. The Reaper was quickly and internationally proving itself worthy of its name. Compared to Grumman's fine F-14 Tomcat, immortalized in the 1980's film *Top Gun*, General Atomic's Reaper was quicker, smarter, deadlier, and safer for our troops who more and more seemed to resemble civilians.

His life wasn't anything like *Top Gun*. He was still single. No prospects. Now and again memories of a brooding Tom Cruise in bluish profile over the ravished and ravishing broad-shouldered body of Kelly McGillis flashed across the screen of his mind. Without realizing it he would start to hum "Take My Breath Away," as performed by Berlin, mouthing Giorgio Moroder's heavy sex synths before shaking off the indulgence of his latently homosexual fantasy.

Almost all of his military hours were logged under ISR (Intelligence, Surveillance, Reconnaissance). An accomplished sensor operator, the Major was instrumental in early development of the nine-camera sensor they called the Gorgon Stare. His earliest missions were startlingly mundane. What seemed like violations of privacy, verging on the pornographic. Patrolling the border for cows and aliens. Watching two women suspected of conspiracy bathe together in the mountains of an island he had never been to, even as a civilian. He started feeling buck. Pulse and temperature rising. Sweat.

IT WAS NOTHING like Top Gun. It never quite felt like sex, masturbating after a mission where nothing happened. Tense because nothing was happening and because anything could happen. Tense because it wasn't much different from reality television, or Jane's Combat Simulations. Nothing in real time could be so inconsequential or convenient.

Only two days earlier had he asked Carruthers what it felt like for him not only operating the bird, but, you know, just being as like a person who walks and talks and feels. Carruthers looked at him and said flatly, it feels like a video game. Like *Grand Theft Auto*.

What maybe saved them from complete monotony was the inextinguishable unknown that made gamblers of sound men—a slight delay in transmission between operator and RPA. Somewhere between a one and two second delay. It was never as immediate, never as synchronized as one assumed in the middle of operations. They were always operating on the back end of real-time, which is often how they grew to will the machine, meld with it in some fetishistic way. When the machine stalled, if the feed froze, the crew (pilots especially) took pride in the resuscitation of the RPA.

Aware of the machine as an extension of self, each of the crew imbued the Reaper with something human, something wholesome and alive. Come on baby, the pilot would sometimes say under his breath, off mic, like pillow talk or prayer. Like talking back to the dot matrix screen, stereo speakers, and candy-coated buttons on the face of a Game Boy. Inputting magic into little black boxes.

He thought he knew he could still fuck if the opportunity presented itself, but he couldn't remember the last time he'd won a fist fight.

How I Came to Love Kelly Sand's Sister

Isle McElroy

With bright little knives the doctors opened her stomach—Julie's—and lifted the kid from her womb. The boy was sent to an impotent couple in Eugene, who named the child Sylvester. Julie named him Liam. She wasn't allowed to contact the family.

The closed adoption was her parents' decision. They were nervous, practical people, who felt vindicated by Julie's condition. It confirmed what they'd always suspected. Their eldest was difficult. Weird. She needed a love that exceeded what their hearts could offer. At least they had Kelly, they thought. Their Supernova. Their scholar. Their second chance—my sweetheart.

Three months after the birth, Julie ran off to find Liam's father: Greg Hayes. She emptied her closet, sold the clothes and her phone to buy a backpack and bus ticket to Whitfield. She sat with her cheek to the window, its glass, fingerprint sticky, gripping her face. The bus careened through the pass. Doug firs speared the clouds. Snow fell. She nodded off, woke up muck-lipped and groggy at the Whitfield Greyhound station, a concrete bunker skirted by cracked plastic chairs bolted to asphalt. Her backpack had been stolen. But her wallet, thank God, remained lumped in her pocket.

Julie booked four nights at a motel called Paradise Loft. Her room smelled like roses watered with bleach. There were cats trapped in her wall. She phoned the front desk. "How do you know?" the manager asked. She held the receiver to the wall: the muffled distress of the mother, tender mews of her kittens. "You will get used to it," he said. "Everyone does."

GREG, GREG, GREG. What did she know about Greg? Got a pen, here it is: . . .

FINE. THEY'D MET at Vicki Lang's grad party when Greg tapped her back by mistake. "Oh, you're not Jamie," he said.

"Even better," she said. "Julie."

He smiled profanely and stuck out his hand: Greg Hayes, English major at Whitfield U. Cropped hair, a mole poking through scruff on his chin, black glasses pinching his nose. They had little in common but drank until who they were didn't matter. Leaning against the aboveground pool they kissed till their lips plumped into painful balloons.

Julie pulled away. "You got a car?" she asked. She'd never had sex with a stranger, and her question—her proposition—stunned and thrilled her.

"A Benz," he said. They drove to someplace secluded. He did not have a condom. Neither did she. He would have to be careful. If anything happened he'd take care of it. Whatever she needed. In the backseat she leaned against the door as he shed her jeans. His fingernails scraped her thighs. Her nose poked the window control, zuzzing it down, zuzzing it up, down, down, up, down, up, down, down, as he sloppied himself on her body. He saved his number into her phone. She deleted it when she got home, relieved to be done with him.

JULIE HUNCHED OVER a wobbly café table perusing the Whitfield student directory. No Hayes. No Hays. No Haze. No Heis. Six Hughes: Amelia, Angela, Daisy, Jacqueline, Lashonda, and Tammy. She studied the students cascading out of the English building. No Greg. She bugged the registrar office. "My brother," Julie said. "Gregory Hayes. He's gone missing."

"Oh dear," the clerk said. "May I see your student I.D.?"

She hadn't seen Greg since the night of Vicki Lang's party. None of the guests remembered him. Cropped hair? Glasses? Vicki had never met a Greg in her life. Julie's parents were even less helpful. If he couldn't be found why bend over backwards? they reasoned. She despised them for saying she'd gotten off lucky. And the most likely explanation, that Greg's name wasn't Greg, felt too dull to consider. So she went after him, fueled by a cocktail of resentment, maternal fixation, and boredom, mixed and poured inside the assumption that Greg might know how to get Liam back and that mothering Liam would make her happy—"Victorious," Kelly would say, with correctional flair, when I proposed this Liamry to her.

After five days in Whitfield Julie ran out of money. With her last ten dollars she hopped a bus to the coast hoping to stay with her grandmother. When Julie was twelve the woman had told her she was always welcome. But a decade had passed since they'd spoken, and as she drew near the coast Julie felt smaller and smaller. By the time the bus let her off she'd sweated through two layers of cotton. She ambled aimlessly, through drizzle perfumed with dead fish and diesel. Two hours later she discovered her grandmother's place: a weathered beach house perched atop a sandy hill messy with weeds and windblown debris. Rusted boats bobbed on the water. Men dragged rattling cages stuffed with crabs drowsily pinching the air. A shed the color of flesh puffed black smoke from a fingerish chimney.

"Hellloo, it's Julie," said Julie, as she nudged inside. Potpourri, wet socks, cigarette smoke. Above bay windows sudsy with grime a stiff marlin was nailed to the wall, its mouth stuck in a scream. She followed coughing into the kitchen.

Her grandmother aimed a shotgun at her chest. "Who are you?"

Julie reintroduced herself.

"You look different," she said, as she set the gun in the sink. She was a compact woman, with floppy, liver-specked skin, and white hair foaming her scalp. A long brown cigarette tucked in her mouth dipped up and down. "Your mother told me you'd come."

"Bet she didn't say I'd stop off in Whitfield," Julie said, with derisive bravado.

"Your momma's a talker," she said. "You staying a while?"

"Just till I get more cash, Grandma. If that's—"

"Nuh-uh. First rule: nobody's grandma. It's Jean. Or Missus Grandma if you're attached to the G-word." She sipped from a Coke can and then spat black mush in the sink. She sipped from a second can, swished, and spat, before ashing in the first can. "I need a system. Ideas?"

"Ashtray?"

Jean cackled. "Youth," she said. "Don't miss it one bit." They looked at each other. "I need a nap. Too much excitement." She lumbered off to her bedroom. Inside, she yelled, "Pick a room upstairs. Any room. But only one's got a bed. TV's out there. And don't futz with the antenna. You'll get used to the fuzz."

Julie chose the room with the bed. Scuffed trumpets and champagne flutes and glittery paintings of horses cluttered the floor. She playfully tried on a pair of wigs. Both were harboring spiders. She left the dresses alone. On the shelf over the headboard sat a family of Caribbean dolls, their black legs like charred little dicks. She lay down and stared at the soles of their feet.

AND JULIE, JULIE, Julie, what did I know about Julie?

She was Ridge High School's primary subject of gossip and teenage hyperbole. Unclassifiable. A confounding mixture of types: straight As and booze on her breath; 1,024 varsity points; red thong glowing through white cotton sweats; boyfriends in faraway places—college professors, junkies who sold sheet metal scrap, astronauts, and corpulent merchant marines—an acceptance letter from Yale, we heard, shredded, confettied, tossed in the trash. Nerds studied her moods and concluded that Julie, when stressed, bought strawberry shortcake at lunch. Jocks tried to do it with her because "one night with Julie could make you fucking invincible." Other girls thought her close-minded, kookily smart, a slut and a prude: chimeric. She scared the stoners and malcontents. They believed her early departures from parties evidenced rougher proclivities, when in truth drugs made her nervous. Rumors escalated after the pregnancy. I wasn't immune to the rumors. They were what had drawn me to Julie. And it was Julie that drew me to Kelly. Dating Kelly gave me access to Julie, the real Julie, and for that I'm endlessly grateful.

HER FIRST NIGHT at Jean's, Julie dreamed she was sitting cross-legged and topless in an inflatable pool. Toddlers in bowler hats danced on its rim. She squeezed her tits, spraying milk at the toddlers, but instead of their mouths she hit their chests, foreheads, their adorable feet, and on impact they plopped in the pool and helplessly drowned as Julie aimed for the ones who remained.

"What's it mean?" Julie asked her grandmother.

"Means you need a job," Jean replied, and then gave her directions to town.

Downtown at a body shop a veiny mechanic dozed on the trunk of a Buick. The pizza parlor tripled as a bar and salon—beefy men in swiveling chairs sucked down Schlitz as clumped hair fell to the floor. Someone named Rhonda sold chowder and bait from her Sprinter cargo van. A handwritten HELP WANTED sign hung from a suction cup on the front door of the grocery.

"Is that true?" Julie asked the cashier.

"I'm going to college," he said. He had a rigid, symmetrical face, which loosened into a grin when he said, "Harvard."

"I think my sister might—"

He cackled. "Not really. U of O. The fuckers."

"It's still a good—"

"My parents say it'll corrupt me. Little do they know, right?"

She smiled. How long had he been waiting for someone to talk to?

"You can work every day?" he asked.

She nodded.

"Well great!" In the stock room he crossed out the *Kyle* written on the breast of his T-shirt and scrawled *Julie* beneath it. Then he took off his shirt and gave it to Julie.

"That's it?" she asked.

"Nope." His tongue squirmed between his lips and gums. "We gotta celebrate."

That night they went to the beach and smoked weed from a pop can. Julie's lungs were a fiery mess. The moon, a white stamp on the sky, looked melted and dripping into the water.

"Are you crying?" he asked.

She touched her face. She was. They looked at the water. No, she didn't want Kyle to walk her back home, but thanks. They reclined. Arms nudged. Feet grazed. Soon they were tangled, clumsily rolling, loose sand sticking to skin. She unzipped his jeans.

"Spit on it," he said. "I think I'm bleeding." She licked her palm, spittered it. Breaths strained. The rustle of jeans cuffing ankles. A fart? Goop on her thumb as his dick twiddled fishily. He crammed wet paper into her hand then ran toward the dunes. "Don't tell anyone!" He vanished into the night.

She held what he'd given her up to the moonlight. A twenty-dollar bill.

A MUGGY SUMMER stretched its legs into September. Life on the coast had compressed her desire to leave until it became something hard and impossible. Walking home from work every day—distractedly tripping in divots, getting honked off the road—she imagined the sequence that would bring Liam back to her. First, she needed to save enough money to return to Whitfield ($1,500, for a used car, rent, and deposit). In Whitfield a week would pass—no, a month—before she chanced upon Greg, sitting alone in that café near campus with maps of the Oregon Trail drawn on its walls. She would tell him what happened. He'd scramble outside, blindly waving her off, but she'd chase him, recounting the story until something—perhaps the scar on her stomach—proved she was serious. Greg would take off his glasses and stare, tenderly, at Julie, before walking her to a café two blocks south of the first. They would drink espresso and work out a plan. Greg's wealth would dissolve bureaucratic resistance. Liam's adopted parents would say, "He never felt right in our arms," as they returned the child to Julie.

At work she further fleshed out the details. Greg would be wearing a red-and-white flannel. His hair would be long, styled with gel. The second café would smell like burnt muffins. Liam's adopted parents, she decided, were florists. They excelled at making funeral wreaths.

This future, imagined, promised Liam's return. And his return would swell her with joy. But leaving the coast threatened that future. What if the second café smelled like chai instead of burnt muffins?

What if Greg wore contacts? His hair shaved to the scalp? If the adopted parents were bankers, instead of florists, would they then refuse to give Julie her son? Until she could guarantee that what she'd imagined was accurate, she would have to stay on the coast.

She explained this to Jean one evening, in late September, as they sat on the couch eating dinner. Jean shut off the TV.

"You need to leave," she said.

"Upstairs?" Julie asked, knowing that's not what she meant.

"It's been three months."

"I could pay rent," Julie said.

"You pay rent you'll never save up to leave."

She had a little more than eight-hundred dollars. Plus twenty from Kyle.

"A month," Jean said. "A month is plenty of time."

"Why don't you like me?"

"Who said I didn't?"

"You're kicking me out."

"How's this? You sacrificed something most people don't get, money for college, to make whoopie with strangers. You give up your kid. Don't want to know where it goes. Then abandon your family who's willing to love you and run off to me, who you haven't seen for a decade, expecting to get taken care of." Jean tapped her cigarette; ash drifted onto Julie's leg. "It's not that I don't like you, Jules, but I just don't see why I would."

KELLY AND I had been living in Princeton for nearly a month. Kelly was going to school. The School. I stocked shelves at a ramshackle Weis and attended community college. I'd declined a few full rides to middling colleges to trail her to Jersey. I was in love with Kelly. Blind, impassioned, predictable love. I expected her to support my sacrifice—my commitment to her—but she got sick of me quickly. Each morning I'd wake up at five to the *clack clack clack* of Kelly typing an essay in bed, coffee already thick on her breath, and she'd point to the door and say, "Out." In the shower I'd tug at myself till I came, thinking, At least I'm not jerking to Kelly on Skype! At least I still had the scent of her hair in the morning. Her legs on my lap as we sat on the couch watching movies.

Was love a good enough reason to join Kelly in Jersey? Love is the right reason for anything—though perhaps we weren't really in love. Perhaps what we'd felt, when we moved in together, was the hummingbird flutter of loneliness and impractical loins. I began to doubt my decision to move. I started pricing flights back to Oregon. I skipped class. I smoked weed alone in the bathroom, wondering what I'd done to deserve such a fate. But pain longs for distraction, displacement, and when Julie started calling Kelly, to talk about living with Jean, my pain was yanked inside-out and morphed into a loving obsession with Julie.

JULIE COULDN'T SLEEP after talking with Jean. She spent the night on the deck. The sky was drenched in stars. She looked for a pattern and saw, in the stars, what she already knew: she couldn't go home. In Ridge she was a fallen celebrity, attracting the gaze of her pastor, police at the diner, her elementary school superintendent—who in Safeway asked, with an eyebrow raised, what the school could've done better—of damaged baristas, lip-licking butchers, and pharmacists who would catch her attention then eye the condoms glowing next to the register.

"You did what you could," some people said. Meaning: "You failed." But had she kept Liam they would've thought her a whore. "He looks so healthy," they'd say, smiling at Liam, "so handsome [for the son of a whore]." Without him she felt like a failure. And the subsequent failure to find Greg compounded the first, absorbing and exposing everything she'd ever done wrong—cheating on Spanish exams, missing overtime free throws, dialing wrong numbers, alienating her parents—until she became, instead of Julie, a list of deficiencies shaped like a woman.

The next morning, however, she watched the fishermen lug buckets of chum from their boats, the air briny and halibut-scented. She thought of Kyle. She thought of the deadline. Her body had been ruptured by scalpels, plucked of her son. What more could she lose?

After two days practicing struts for the mirror, Julie offered herself to men at the dock. She paced beside the flesh-colored shed, wearing jeans she'd cut into shorts and a gold, cropped-top T- shirt. She stained her lips pink with Jean's chunky makeup. She batted her eyes at the men squelching past in their rubbers. A middle-aged fisherman asked what the hell she was doing.

"Whatever you want," she whispered, but had to repeat it.

"Unbelievable." He shook his head. "Had to hear it myself."

Some gangly guy, Wes, who owned a trio of boats, took up her offer. He had childish teeth the color of stones and a wallet swollen with cash. Julie handed him an index card:

$100 hand job
$200 blowjob
$500 all the way

They went inside the shed. She leaned against the stove and hooked her fingers in a frayed net nailed to the wall. Wes licked circles on her neck. He nuzzled her shoulder, face prickling skin. She was trembling. His calloused hands rolled up her shirt. The tremble gave way to shaking and shortness of breath.

"I can't," she muttered.

"I didn't think so." He picked up her shirt and turned away, handing it over blindly. The courtesy struck her, and she flinched, nearly dropping the shirt.

"Here." He handed over a one-hundred-dollar bill. "Come visit sometime."

She spent a week in the shower. Afterward, she called Kelly.

Kelly listened, enchanted and dazed, then hung up and screamed, "You will not believe what my sister's been doing!"

But I did believe. Julie was doing whatever she could to regain what was lost.

"What the hell does that mean?" Kelly asked.

"She loves her son and she misses him. If she has to—"

"Whore. If she has to whore herself out, that's okay?"

"She never intended to do anything."

"She's bi-polar, you know. I've been learning about it, in Professor—"

"You'd know if she were schizophrenic."

"Bi-polar, Wilson. I said bi-polar."

I reached for her hand but she yanked it away.

"It amazes, me, Wil, the things you don't know. You'd be perfect for

Julie. With your stories, rationalizations, trying to make the world what you want it to be."

"Are you setting me up?"

"Why are you here, Wil? Why did we do this?"

"Because love," I said, "conquers all."

That night I slept on the couch.

KELLY WAS SCARED of her sister's potential. Julie was the smart one. The genius bored by the ways of the world. She'd aced her SATs. Valedictorian. Mensa begged for her membership. Kelly? Her mind was a mechanical ox, endlessly plowing. She memorized two dozen SAT preps—a mere 2260. She stampeded through book after book, writing cramped notes in the margins, filing chapter outlines in folders coded by color. She cut back on sleep—in bed at eleven, breakfast at four—and pounded kale-colored pills that promised to "double her memory." She was embittered by overambition. And because we both knew that if Kelly were in Julie's position she would've caved, my job after their phone calls was to offer Kelly pessimistic comfort: Julie'll be fine—but not that fine. She would overcome most, but not every odd. In the end, she'll live a practical life of domestic travails. This prediction nearly came true.

JULIE AND WES struck up something like friendship. But he was in love with her. He proved it with gifts: dinners, necklaces, dresses and shoes too nice for the coast. One night he took her out on his fanciest boat, Prescylla. She hadn't told him about Greg or Liam. They were part of a fragile, parallel world that would collapse if it bumped into the salty, sumptuous world furnished by Wes. And on the boat she imagined a life without Liam, a life in which she gave up searching. A tranquil life. A life where the future didn't emerge from the past, where she would learn to love her homely, generous husband, and be happier for it.

The next morning Wes asked her to marry him. "Sure," she said. Wes ran to the prow, joyously screaming, and Julie, realizing what she had done, began to see herself growing old in a prison cell papered with money. When they docked she kissed him, lengthily, and told him she needed to put in her notice at work. She walked to the auto body shop. The mechanic wanted seven-hundred for the Buick. "But I've heard some things that might make me go lower." He smiled tightly, lips chewing teeth, as he dropped his hand to her waist. She slapped him, and paid $450, plus whatever he charged for new tires.

Jean was right. She had stayed on the coast for too long. She reminded herself that she'd only come here to leave. To then find Greg and Liam. Little Liam. He was six months old, now, and she longed to feel his fingers gripping her fingers, to spoon mushy peaches into his mouth, to lather his hair. Did he have hair? she wondered. When did babies get hair? She called Kelly to ask.

"That's just like her," Kelly said. "Hair? Of course he has hair! I swear, if she finds him—"

"Liam," I said.

She scoffed. "If she finds Liam—what next?"

"What's next is she raises her son."

"You know she wanted to kill it."

Was that true? It couldn't be true.

"Mom and Dad made her keep him. What if she'd gotten her way, Wil, would you cheer her on if she were diving in dumpsters at clinics, looking for the Ziploc filled with chunks of what—"

"Jesus, Kelly. What's the matter with you?"

"Me? You're the one who's obsessed with a pariah."

"She's a *pariah?*"

"Oh, look it up, Wil." This fight, our tone, it was normal, and rather than press her I waited for Kelly to say: "I'm sick of you. Your smell. The TV shows that you like. Of your questions—*How's Julie? Did Julie call? Are you sure she's okay?*" She paused to catch her breath. "What do you want out of me?"

"Want?" I asked. "Nobody knows what they want, Kel. The heart is a corruptible organ. Infiltrated, manipulated, by the swirling glaze of the world, by glistening ads, the grunts of incoherent malaise, and the promise of love, that regenerative, slimy, jewel-encrusted carrot that I trailed to Princeton, New Jersey."

That night Kelly and me fucked like sedans in a head on collision. We broke up in the morning, about the same time that Julie, over in Oregon, was dragging her stuff to the Buick. Jean followed her outside. Late dawn. Sunlight marbling clouds. They hugged—their first time. "I can't thank you enough," Julie said. She was crying. They both were. And as Julie drove off, she peered in the rearview. Watching Jean's cigarette pulse, something inside her unraveled.

KELLY KEPT THE bedroom. I slept on the couch. I did what I could to stay friendly. I vacuumed, paid the electric, took out the trash, and shared all of my groceries—not just the milk. Some nights, over dinner, I worked up the courage to ask about Julie. Kelly might say, "She's fallen in love with a hippo. They're moving to Kenya to be near his family." Or, "Screw you, Wil," and carry her plate to her room.

A month passed in this manner. Kelly took a lover. A brickish man with veins lashed to his arms and rifles tattooed on his neck. They made love every night. So I took a lover as well. A co-worker with wonderful breath. My unique situation disturbed her. She left me. Kelly's lover started coming over for dinner. We would sit in the kitchen, scarfing spaghetti, Kelly and her man saucily kissing and groping under the table. One night he carried Kelly to the stove, swept the pots to the floor, and tore off her skirt as I twirled spaghetti around and around my fork.

I went for a walk. The sidewalks were crunchy and orange with leaves. I could feel a crack opening up in my life, widening, widening, into an empty crevasse. The crack wasn't Kelly. It was Julie I missed.

She hadn't called for more than a month. And that night, with Kelly distracted, I copied Julie's number into my phone. I called on my walk. It rang ten times. I hung up. Tried again. Twelve rings. I walked on, dialed again, ten, twelve, fourteen rings before the clatter of a phone lifted off its receiver. "What?" someone groaned. Coughing consumed the voice.

FROM JEAN'S HOUSE Julie had driven to Whitfield. She planned to reassert herself. She wrote *Liam* on an index card and taped it to her steering wheel. She moved into a windowless studio. She waited tables at a sushi restaurant called Raw. Each morning she slipped into one of the dresses Wes had bought for her—baggy sacks patterned with flowers—before walking to campus. She tried delivering fake telegrams to English classes in session. She'd knock politely, enter, and assuage the scorn of professors with, "I have a letter for Gregory Hayes."

The professor would ask, "Is there a Gregory Hayes?"

There wasn't.

The registrar gave her a stack of outdated student directories. No Greg Hayes. But in the 2006 directory she found a Nicholas G. Hayes. She got Nick on the phone. "Did you ever make love to a woman named Julie?"

"Who is this?" he asked.

"Is your middle name Greg?"

Nick Hayes hung up.

He was hiding something, she reasoned. At the library she searched through the yearbooks. Finally, she came to Nicholas Hayes: cropped hair, black glasses, tick-like mole on his chin. Class of 2008. She flipped back a page. Returned. The face hadn't changed. The past six months swelled up inside her and popped. Julie searched for his address in the student directory. 21995 Rickard Road, Bend, OR. She called in sick the next day, halfway to Bend.

The iron gate at the end of his driveway was locked with a rusted chain. She stuck her foot on the ornate H in the center of the gate and gripped the bars, pulled up, and rolled over the top, landing with a pitiful thump on the pavement. Spruce squeezed the serpentine driveway. The forest flattened to lawn gone marshy in the Oregon winter. The house resembled a church crossed with a frat. Tall, shattered windows. Bone-colored columns rimming the porch. Julie marched across the yard, footsteps splattering mud on her calves.

Inside, dust moats curled and hovered. Julie pinched her nose. Dead mice stacked in the corner smelled nearly as strong as the black Xs and anarchist As spray-painted over the walls. A mangled chandelier lay at her feet. She heard music blaring upstairs and chased the sound to the master bedroom. Two men in Guy Fawkes masks were tagging dicks on the wall. Metalcore blasted out of an iHome. She unplugged it.

"What's going on?" she yelled.

Both men lifted their masks.

"The economy," one said. They put on their masks. "Do you mind?" he growled, and pointed at the iHome.

She explored the house. Its drawers and bedrooms were empty. The bathroom mirrors were cracked. The couches were shorn, their stuffing fluffed all over the floor. As she walked to the car the sky opened up. Rain soaked her dress; the fabric sucked on her skin. She tore the Liam index card off the wheel, dropped it in the street, and drove back to Whitfield.

KELLY KICKED ME out in November. Her lover moved in. To save face I told her I found a studio across town, that I planned to stay for a while, but that night I hopped a redeye to Portland. Was I embarrassed? Yes and no. Kelly and I, we failed as a couple. And I'm grateful for that. With her I learned that love cannot conquer all. It is not a perfect, eternal connection, but being what somebody needs. Kelly needed a lunk, a man double my size who did pull-ups in doorjambs. A man with guns on his neck. Me? I was emotional. I was, ironic enough, the lover. And though I wasn't what Kelly needed, I was—or would be—exactly what Julie was missing.

JULIE WAS FOLDING napkins at Raw when a man hurried past on the sidewalk. Had she seen him correctly? Cropped hair, the black smear of his glasses? She ran to the sidewalk. Greg was two blocks away. She untied her apron and carried it bunched in a ball, jogging, gaining a block, before slowing down to keep from getting too sweaty. A traffic light stalled him. Half-block away. She lengthened her steps. Quarter block. Eighth. Sixteenth. Thirty-second. She grabbed his shoulder.

"Yes?" the man said. He must've been fifty, glassesless. "What is it?"

"Here." She handed over her apron. "You dropped this."

The *Raw* stitched on its pocket matched the one on her shirt. "I think you're mistaken."

"I saw you drop it."

The man stuffed the apron in the nearest trash bin. Julie walked to the park adjacent the Greyhound station. My bus had just let me off. She sat on a swing, rocking forward and backward, thinking that everything about the last year was a waste. Was she any closer to Greg? Probably not. Liam? Not at all. She had made a fool of herself, searching. It was time to go home. Her parents would forgive her, Kelly had assured her. She stood up, planning to put in her notice at Raw, when I caught up to her, shamelessly winded, shouting, "Julie! Julie! It's me!" I pinched off my glasses—the square-rimmed fakes I bought at the airport—and wiped the lenses. "It's Greg," I said. "Gregory Hayes."

She backed up, crossed her arms, and considered me. The irony of fate, she thought, delivering that which she no longer wanted. Had she and Greg spent the past year in search of each other? Should she be angry? Elated? And could Greg, this Greg, help her find Liam? Her mind rewired itself, connections were severed—which explains why when she finally answered she didn't leap into my arms or pound on my chest or even call me a jerk. No. She tilted her head to the left, suspicious, and muttered, "Who?"

Man, Water, Dignity

Caitlin Palmer

The West: rim of mountain, some dusty surface scratched. *I will die here*, I thought upon arriving. I just wanted water, a pool, a large rushing river or a lake to submerge both body and spirit. Everywhere I had ever lived there had been water. Yet my bleating GPS showed none of this. Electric signs recommended no recreation, only numerous places of banking.

The truth of it, and I knew it then, was that I would forget about excess here. I would be stripped of all but the barest elements. What of me, was me.

First went remembrance of water, then green. The long land ridges sloped, everywhere in wheat. Like the bluffs, the phone calls between my ex and I dropped off slow, then suddenly.

In my new house, the dirt that blew in was black. The grass coughed, embarrassed, in the yard.

I asked shopkeeps and clerks at desks about water. I needed it. I was limp, overheated, the skin was peeling away from my nails. I asked the hardened faces of construction men, who looked at me suspicious of the request's practicality. Their sharp eyes chastised me, for my need was not for work, not for survival. I was showing them a soft spot, at the throat. Someone at last showed me a picture on their phone. Some creek, a dribbling over rocks. I tucked back into my vehicle which groaned, disconcerted, at the slopes both ascending and descending.

The directions took me to a new state but it was the same. The highway ribboned along for eight miles to another town that straddled the government line. If I thought Washington would be different from Idaho, and show fields of green (I seemed to remember from childhood studies of geography, maps that named *The Forests of Washington*), then I had another thing coming. The thing was muted acceptance. A path went along that stream, marsh grass choking and no love for lushness. I sat and threw an already withered stalk into the water and tried a sketch, but it was disheartening.

On impulse, I entered a darkened bar. The first place I'd come across with decor that didn't revel in rusticity, but settled for what passed for style in other places: dark curtains, tinkling chandelier. It felt like an old bar I knew, maybe the one where I plotted this foolish move, where one man I had waiting on me said, "I will not be coming." Well, what of it. In Washington I was grateful to pay the extra dollars for the cocktail but I realized, with the drink's burn, that a place reminding me of what I left could perhaps only make me regret each new quality.

What he'd said was, "If that were the point we were at in this relationship—"

And I'd said, "If we're not—"

And he said, "I might not be that type of man—"

And I said, "That is evident."

And so with that drink I started cutting things from me, the out of place characteristics I wore about me, and the first was that happy solicitation of partner and known acquaintance and in its place was the looming university, its brick and lawns, its tiles and offices, and others solitary like me, who did their studies' ungrateful reflecting, surrounded by no rivers of blue. I was a snake, I thought. I once would have said a water snake, but now, how could that be true, when around me there was no water, yet here I was? I needed element from outside to reflect upon what was within, like how the sun, the cool night, modifies that reptile's temperature, tells it when to hunt, when to sleep. What was I now, so far away from what I had known? I had shucked one skin off, wondering how many others lay underneath.

MY NEXT SLUICING happened while getting accosted in the street. Walking to the Idaho downtown, I had the light given me and the little electric man, so I began. The driver of a load waiting shouted, strangely amplified, for me to continue to take my time. Invoking my sex and the low nature of it, being female. And so, perhaps, not one supposed to make a large trip across the country, or even to walk about on my own. I turned, much, I'm sure, like the deer that startle, and the large truck made a turn crosswise at my heels, I had to step back to avoid dust on my shoe. Across the top of this truck was a megaphone speaker that had blared at me. The driver, mere feet away, grinned and wagged his long tongue, his bearded face and eyes strangely empty behind tinted glass. His open mouth morphed into a roar. It would swallow me. This bear-man bearing down raised his middle finger, slashing up, while using the other claw to steer the wheel and be on his way and gone. Two balls that looked to be tennis-sized swung in a sock on the tailgate signifying I knew exactly what, and I stood in the street, stopped, and he yelled, "Bitch!" Gearing on, he let me know what I was; exactly what. He moved too fast for my forked tongue.

MY THINKING IN this place would become over time: that I had Skin and Bones and if these were unadulterated then I must continue on, and if they were adulterated I would wear them no more. *Bitch*, no, that skin I took off. The one that balked in the street, too, in a fear, or perhaps just innocence. But I did not have this strength then. Coming upon the main avenue, I turned as if looking into the window of a storefront solidly shelved with goods, and I looked for myself within it. Tried to see where the length of me started and began. If I swallowed myself, could I spit myself back out, in a stronger, more intentional form? Men have always yelled at me. It is not a thing dependent on location. I knew I carried myself with something enough like pride that some feel the need to call it down. An educator of mine, a clergy. A bossman who quickly fired me. The partner who left me or rather chose to stay behind, he would have felt a righteous anger there in the street. He would not have had to hide in the grass. He would have looked sideways at those men, and not called out. Not needing to. But he too was gone and so I pressed the tips of my fingers under the rims of my eyes.

The downtown consisted, on all sides, of one-way streets. I argued for a moment that perhaps the driver had gotten confused in his navigation, therefore left waiting a long time at his light. This made me feel no better, nor did the sight of the cheery downtown storefronts. Yet I knew soon they would have an encouraging effect. I told myself Blink and have renewed eyes.

A snake must take its time to know what to do, lying curled in the grass. When to strike or retreat, when to lie curled or luxuriate in its full length. It watches those that move. And there were so many that moved around me there, a mixture of people I would not expect to see, so removed from other locations in such rurality. People with long hair and iron in their noses, ink along their skin. People with thick tortoiseshell glasses, and collared fronts. People in leatherhide boots and bow-brimmed hats and dirt under their nails. All sharing sidewalks in this place, an odd and, I ventured to hope, beneficial marriage. Crow, Jay, Quail. I watch you.

THE NEXT SKIN I cut from me, the colored scales I could wear no more, after Man & Water & Dignity, was a liquid type of Comfort. I went into a diner specifically to sit, and gather myself, and I would do it with a Whiskey & Coke. The server said, as if I might take the news badly, that they did not offer such commodities. I asked what sort of place was this? For I was used to, I suppose, getting a lunchtime drink at any venue, and thought I deserved it after my greeting. Very much sorry, ma'am, it was that he continued, but the town only had two liquor licenses for all of the places of business, an old law based on population of counties, and that one family owned both liquor licenses on both places and that other owners lined up in petition for the hoped-for eventuality of a third license, or that one branch of the owners may die. By this time I had accepted whatever he would say with steadfastness. I settled for just the Coke.

LATER ON, RETURNING to the new house, I was ever losing my way, moving in S's, closer and yet not close. I looked up and immediately realized I was lost. I had been talking on my cell, distracted, I had wanted a friendly voice. I knew there were hills around me and that I lived at the base of one and that it was such and such a distance from a water tower. In my mind I had thought that the water tower would protect me, as water had always done. But when I put the phone away, and looked up, it loomed in a direction I hadn't planned on, far away. And I realized, I could live at such and such a distance to it, at any point on a large circumference, that took in all the streets I could see. Where was my street? Where the downtown? Dusk was falling, and I knew it to be a small, homely sort of town, but I felt that any around me were enemies, they would sense my weakness at a glance. I didn't want to be seen. I wanted to hide, to withdraw, to have enough to get by within my own self. But this was false. Night would come and I needed to move, to take a chance, one direction or the other. My phone could have been of use but I had talked too long and the battery was low.

I remembered then, how once I got stuck in a cave. This is no Platonian observation, just the consequence of some drink on a night of camping. The cave was called "Old Man Mountain," and it was popular to go through the narrow labyrinth at night while wearing a headlamp. Many people had done this, including those wider in girth than me. So, though I faltered, I followed some who had gone before. Then in front of me, they just disappeared. I looked for a turn I had missed but there was none. Only a crevasse in the wall. One had to slide across its length, on their back, using the fulcrums of elbows and heels of feet. Then the crevasse steepened in incline and you were holding yourself up, alternatively, wrist to knee. When this ended, I heard voices ahead telling me what to do. A pit was what remained. You had to fall. Or let go. The drop was short, you could land on your feet. If someone were there, if someone had not stated in simple terms that it would be inconvenient to see it through, as my ex had done, leaving me here. With no one to call out to as I hovered at the edge of darkness to let go.

A teacher once wrote in a margin, where I was writing about death, over those words I had typed - *let go* - "Why not dive?" Why not? There was no one here to help me in this new town, where I didn't even know where my house was. There was only me. What did it mean to throw my long body into action, to make it an arrow?

What did it mean, then, to dive, to let go of all that held me? Even now I could not tell you. The me that could have is dead, that snake. I snapped its neck and swallowed its body, devouring it from the tail. Behind my gnashing head my length grew resplendent, shimmering, a mirage of heat and dust. What is the least amount you can survive on, of water, happiness, love? That is what I became. I no longer even hiss before a strike. This I warn you.

So the point that I wish to pass on is not that I learned to conquer a thing. This is not about the jumping, or the being left, or even the striking out with bared fang. It is about that moment right before: the standing, the stillness in the dark, the coil. The point is that there are things in life that insist on a continuation. Once you have started, you cannot go back. Old skins will not protect you. You may never come across water. You must accept some losses, you sweet, poisonous thing, to become a different thing. You must hold the things inside yourself, secret and whole.

A Billion Miles from What Was Home

Phoebe Barton

The first time I saw you, you were crying for the dead city. The rover's thick windows and air conditioning kept it at arm's length for the tourists, but I could taste its grit and blood on my tongue. All dead cities taste the same: hubris and disbelief and abandonment. It's only in the dying that they're any different, and tasting that once was enough for my lifetime.

I noticed because you were the only one crying. The other twenty-six people in the tour group stared outside, took photos, and talked about how amazing it all was, the same way people acted at Mycenae or Tranquility Base. You were acting like this was more than a place, like it was personal, even though it had been sand-choked for two centuries. Like you'd walked those streets yourself when they'd been full of life.

"They're not a vampire," Wiseacre said when I mentioned it to him later, while he curled atop a shoulder he considered as much his as mine. "Don't even think about it."

"Of course they weren't, it was the middle of the day." I gave his head a good scritch. His sapience didn't override his catness. "Too weird, though. It's not like there's no more casinos. Who gets teary-eyed about that?"

"A really dedicated gambler? Or maybe just someone who never heard the world always wins in the end."

"I thought it was the house that always won."

"I'd like to live in that world." Wiseacre purred, and it made me feel a little better even as I winced from my words' sour residue. They tasted like a freshly dead city, like batteries gone bad, like a rotten garden. Maybe that's what you tasted, too.

At least the sand let Las Vegas hide its shame.

IT'S EASY TO find cities built on myths: they're the ones that aren't cities anymore. From the shattered domes of Marsopolis to the sunken wreckage of Libertalia and the tourist-trapped echoes of piratical Port Royal, they only endure as examples or as warnings. Las Vegas, I think, is both. It's what happens when your myths tell you the future will be the present endlessly renewed, that you don't have to think about consequences, that your debts will never have to be paid.

That the house would never win.

The city's old spine was preserved like a trophy, with three kilometres of cracked asphalt and real money casinos freeze-dried under a steel-and-diamond sky for the tourists. I moved through it carefully, as if one wrong step was enough to shatter the illusion. Only the palm trees, stubbornly reaching, hinted at nature. The rest was a facsimile, maintained by people from well-founded towns in kinder patches of desert. Only true believers and lost souls still lived outside, among Vegas's bones.

I envied them that. Here on Earth, with its plentiful air and aegis sky, when a city's skin split there were still ways to survive.

"You'd think capitalism never fell with all this," Wiseacre said, still clamped onto my shoulder. Around us, the preserved Strip's neon signs and LEDs and holograms shouted to catch our attention, our approval, our avarice.

"It's what it is," I said. "It takes a while for the echoes to settle."

The bottled Strip ended where it had always begun, with a bright, gleaming, unmissable sign of stars and bulbs and rounded corners that welcomed visitors to fabulous Las Vegas, and that was where I saw you for the second time. You were kneeling next to it like a knight supplicating before a king, and as I watched you set down three flowers on the grass next to it, blue and white and red. When you stood, you carried yourself not like a groundpounder but a fellow habitat dweller, braced against centrifugal spin.

When you saluted the sign, I tasted the sourness of a myth overtold to rotting and I knew you had to be from Yorktown. It had been a long time since red and white and blue were the colours of Las Vegas, and few habbers cared about lines drawn in shifting sand. Yorktowners, though, they defined themselves by those colours the way some people defined themselves by one particular grandmother's grandmother's grandmother.

I wanted to ask you why, then, but Wiseacre knew me well enough to dig his claws into me. Enough to remind, not to hurt, and he was right to do it. As much as I'd come looking for stories, I didn't have any right to yours. As long as I kept my distance you could be a reminder that some myths endure, despite it all.

Those colours had made the myth that built Las Vegas, and by the time Las Vegas had fallen they'd been bleached to bones.

BOULDER DAM WAS a work any habber could respect. Here, in an increasingly harsh environment on a world that encouraged laxity and drift, concrete flanks and spinning innards built when spaceflight was an impossible dream had been maintained in working trim for three and a half centuries. It was why I'd come to Las Vegas at all: to breathe its air, touch its walls, and be reminded that collapse was always a choice, never an inevitability.

I needed to understand it so I could help others understand it.

"You've got the water, right?" Wiseacre sounded almost hopeful that he'd catch me in a mistake, that I'd have to go back and try again another day. It was no wonder he'd picked that name for himself.

"Only because you didn't let me leave without it." I patted the flask that hung from my hip. The water inside was mixed from the ice of Saturn's seven great moons. It had never been sweat, a river, or rain. Offering it to the desert was how I would ask for enlightenment and forgiveness.

"Just making sure it didn't disappear on the way over," Wiseacre purred. "I heard people tend to lose things in Las Vegas. Now have fun in there. I've got stuff to do out here."

There was little trace of desert heat inside Boulder Dam's turbine hall. I wondered how many people looked at the gleaming generators and polished walls and saw the commitment and endurance that had saved them from rust and ruin. A few large flags hung from the ceiling, but where older photos showed the striped and star-flecked banner of the United States of America, the colours of the Four Deserts Confederacy were unfurled there now. How many people aside from you cried over the end of that myth? Even the dam's name had been changed long ago, to strip one more unearned honour from an imperialist colonizer. Would you, I wondered, salute the ghost of Herbert Hoover?

At least I was at peace inside the turbine hall. It reflected the boxed-in world I'd grown up with, without that vast and daunting sky, and felt like hallowed ground. How many generations of technicians had worked here, changing out worn components for fresh and cleaning away grime, so that millions of people they'd never meet could live another day?

I stayed there as long as I could, basking in its example, until they ushered us back under the sky. That was when I saw you for the third time, leaning against the walkway's chest-high wall and facing the lake behind the dam, as Wiseacre ran up and leaped onto my shoulder.

"Our friend's been busy." Given the choice between looking at turbines and being the centre of attention outside, it was no wonder Wiseacre hadn't gone down into the dam with me. "Screaming at the sky by those green angel things like someone was dead. People were taking pictures. I tried to calm things down, but one cat can only do so much."

I winced. The two sculpted angel-sentries that guarded the western entrance to the dam flanked a towering flagpole that flew the Four Deserts' colours now. Was that blasphemy for a Yorktowner, a knife in the heart, or both? The idea of gawkers only made it worse: *Hey everyone*, the echoes said, *come look at the ridiculous habber.*

I figured you were having a hard time, gazing down at the long fall to the water below, and I couldn't stand back and watch it happen. Habbers have to look out for each other, to keep ourselves and our worlds from falling apart. That goes double on Earth.

"Hey," I said. "Are you okay?"

You looked at me first with surprise—the accent, I figured, with few Saturnians on Earth—then with a controlled face that tried to hide everything beneath. It might've worked if not for the whole "screaming at flags" thing.

"You're a long way from home," you said.

"No more than you. But I guess you don't think of it like that."

"This *should* be home, dammit!" You gestured at the weathered pink rock, the wide blue sky, and the penned-in lake behind the dam. "My ancestors built this place, and now they've been erased."

"You think they should get more respect, then? Some recognition for building all this?" I gestured at the dam, to the shallow lake where there had once been a canyon, and toward the baking remnants of Las Vegas.

"Yes!" You punched the dam, hard and solid, and there was a true believer's certainty blazing in your eyes. I'd seen Yorktowners approach that during arguments a billion kilometres from Earth. Here, it was the sort of fire that burned everything down.

"Is that really something to be proud of?"

You gaped at me, open-mouthed, trying to decide whether I was a fool or a blasphemer or something else entirely. Too many Yorktowners approached their American legacy like divine commandments while ignoring the facts on the ground. After a few seconds, you turned back toward the reservoir.

"Look at that," you said. "All that water. What do you think it'd feel like to dive in?"

Wiseacre leaped onto the wall in front of you and started purring. Cats were great distractions. "Probably hard and cold for an instant," I said, "and then you'd never feel anything again."

You wiped sweat off your forehead, and I mirrored it. The sun had only been up for a couple of hours and the heat was approaching the danger zone.

"It shouldn't have been like this," you said after a long moment.

"A lot shouldn't have been," I said. "It's all right to mourn a story. They're always softer than reality."

You pressed your head against the wall. "What was it all for?"

"When people write a story to make themselves feel better, sometimes they don't care who they overwrite along the way," I said. "Sometimes they forget there are plenty of storytellers."

I offered you a flask filled with seven moons still writing their own stories. Wiseacre gave me a sharp look but said nothing. An offering in the desert was as meaningful as an offering to the desert: maybe even more so, letting a little more of its own precious water flow on.

"So why'd you come here, then? To gawk at the ruins?" Your eyes burned into me like lasers. "You don't know what it's like."

I closed my eyes, and instead of desert wind I heard the emergency klaxons again, shrieking and wailing a tale of catastrophic environmental failure. Instead of sand and grit and life enduring, I smelled the sour stink of a vacsuit worn for six days straight and tasted the freeze-dried blood of a habitat split like edamame.

"I'm from Steelwall City," I said, and your eyes went wide and deep. It was rare to meet a survivor; there were so few of us. "I know."

Five years were enough to dull emotions so that they wouldn't cut, but habbers knew that even butter knives could kill. Habbers understood what it meant for an entire city to die choking in the darkness between orbits. Even the desert's cruelest strikes were kind by comparison.

"I'm so sorry," you said. "I can't…"

"I'm here to understand how to keep living when the world wants you dead," I said. "Maybe we could both use some understanding."

"How do you mean?"

"Water," I said. "You look parched."

In the desert, water was a boon worth any myth. The flask was smooth and cool in my grip. I waited to see if you'd take it.

Once Called California

Enotea

1. Hatches in a Wet Cave

Crack. Shell-breaker. Sparkling mud in gurgling caves. Deep down far under dry land once called California. Dripping wet way-paver. She opens eyes. Faint embryonic cries. Slithering damp moist in spittle drool saliva echoes with plastered slimy scales on glassy greased oily toes for slippery joint muscles try out. Damp moist in spittle drool saliva echoes with plastered slimy scales. Plastered slimy scales on glassy greased oily toes for slippery joint muscles try out. Slithering damp moist in spittle drool saliva echoes plastered slimy scales on glassy greased oily toes for slippery joint muscles try out. Tiny pools of water on her back. Tiny pools of dripping water reflections on her scaly greased oily slippery back. Tiny pools of dripping water for joint muscles try out. No later than immediately, she smells in the fungal cavern air her own mortality. The life ahead. Surf church. Tactile organ pump. Timeworn wheels of dogma always already on new lands grinding.

2. Infant Movements

In sprawling space of upper cave system, she begins to move. She runsh. She jumpsh. She slithersh. She spinsh. She's dizzied with freedom of movement. Hollow caves tower. Black wet stone. Black wet stone. Walls move too. Dancing for her, showing something to her. Shadows of her fore jangle in the dark wet corners of black moist stone with glistening minerals that are eyes of past evolutions trembling in awe of the primordial drive of New. She seesh. Other beings. Metal in stone. Ages past and distant civilizations. Plucked strings and nimble wood clacking. Symphonies of insecurities. She crawlsh on glassy greased oily toes and reachesh a ledge and readiesh a jump. Insects make way for her. Jumble cave life scramble to see what next. She swingsh her tail in spangled circles of slimy light flashes. Moist fall through gleam in hitherto unknown symbols. The air drops its weight and goes simpler. She catchesh breathsh. Counts down drops of soak falling on ledge across the empty space of her infancy. She jumpsh. She sailsh through the air. Damp water dripple hang still-paused in space. She is fly. Slow motion proud. She landsh on stone embodied. Findsh light cascading down black wet walls from somewhere else. There is above. One of infinite tunnels illuminated with the promise of daylight. It tells her to move. Up. Out of caves.

3. In Her First Sun

Rays lift grains of sand above scorching desert floor. They coagulate in radiant heat and become flickering mirrors of the world. They gain weight when glass and fall back in the dunes as orbs and flakes bright melt. Naturally occurring diamonds of dry. This place was called Zzyzx. Zzyzx. Very last word of humans in the ages. Now, burning noon air rolls like ocean waves and swell with distortion. Mirages in the orbs. Solid sandy floors. Glass furnace. Shine pushes down upon the land like gravity. Bones are floured. Dust is burned. Where once were drops, only dry salt is left. Even dry salt. Blown away with wind on barren stones. Lonely cries of against all odds still-alives. Even cries are distorted and prolonged on the event horizon of heat hallucinations. Zzyzx. Dry viola loop. Animal calls. No ideas. Shell-broken in the wet caves under this place once called California.

4. Onto Vast Open Spaces

Electricity. Currents in the heat. Magnetic crunch gyrates whirl-drone beats from somewhere off revolving. Wind turned swept. She mountsh a dune with strain. Bye Zzyzx. Coil winds dry her plastered slimy scales. She seesh. Electric storms move past on far out titanic plains. Limitless oversize. So immense she feelsh falling. Onto vast open spaces. She slidesh dizzy down dune, far down falling low toward cracked rock-hard terrain, the fissure cracked territory once called California. She is onto now. No back way-paving. Electric storms move past on far out titanic plains closer. Charred cluster clouds of pull slip burned above this glass furnace. Down here spun sounds. Endless voices in the wind turned swept. Ghost of humans past trapped in barren landscape for atonement. No left or right, only charred clouds atop eternal dunes. Giant nothing. She lands on rock like dropped. Okay. Magnetic drone beats again in drummed ear that catches dust crunch. Cricket beasts and power harmonies break off in charged currents. Wind turned swept. Time-voices turn into crooked curvatures of twist warp. Twist warp to one-tone sirens of infinity. She treksh forward in arid long line. What else. Polished phantasm drones of deception. Trust not bend metal tuning to sirens. Trust not bend visions of green. Trust not magnetic skies. Glassy greased oily toes in sand burn dried.

5. Reaches an Oasis

Excited twine and chaffs of jade spring forth in emerald abundance. From dry to damp in sensory vivid. She arrivesh under juniper crowns, her glassy greased oily toes soft on grass carpets and wildflowers. Avocado chollas and lime olives ripe and sprung. Hung yuccas and dense waterfellers make her body go back replenished. Celadon pears, rich malachite pistachios and screwbean mesquites. Elders feast in the Mid Hills. Strumming youth dance under alluvial fans by the Salt Marshes. She jumpsh and wagsh, mesophylls the water-flesh acids. Soil health. Poppyflies and cream viridian in hypnotic leisure next to racing daisies and deep filaments of meditation. Firebugs crouching on long arched asparagus stalks drip tiny pools of milky mint on her scaly back. Teal and a thousand tongues talking at once. Lives uttered and tales traded in another green world, where the oldest living things live in creosote rings. Chords up, chords down, catch everything never once, so give up and give in, ghosts do not reach. Night break and lunar layback cast cold, refreshing blanket of space on asylum. Violas light-mark the pathways to the Underground Pools and to the Ash Meadows at dusk, where lemma pods whorl the dew into tufts for all sleepy things. Ripened ovary florets and bract succulents bow for the cool night shade. Deep sleep breath calls into calyxed culm. Pacific honey drops linger. Rest on epiphyllum slippers her glassy greased oily toes now wet once yet. And lullabies in softer lands. Love abides in softer lands. Love is with the living.

6. Breeds At The Underground Pools

First thing she hearsh, as she descends beneath the oasis, are wet echoes of water dripping on dark stone. Reminds her of Zzyzx, way back birthplace. Then. Peculiar shapes and shadowy blobs come into vision. Rhodamine dyes the farther pools fluorescent red, slow glow illuminate reveal thousands of mating beings on bedrock. Spongy tufas, arthropods and millipedes in dry repeating. Selenite shawls veil the orgies, but hoarse mating calls and hesitant hushed cries tell her caves are deeper than she sees. Moonmilk. Inter-species breeding and violent secrets. Aeolian limestones pierce the ceiling, hanging like killing. Water makes weird. Lonely cries of mid-life. No more fantasies. Orgies of wetness. Slow glow fluorescence fade, all goes back to gloom. Fine glass orgasm. Silence between. Death is watching life and gives it energy. Birth spirits soar around the cave ceilings like metal disks. Plunge pool swirlhole whirls downward spiral, many levels deep under dry land once called California. She peaks over edge. Leucophors, the colorless water tracers, fluoresce blue. Reveal. Water-fat relict species of cryptozoas, colonizers of caves, in hollow runnels deep down been here ages. Rulers of resource, cave pearls and crystal pools. Karstic privilege and salamander soft living. Comfortably crystalline. In the tafoni cavity, a tegu moves on clay soil, catches her from behind. Halite fornication. Rimstone breeding. Calcite blowholes. Dolomite silence. Water makes weird. Her fine glass orgasm rings out with the thousand others. Mid-life.

7. Hunts Through Time

Sun rise on shades of palm. Cool winds dawn. Finely grained tactile organ pump for morning rituals wind the world up. Desert life awaken. Shine warm on skins and small teiids open eyes. Slithering damp moist in nests of rock. Morning hungry squeaks and squishy peeps. Proud mother. Shine reminds her that time is to hunt and wait is death. Slithering damp moist belly and plastered slimy scales over dry desert floors. Dune rabbit moves on sands remote. She glimpsesh. She pouncesh. She runsh. Faster quicker nearer. Dune rabbit turns head to see her. It runsh. She runsh. Faster quicker nearer. Her vision pierces empty spaces of dust and sand, her mother eyes lock on prey. She must feed. She must runsh faster quicker nearer faster quicker nearer faster quicker nearer. Sound of glassy greased oily toes trampling stomping running hard faster quicker nearer on sandy desert floor make rhythm then faster rhythm, quicker nearer faster rhythm. A mirror breaks her ran through invisible, shatters in billions of fractal pieces scattered up and around in glass furnace and slow downs faster quicker nearer. She breaksh through. Breakthroughsh. She runsh backwards in time. She runsh all the hers before. She runsh all the teiids ever ran. All the teiids ever prey. All the teiids ever feed across hard desert floors. She is all that ever ran. All that will ever run. Mirages in the orbs. Past and futures in flakes of bright melt. A mirror breaks in billions of fractal pieces and scatters time in the glass furnace. Faster quicker nearer. Portals to the past. She sees. Pink Tulip Trees. There used to be cities. Bipeds on gravel.

8. In Upper Paleolithic

Something is different now. Now. Now is different. Now is a different time. Ancient but fresh. Archaic but new. A time out of time. She is on a cliff plateau. A whiter, calmer sun shine on down land. Not angry. Not scorching. Caves behind her hold paintings. Someone lives here. Someone summoned her. The plateau extends out over vast valleys, where mammoths form vernal pools with the weight of feet wallowing in the grasslands and coastal prairies someday to be called California. Strange birds crease lapis lazuli skies. The dune rabbit is dead in front of her, the white fur on its neck stained by the dull and brownie red of her bite. Blood on ancient stone. She was brought by the biped by the pillar ledge. A white sun is setting, a papaya fire is burning. Bipeds are singing in Upper Paleolithic. Bipeds are singing in Upper Paleolithic. Summoned to unveil for the bipeds of curiosity. Mycological prayers and passed knowledge. Dusk shines on cave paintings of grazers, browsers, scavengers and prey. Archetypes return. Mantles are passing. Amniotes bite own tail to tip of tongue for the bipod chanting. They see what she seesh, they see what she has seen. Glass furnaces. Magnetic skies. Zzyzx. Winds turned swept. Horns of eternity. Soft steel tick-tocks at time's crossing. The low rumble of unsolved symbols, changing the timbre of all else. Now the Mother, the mystic. Jungles extend far beneath and smells soil ripe and unspoiled.

9. Dreams of Electricity and Ice

Electricity crackles and falls onto spacetime as elemental balls, then electrifies and shoots like thunder upwards, crackles and forms metal balls that fall back down onto spacetime, then electrifies and races up in lightning, crackles and falls onto spacetime as metallic balls, becomes thunder that crackles then collapses into matter balls, then shakes like metal and falls onto spacetime breaking like ice, shakes then breaks like ice, shakes then falls under spacetime like ice broken, down into under spacetime, shakes becomes breaking of ice, electric movements under spacetime then rapid ice breaking then moving slower and slower under spacetime, then ice breaking under spacetime, slow break sounds of ice cracking and breaking under spacetime, where the excess of math, discorded and random, hovers.

10. Expires in the Highlands

When she awakesh, thick rain and thunder shower the rocks and turn them deep in color. Last vibrant smells of fresh desert rain. Hummingbirds. Cicadas. She liftsh old body off cold stony floor, moves old lizard head gazing out cave emerita. Electric storms move past on far out titanic plains, far down under rocky highlands she dwellsh atop. Retired high. Deathrock. Somewhere down in hard shine lands once called California, her daughters are hunting. She will see them again. She will be shadows of their fore jangling in the dark wet corners of black moist stone. She crawlsh out of dwelling. Dusty belly scratching red wet clay, her glassy greased oily toes old and wrinkly. Her weary scales wet. Rain imbues youth one last time. Bird eggs in rock nests, but hunger has left. She crawlsh toward white high rocks. Zzyzx but a dream. She is weary. She breathsh deep and slowing. A life lived. Surf church. Timeworn wheels of dogma always already on new lands grinding. Timeworn wheels of dogma always already on new lands grinding to a halt as old age shatters all, like the bolt to the rock. She stopsh. Her breath cannot carry her any extra. She turnsh moist in grass uplands. Electric storms move past down on far out titanic plains. Breath slowsh down, slowsh her mind down, slowsh all down. Magnetic skies. Thunder and rain roar in her ears, then break into fractal harmonies. Slowing down. Rasping breath expiresh her body. Slowing down. Insects and humming birds. Slowing down. Slowing down. Thunder in the distance.

The Objects

Yuri Herrera
translated by Lisa Dillman

Every night Rafa stares at the vestibule in hatred until those in line protest. Then he crosses it and is transformed.

But sometimes, no matter how much we pressure him, he keeps staring at the vestibule as though his scowl could destroy it. Last night before entering he turned to me and said:

"I can't stand it."

I know, we all know. But Rafa, he can't adjust.

I pointed to one of my ears and said:

"Wait for me on the other side."

He entered the vestibule. I closed those eyes, while I still had them, and followed: a fleeting gelatinousness, a flash of disintegration. Then I emerged from the building transformed into a rat. The moment I felt Rafa-louse jump onto my ear I started to run before anyone from the upper offices appeared transformed into a dog or cat. And because that's how I cope. Run, run, run, scurry along pipes, climb walls, inhabit my new body by running. Then eat. That's what we come out for. I let Rafa feed off of me, but I myself search for food scraps discarded who knows when or by whom. Detritus. Delicacy. When you're a pestilent creature the world is no longer pestilent.

After that I start greeting the others. So to speak. I say, inwardly, when I bump into another scourge, "That you, so-and-so? Looking good today, so-and-so." And I laugh. Inwardly. After crossing the vestibule a rat is a rat is a rat, even if at times it's still capable of people-reasoning.

Then I go back to ratting. Rats can't concentrate on anything.

After that I sleep (that's what we go out for) in a basement warmed by a mechanical afterthrum. This time I dreamt sounds: footsteps on upper floors, eyes shutting with a snap. There are no words in rat dreams, only residues of lives you more or less remember.

"What do you think the higher-ups are transformed into?" Rafa asked. "What other *thing* could they be?"

I say nothing. Rafa says one day he's going to go up and find out. We already know those right above us are transformed into cats and dogs. I imagine those at the very top are transformed into lions or elephants. Or sharks. Maybe when they emerge from their vestibule crystal-clear pools await and they swim all night and then cross back at dawn. From below all we can see are enormous balconies.

Dawn. Before returning to the building I climb a desiccated tree or a pile of debris to watch the day dawn. I sprawl snout-out in the sun and watch it rise as it warms my claws. Today for a moment I remembered why day used to be called *all the blessed day*. Then I went back to the building to spend all the dark day at work until it was time to cross the vestibule once more.

I didn't see Rafa when I got back. Not the first time it's happened. He's often so anxious to stop being a louse that as soon as he crosses back he immediately dons his work coveralls so he can be a person as long as possible. Regardless he'll have to undress and go through the vestibule again sooner or later (even those who manage to do double shifts have to sleep and eat occasionally).

At breaktime I went to find him. On the floor immediately above they gave me a scornful look, perhaps because they've owed me a raise for quite some time, to squirrel at the very least. Still, I asked if anyone had seen him. No one replied. Until I said loudly:

"Ask you to speak and you won't speak, as though you had the option whenever you wanted."

Then one of them stood up to me, said:

"Maybe you haven't heard, but despite our best efforts to prevent it, the building is falling down, there's less and less space so who knows—maybe they wouldn't let your little friend back in."

He was smiling. Smiling a lips-only smile. Like the animal he was outside, perhaps.

I couldn't find Rafa.

At the end of the day, when everyone started heading to the vestibules, I went upstairs again, not to the next floor up this time but higher and higher: more and more stairs, emptier and emptier. For the last few flights I saw no one at all, and the top floor was equally deserted.

There were no guards, only a frosty solitude like a giant sign saying I shouldn't be there. I walked through increasingly dim storerooms. And then I thought I heard something, a click, a clack, one hollow sound and then another. So I said:

"Rafa."

I don't know why. Or I do. Because it was the one remaining possibility, if he hadn't stayed outside. That he was there, among the carnivores.

The sounds were crystal clear now, coming from a storeroom where finally light could be seen coming in from behind the door closing it off.

I opened it and saw not a soul. *And saw not a soul.* Only an ocean of objects in silence. Suddenly I heard the clack I'd heard before and, from the corner of my eye, saw one of them fall, pushed from the other side of the vestibule: an armchair or a pane of glass or a hatchet, doesn't matter. Another object, in from outside, and then, on one side of the vestibule, Rafa, crouched down, head between his thighs, waiting for the moment to start his new job and push the bosses out of the building.

Crepuscular

Tessa Fontaine

I never knew there were mothers who slept in beds. All tucked in, apparently, wearing pajamas or sipping tea, mothers who peed in the pot at night and slid their worried faces into the open bedroom doors of their sleeping children to make sure all was well, and all would be well.

Mine was not this sort. My mother and I lived in a small wooden cottage at the top of a golden hill, right at the tree line. The trees were redwoods, biggest in the world, so big they made their own damp world where the fog they drank and light they blocked cast perfect shadows for the sword fern below, azalea and salamander, for the shy deer and elusive fox and all manner of other creatures for whom the wide, open world was just too much.

We were half in that world, and half in the world it broke open into, where the edges of the redwood groves gave way to hills of grasslands, scattered with the occasional oak or madrone trees, but mostly wide open and covered in grasses that remained dead and gold for most of the year. Here, the rattlesnakes sunned and blue-bellied lizards scuttered about in huge colonies, hawks caught hare and the creatures of the sun and wide-open spaces thrived.

This was where we lived, my mother and I, right on the break between these two worlds. We ate well from the land and water and sky and drank cool clean water. We gathered beautiful items for our cabin, bones and feathers and moss, and carved tools from the abundant life all around. I was vaguely aware of another way that others lived, but it didn't much concern me when I was young. We worried about one thing only: the beast who also lived between these worlds.

I didn't go to the kind of school I'd later learn most kids went to. Instead, in the crepuscular hours, we set out into the deep woods or open hills, the veil of lilac dawn thinning as the sun pressed against the morning fog, or returning as evening arrived. My mother taught me how to identify tracks and evidence of past kills so I could keep count of who was around, but we also discussed the unfortunate politics of Dr. Seuss, and the awakening in Kate Chopin, and steel drum melodies of her favorite musicians. In other words, I received a proper education. And as we walked and gathered and hunted, we were always keeping an eye out for signs of the beast.

Sightings of the beast were extremely rare. In fact, I'd never seen her. She was elusive, hardly glimpsed, my mother explained. She had a nose that could smell prey a mile away. A voice that could imitate the sounds of many other creatures, calling them to her. Teeth that themselves could sense when her prey was alive or dead and would keep it at the precipice. We would always know when we'd come across something she'd killed, my mother would say, by a bite at the base of the skull. That, and how she stored it, half in the earth. Once we saw a deer carcass, bloodied head opened at the back, and body half-buried in the dirt as if it were falling backwards into a lake.

It was our duty to keep watch of the beast. To avoid her, of course, since she could kill us dead, but also to know where she'd been and what she'd killed. It was what we kept track of every day. To keep us safe, my mother kept an axe strapped to her back. We would never use it except for the direst circumstance, my mother said, but I felt safe, when I was small and would glimpse its metal pressed against my protector, and I'd slide my hand into hers, feeling the thin golden rings she wore on her fingers, spinning them around when she'd let me, the golden rings like the golden sun's halo above the endless roundness of the golden hills. I felt good, and also a little scared all the time, a little on guard, watching, paying attention, and this, my mother said, was exactly how to be.

In the evenings, my mother made notes in a small book to keep track of the beast, and then tucked the book into a wooden box which she locked each night before she locked me into my room. I was never quite sure what she was writing in the book, since we found only the rarest indications of the beast.

We lived like this, frost on the yellowed grasses on winter mornings, the blazing midday sun cracking the dried dirt on summer afternoons. I was small and then as tall as the sage bush and then long enough to climb over the fallen redwood trees and then big enough to wake in the night and hear the creaking wooden floor boards and sneak to the sliver of space beneath my locked bedroom door that let me peer into the dark room beyond and still my hammering heart and watch my mother, each night, head out into the darkness.

I knew what she was doing, even though I would never ask her. She had a duty to track the beast, even at night. I knew, too, to never startle her in those moments. It was one of the oldest lessons. To surprise an armed woman was the quickest way to become prey yourself. I had to remain locked in, and quiet. It was my only rule. Once we were inside our cottage at dark, I could not leave. I could not go outside my room.

And so fallen redwood trunks sprouted new ringed growth and waves of orange poppy's bloomed and died again and again and we lived. I was content, and a little afraid. As it should be.

But as I grew, and would stay awake longer into the night after I'd been locked alone in my room, I listened more carefully to my mother leave and then to the hoots and screams and chirps and groans of the nighttime world, straining for signs of the beast, and then, for anything at all. Occasionally, on nights when I thought I'd go mad from captivity, I did hear something thrilling. It was the sound of claws against wood, scraping. I shivered in terror and pleasure, to be so close to the unseen threat.

I was as tall as my mother by then, with strong, lean limbs and quick reflexes, like her in many ways though I would never have told her this one small truth: I was lonely. I cherished her teachings and company, but there were long dark hours of the night when she was gone and all I could do was imagine where she was, how she was tracking the beast. And then I'd imagine what else I would see at night, more like us, perhaps, also walking through the darkness to complete the tasks that they were meant to complete. And thinking this, my stomach would expand with a kind of ache I hadn't known before, not hunger, not pain, but a certain kind of longing that grew in size the more I thought about it.

One night, after we returned from our crepuscular twilight walk, and she was preparing to leave while I was readying for yet another night in my room, I asked if I could come with her. She did not respond. I asked again, louder this time, and she spun quickly to me, shoved me back into my bedroom and locked the door. You are not ready, she called from the other side, her golden rings tinging as she hit the door.

I seethed, but did not talk back. The next night, I asked again, and again my mother had the same response. Same on the third night. But by then, I'd already made up my mind.

I waited until she had been gone for some time, and then took the knife I'd stashed and used it to break the lock on my room. Our house was dark except for a faint moonlit glow, but I was surprised by a familiar shadow by the front door. It was the axe my mother always carried on her back. For some reason, she hadn't brought it with her even though what she was undertaking at night was the most dangerous tracking and record-keeping of all. She must have forgotten it, I figured, with a mild panic rising inside, imagining the beast's nostrils flaring from miles away, its voice calling to her. I strapped the axe to my back, shoved a few supplies into my coat pocket, and went out into the night.

Though I was accustomed to our twilight walks and the purple-blue sky, I was unprepared for the depth of dark that night brought with it. I wanted to walk quickly to get the axe to my mother as soon as possible, but I did not know the ways to move through the darkness with confidence. I stumbled and tripped. I went slow. But I went on, trying to sense where my mother might be, feeling the weight of the axe compelling me forward. I walked until I shivered and my shoulders ached. The moon was just a thin smile. I walked and walked, and then I heard her voice.

It was coming from the small valley between the hill I walked and the next. It was her voice, laughing. Or crying out. I wasn't sure which. I hurried, needing to get her the axe as soon as possible, needing to know what was causing her to make these sounds. I was excited and afraid.

I stumbled down into the valley, moving quickly, the moonlight casting just enough light to see the shadow of a body against the dirt. I came closer still, and called out to her. At that, the shadow turned and began coming toward me. I pulled the flashlight from my pocket and clicked it on, prepared to hug my mother, prepared to slap her for her recklessness, but, you might have guessed this by now, the shadowed figure coming toward me was not my mother. It was the beast.

She walked on all fours, her fur a deep tan, her ears back low against her head. She was enormous, her shoulders as tall as my own, her bared teeth each as long as my hand. My mother had described to me the sharpness of her claws and length of her tail, but I had never fully imagined her as she was: a giant mountain lion, queen of forest and hills. And covering her face, dripping down her chin and onto her paws, was blood.

I unharnessed the axe, my heart almost exploding, for I heard once again the cry of my mother, and knew, with perfect clarity, that she must lay just where the beast had been feeding, her head bleeding open from a bite at the base of the skull, her body half-buried in the earth. I had to save her. I had to kill the beast.

The axe trembled in my hand. The beast approached. She sniffed the air, and walked forward, head low, muscled limbs and back rippling with each step. I yelled at her to stop, to hold still, held the axe above my head to make myself look larger, as I'd been taught to do by my mother, but still she came closer. The blood had seeped into the fur around her mouth, and she licked her long tongue, taking in the juice. My flashlight then began to flicker—we hardly used it—but I heard, clear as a hawk, my mother's voice calling again, yelling out *stop*. That was the last push I needed. I dropped the flashlight and charged at the beast, swinging the axe from above my head and bearing down upon the lion. The strangest thing happened as I ran at her. She did not turn to flee. She did not rear up on her hind legs to fight. I braced for a blow but no blow came. The last thing I noticed, just before the blade sunk into her neck, was a glint of light down low.

Her body collapsed onto the ground, limp. The axe stuck halfway out of the beast's neck. I did not stop to check whether she was fully dead—rather, I ran as fast as I could, down to the shadow on the ground where the beast had been feasting, to save my mother. But when I crouched low, I found, bloodied and mangled, skull busted open, half-buried in the earth, a doe. It was not my mother.

I turned slowly around. Lying halfway up the rise was the beast. Still, on the ground. I approached the beast slowly, then. The air was as cold as I'd ever felt it, the wind making a racket in the trees but I could hear only my hammering heart. I gave the beast a wide berth as I walked around her. Blood pooled on the dry earth. Out from her neck stuck the axe handle. And when I reached the front of her body, I saw what had made the glint of low light just as I'd charged at her. Upon the thick clawed toes of her front paws, the beast wore golden rings.

I fell to the ground, right beside her. I could neither scream nor gasp. I wiped blood splatter from my face, and found there, too, tears. My mother had been leaving each night not to track the beast, but to become her.

I sat by her side through the night, holding onto the slimmest hope that she would change back, and in so doing, awaken. But the body of the beast did not twitch or transform, and through the long hours of the night, I sat beside what I had done.

When the dawn's crepuscular hour arrived, I noticed we were close to the boundary of the redwood forest, that I had slain my mother in the place we loved best, between the two worlds. I waited still until the sun was higher to see if, somehow, she would return to her human form and come back to life, though I knew it was a foolish, childish desire. She did not. I pulled the gold rings from her paws, surprised by how easily they came, and slipped them onto my own fingers. I ran the pads of my thumb over her sharp, bloodied teeth, telling her how sorry I was.

I did not want other animals to have her body before I was ready, and so I knew what must be done. I rose and found a flat rock to sharpen. Then, I began the difficult work of peeling her pelt away from the flesh. It took all day and into the next night, big as she was. I cut sinew from muscle, went slow and careful at the joints and small bones, meticulous so I would not nick the tender fur. All the while, as I worked, I looked down at my legs and my arms, watching to see if I too would transform. If her death meant whatever she was would pass to me. But my fingers remained hairless, my arms thin and brown. I did not have my mother's gift.

By the next crepuscular hour, as darkness took the earth, I had completed my task. I draped her pelt across my shoulders and let the rest of the animals have her flesh. Already the vultures were circling. I knew they would begin with her eyes.

Back at the cabin, I lay her skin out to dry. With the knife I'd used to break out of my room, I opened the box where she kept the notebook into which she recorded her observations about the beast. I had to satiate my curiosity. If she was the beast, what had she been recording in the notebook all these years?

Inside was a ledger of sorts, organized by date. *Two condor pairs, jackrabbit family beneath the holly on buckeye ridge, nine banana slugs but not recent rain.* It was an accounting of how many of what species we saw evidence of each day. Beneath the lists, on some days, was what looked to be a plan. *Three nests of broken blue jay eggs in a row, correct for boom in raccoons.* It recorded what animal needed to be kept in check. She had been planning her kills. But in between these kinds of entries were those of a different sort entirely. *Daughter appears distracted today,* one entry read, *told her story about how the beast's teeth know when the flesh is alive or dead. Daughter is lonely. Scraped claws against her window at night to gift her fear.*

She had been keeping a record of how to raise me right, with enough questions and fear and excitement about the beast that my life was shaped by purpose and meaning. It had been a gift.

I remained in our cottage, living out my days much as I always had, though they had a dullness to them I'd never before felt. I knew some of this was from missing my mother. But there was more to it, too. Without the ever-present threat of the beast lurking unseen and ripe with potential devastation, the days felt easy and I was prone to distraction. I did not have to pay attention in the way I once had. I did not have the skill to hunt the animals whose populations needed to be balanced, nor the interest. Even the thrill of watching my own body to see if I too would become the beast grew tiresome. I had killed my mother before she taught me how to become my own beast.

This is how I have come to the place where I now live, to the place where you might have seen me. Just as a flash, probably, a shadow, a prickle on the back of your neck. I left the place between forest and hills, which became too lonely. I've come to the city, your city, where I can watch mothers in their nighties, peeing in pots in the moonlight, looking in at the twitching faces of their sleeping children. In the crepuscular hours, I drape my mother's pelt over my body and slink into their yards. I hardly let them see me, these mothers, these children. Sometimes I hear them talking about how the mountain lions have started coming down into their cities, about human overpopulation and habitat loss, and I smile at how little they know. Sometimes I snatch their dog or cat to help them with their own awakening, so that they too might feel something big. When I see one who is particularly bored, or deeply lonely, I will do something special for them. While they are sinking into the brutality of the mundane, I offer them a new gift. I remove their child. I eliminate their confused, wandering old mothers. Then, they have something truly special, truly enlivening. I wear the heft of my mother and, as she'd done for me, offer these mothers the pleasure of panic under the vast night sky.

Kafka-san and the Happiness Machine

Karen An-hwei Lee

Dear Max—

Is there any invention
as a happiness machine?

With our modern cures for polio
and pox, even the plague, tuberculosis—

are we still happy, as you say, in unhappiness?
When we toss our bitter shreds of tragedy
and neurotic civilization into one gullet,

out of the chute
slides a packet, no, a fragrant satchel of happiness—
dried lavender from the field,
sun-perfumed grass
or strawberries

while the happiness machine,
a sentinel cat or a vendor of knick-knacks,

abolishes the woes of urbanity
in our living room. The day curtains are open.

Max, I can hear your voice, a prayer—
Es war nur ein schöner Traum.
Only a beautiful dream.

LITTLE URCHINS, SAYS Kafka-san, opening the door to his room. Bedraggled rough-skinned urchins arrive in the night and stand outside my sill, hungry-eyed street urchins in Los Angeles, anonymous starved urchins clothed in rags of Amerikan industrial cotton woven in nameless typhoon-blown factories overseas. The typhoons are named while the urchins are not. Ida. Noel. Olga. Sebastien. Katia. Otto. Claudette. Do we have any rolls or buns I can give them when they show up at nine o'clock each night?

What urchins, Mister Kafka?
Wide-eyed, famished little urchins.
Where are they, exactly?
Under the street light.
Where else?
Hungry on street corners.
And?
Outside my door.
How many, would you say?
One night, only two. Other nights, hundreds.
Urchins as in children?

Yes, malnourished urchins who roam at night, scavenging for scraps in the dumpsters, the alleys, and gutters. My chafed epiglottis and perforated ulcers burn to witness their ravenous grief at such a tender age.

Mister Kafka, did the mice ever return?
Not mice, Miss K. Urchins.
Yes, Mister Kafka.
What about mice?
Do you suffer from insomnia, Mister Kafka?
Yes, terribly, from insomnia.
Are all eyes on you?
Yes, paranoia, yes.
Mister Kafka, the urchins are symptoms.

No, Miss K.
I'm sorry, Mister Kafka.
Miss K.
You're welcome to ring the operator for a sleeping aid, Mister Kafka.
A sleeping aid?
Sleeping pills from the concierge or a white noise machine.
White noise!
Sea waves. Foehn wind in the trees. Or an airplane.
How big is the machine?
Only a box.
Like a radio?
Yes, a radio.

White noise box. *Kästchen*. Box. The whistling of a storm arising, of hundred-page insurance reports when an angry supervisor tears into a file right in front of you—white noise. Sound of milk of magnesia poured into a chilled glass after midnight when one cannot sleep. White noise. The hush of a moonbeam on the first day of winter, the solstice. And the days lengthen thereafter. Or the sound of calamine lotion massaged into a mosquito bite on a boy's arm. Mine. What would we name this? *Weißes rauschen*. White noise, the transitory foam of existence vanishing into an ever-widening spiral of history, a clogged sink vortex in the universal goose-neck drain, with God uttering your name at the other end, holy broom of light cleansing us of dark matter and everything mortal whispering my name, Kafka.

KAFKA AND THE STRAWBERRIES

Dear Max—
Remember the old postcard
I sent you from Berlin?
I wrote,
The difference is this: in Paris,
one is cheated—here one cheats.

So ironic at twenty-seven!

And now this happiness,
a cup of strawberry-leaf tea,

an offering of ripe berries, yes,
erdbeeren, Max—
    even in December

with a light blancmange
at a café. Over this
                I forgive you, Max
for printing my works,
    not burning them.

Max, a fragrance
of peace rises from here
                to Tel Aviv.

Shalom—peace among us.
Adieu.

ONLY FOUR OF the wasabi chocolates, *omiyage* gift from Kafka-san, are left: a humming chartreuse quartet robed with plumes, lattices, and dots, marbleized and garnished with mini-rosettes. Kafka reaches over the decoratively S-shaped, gold ogee-adorned table in the hotel lobby. Orange blossom and wasabi, he says, enrobed in dark chocolate. His fine-boned hand, light as a sandalwood fan, does not melt the chocolate. He cradles it tenderly, then carries it to his nose as though sniffing a prize truffle dug out of a German forest's loamy wilderness, a Pfifferlinge. Gold chanterelle. Sumptuous champignons of the meadows or a sumptuous panoply of mushrooms in the Black Forest.

Tell me, Miss K.
Mister Kafka?
What else has our rapscallion, Max, printed?
Of your works, you mean?
Asked him to burn everything.
Don't worry, Mister Kafka.
He acted against my dying wishes.
Isn't it true that Max Brod told you otherwise?
I was so ill. Dying.
I thought you forgave him?
He didn't listen.
What are you going to do?
Hire an Amerikan lawyer!
About Max, I mean?
What about old Max?
He is dead, Mister Kafka.
Silence.
I'm sorry, Mister Kafka.
Silence.
I apologize.
Silence.
He lives on, Mister Kafka.
Silence.

WOULD YOU BE interested in taking a course on Kafka Studies?

Yes.

What aspects of Kafka Studies interest you? A. Actuarial Ants B. Bohemian Ballads C. Canned Coffee D. Dueling Data Analysts E. All of the above F. None of the above. All of the above. *On a scale of 1 to 5, with 5 the lowest and 1 the highest, please rank your interest in Kafka Studies.* Three. *Would you prefer A. K-cup B. Bottle of Bureaucracy C. Cake of Streuselkuchen?* None of the above, if possible. *Optional questions. This information is confidential and used only for information-gathering purposes. What is your age?* Not yet forty. *Male or Female?* Female. *Marital Status?* Single. *Race, ethnic-*

ity, nationality? American-born Japanese, Nisei. *Why are you interested in taking a course on Kafka Studies? A. All of the above. B. None of the above.*

Did Kafka ever write a love story? A. Yes B. No C. Maybe D. Depends on how love is defined E. All of the above F. None of the above G. Other–please comment. Kafka had liaisons with various women, ending with Dora, but I don't know whether he would consider those true loves or otherwise. In his works, I mean. To the extent that his work is fictionalized autobiography, that is, in an allegorical sense, about his domineering father, for instance. What he could not bemoan in life, I mean, rather than resorting to rose-colored fantasy, he personified elegantly in allegorical prose. Which is not responding to the question about love at all. *On a scale of 1 to 5, with 5 the highest and 1 the lowest, please rank the similarity between the Japanese language and German.* Three, I suppose. All the consonants are pronounced in Japanese, as they are in German. The same is mostly true for Spanish, however. And the vowels in Spanish and Japanese are sisters, too. *Arigatou gozaimasu*, for instance. *Muchas gracias. Danke schön.* Thank you. *If Kafka were a perfume, would you describe him as A. Actuarial B. Bookish C. Comedic D. Doctor of Law E. All of the above F. None of the above G. Other–please comment.* What is an actuarial scent or comic fragrance? I find these descriptive terms irrelevant to a question about Kafka, but there is no response box where I may type an original narrative reply.

Prague doesn't let go.

A recurring dream in the hotel, Kafka says to me, derives from one or the other, namely, either from the oval-shaped pills with a single groove dispensed by the concierge or the abhorrent Los Angeles toxic smog. Or the caramel-colored boba drink with spongy tapioca balls I ordered yesterday. Or the curious air in the elevator ride to the nineteenth floor, which seems to expand and shrink noiselessly as it passes each floor. In the foul dream, my father, the giant Hermann, picks me up sideways as though I am a freshwater trout and throws me in a lake. Swim! Swim! My father commands in German and in Czech, his brawny, hirsute arms in the sky. His shadow is longer than our house at four in the afternoon, and I am chilled to the bone, a skinny boy, reedy as a cattail, naked arms flayed and thrashing about in the water where. There. Is. No. Lake. Bottom. Drowning. The cold dark swell of water closes over my head and pushes me down, the pendular weight of my body drawn by gravity to the murkiness where no lake bottom exists, nothing underfoot, only stairlessness. I open my mouth. My lungs fill with water. My mouth opens. Drowning. I cannot see my father. Roaring in my ears, the world enfolds it petals overhead. I cannot see my mother. My eyes and nostrils and my mouth are open and my lungs are closed, two broken peony blossoms crying for breath, none. Zero.

When I wake, I see the rented sallow light from another hotel falling through the window of this one. Into my room. Where I was sleeping, my bed is soaked with cold sweat. A glass of water I keep on the bedside spilled on the clothes. What a mess. Yet transparent. The hotel carpet. And the liles and cyclamen, cut aslant as I like them to be, swilling, as I say. Drinking without motive or desire, purely free of will. Then I realize, my interpreter, Miss K, told me those are cyclamen. She did not buy cyclamen, she says. Mysteriously, only lilies. When I spoke the word, *cyclamen*, the flowers appeared. My interpreter echoed me, *cyclamen*. Upon a closer examination, I see the lilies for what they are, true lilies. The cyclamen, in fact, are streaked coral-colored tulips in the night.

Tulips, I say, grateful for tulips.

Mister Kafka, your nightmare was real.

What do you mean?

I mean, your father threw you into a lake.

Did I drown?

No, you learned to swim.

I could swim?

In fact, you mastered swimming. An excellent swimmer. You even rowed well.

A great outdoorsman!

You rode horses, too.

I swam, rowed, and rode.
You did not consider yourself a great outdoorsman, however.
I undersold myself.
Silence.
Miss K.
Think on the beauty of streaked tulips, Mister Kafka.
Lilies and cyclamen, you said.
Tulips, you see.
Tulips, yes.

WINTER, HE SAYS.

No, Mister Kafka. Winter rarely means snow in southern California. At least, not in the decade I've lived here. I grew up in a place of snows, but it has never snowed. Once in a blue moon, one might say. Only once in a blue moon.

How does the winter announce itself, then?

In late November to early December, the afternoon darkens after four-thirty, and the street lights come on. One by one, in the distance, in the sloping estates and hills, the coastal brushfire homes of millionaires, their Spanish-style ranches and villas, their arch-terraced stucco mansions perched on the creosote beach bluffs, alight. One wears a sleeved watered silk dress, even a rayon scarf. A vest. Nothing like a double-breasted wool overcoat, though, although some wear parkas in the late year.

How does one feel about the year, so long without seasons?

We do have seasons with nuanced transitions. Four of them, like the rest of the world. Or like Prague, I should say. Berlin. Paris. Rome. Beijing. Tokyo. Seoul. The changes from season to season, however, are subtle. The days lengthen, the rains are more frequent, and one feels the rain, more chill, in the bones. Not the rare summer rains, though. No fires in the hills, no creosote ignited by a dropped cigarette. Winter comes quietly without snow.

How does one mark time in the course of a year without seasons?
There is a subtle change, Mister Kafka.
Does the smog abate in winter?

Only slightly, mixing after a cold rain. It sends the ash and aerosols back to earth. *Aki no koe* colors of insects in the air, autumn's voices above the Japanese red maple and the walnut tree, are brighter. Vivid. The sparring hummingbirds fly sharper and livelier in the eucalyptus grove. Whether they migrate elsewhere to winter in a warmer climate, I do not know, but fewer hummingbirds are seen warring in my yard than in the summer.

Does one ever long for a real winter of snows?

METAMORPHOSIS OF SATSUMA ORANGES IN SNOW

4 egg whites
1/4 cup sugar
1 cup orange juice
2 cup lemon juice
1 envelope gelatin
satsuma oranges, sliced
salt to taste

Boil orange juice and gelatin.
Remove from heat. A chilled bowl –
Add 2 T. sugar and lemon juice. Stir.
Beat egg whites, folding in sugar
until stiff peaks form. Fold whites
into orange juice and gelatin.

Serve with satsuma oranges, sliced.
Metamorphosis or *metapoetical*,
says Kafka, an observation, not
a question. Or neither, *nein*.

TOWARDS THE END of the fourth day, I invite Kafka on an outing to a local parfumerie near Pico, hoping the aromatherapy will soothe his nerves, rankled after his encounter with the two film*Menschen*. Perhaps it will heal my psoriasis as well as any neurosis, adds Kafka, as we cross at the intersection.

You don't have dandruff, I say to Kafka-san.

Dander or none, I am a hypochondriac, he replies. Won't heal my psoriasis, maybe anesthetize my ulcers and loosen the stubborn entrails. As he says these words, however, he is smiling. Kakfa is curious about the parfumerie, neither an apothecary nor an opium den nor a nocturnal bordello of ill-repute, rather, a vendor-laboratory devoted to the olfactory sense, and looks forward to naming his own fragrance therein, as I promised.

With a ringing of hand-tuned Tibetan chimes, the tiniest of bronze coins, bells, cymbals, we enter. Hundreds of essential oils and extracts wait in vials with eye-droppers, bottles with glass corks, flasks and mixing bowls await us on sanded pine shelves. The boutique reeks of heady vanilla musk, linseed oil, dew-grass accents, cinnamon, balsam fir. Rose oil and salt clay. Yes, I would love to design my own perfume, says Kafka-san. What essences shall we choose? *Ach*, the vigor of a scent as it swirls out of a vase to pervade a room, spiraling, unfolding, diffusing the intoxicating notes of a lyric aroma. What about the odor of a bookshop in Prague, the toasted melancholy of aged paper in a leather-bound journal, a touch of brown sugar, and a dash of—what is this bright, mingling scent—ylang ylang or ginger and this, only for the name, *patchouli*. And what is patchouli? Kafka rotates the vial on its side to read a label, where an employee has written in a succinct cursive—*mint or basil but not either. Patchouli is patchouli*. This will do, he says.

Top notes: Ginger.
Heart: Patchouli.
Base: Rose and almond oil.

How will you name it?
After me, I suppose.
Kafka?
Kafkaesque.
Kafka's Arabesque?
No, Kafkaesque.
Kafka-san?

Soundlessly, Kafka leans over to pick up a glass atomizer, exhales on the unlabeled surface, and lifts the bottle up to my face. I take a careful look. Etched on the fogged glass is a poem, "A Short Autobiography of Perfume."

I was a flash-fire in darkness.
I was glacial phlox.
I was ambergris in a whale's belly,
a bone-spear,
kilos of roses distilled in Asia Minor
                roiling in copper florentines,
a fixative washed ashore—
not an otolith, not ear wax of whales.
I say to ethers and esters—
not yet the skin of a vanilla bean
or red tears of migrant workers.
Not a cuttlefish
  sliced for birds to take home.
Not stolen blood of pines.
Not amber. Not even beeswax
where I survived
as sea-light, as fuel,

pollen oils of *rosa centifolia,*
                    your stark rooms of musk,
your lavender on the waved mile,
your edible field on an ear,
your covalency of desire
   sung and decanted, my love.

I look away, then glance at the bottle again. Inexplicably, my girlhood in New England arises in the early morning mist as I rode my bicycle to flute lessons a mile away. In this day and age, a child would never be safe riding such a distance alone, unchaperoned by a relative. On the way to my flute lesson, I would pass a creek, a field of tall bright grasses edged with gold dandelion turf, and roadside vendors of peaches. I was told to ride my bicycle straight to the flute lesson and back home, not stopping for anything, in particular, dogs and strangers. I only stopped once, when I fell on the dirt road by my house after a rainstorm. The name of the fragrance in the air after the rain, *petrichor*. On my left knee, to this day, a dime-sized scar marks the place where I bled.

The poem, with the fog, has vanished.

KAFKA AND A BEAUTIFUL NUMBER OF EXILES

Dear Max—
In exile for twelve months of the year—
In exile from a ramekin of berries and cream.
In exile from the Germanic mother tongue.
In exile from an Italian briefcase of insurance.
In exile from women named Felice or Dora.
In exile from the sanatorium near Vienna.
In exile from from the frailness of my body.
In exile from posthumous reviews of my work.
In exile from anagrams of metamorphosis.
In exile from ash scattered over a vase of lilies.
In exile from my ursine father in moonlight.

In exile from the parfumerie of ylang ylang.
In exile from light-and-air cottages.
                    In exile from exile,
dear friend, house me in aromatic fumes,
the unbottled flames of our memories.

ON SUNDAY, NEITHER the *shibboleth* nor the *Sabbath*, doused with the patchouli fragrance named after himself, Kafka-san meets again with the film director and film producer, whom he has dubbed Mann No. 1 and Mann No. 2, two doppelgängers. Mann No. 1 desires more *edge* in the film. Mann No. 1 and Mann No. 2 are silhouettes, no, mere puppets whose images are sliced from an old-fashioned kinetoscope. One whispers *sotto voce* as the other nose-whistles, *wheeeee*, his coat-hanger shoulders casting a Sierra range on the rear wall. Their words, syllable on syllable, brush each other, cindery tall grasses in burning in a high desert wind. No eyes in the shadows. What sort of edge? Edge as in edge, says Mann No. 2, shrugging. Mann No. 1 says, edge we would see in, for illustration, avant-garde film noir. What sort of genre do you mean, says Kafka. Mann No. 2 replies, the same we see in film noir nowadays. Can you give me an example, says Kafka. Mann No. 1 says, you see, film noir must still offer the mystery, the man with an aadvark under a street light with a trench coat, the ravishing linzer-torte dame in distress as an undercover cop, the private eye dective with an armadillo, all that bizarro business.

Kafka scratches his chin.
The work demands an edge.
What sort of edge?
Razor-sharp. A rhinoceros in love.
Here we go again.
How about we write this for you.
Nein. I don't like it one bit.
Why not?
This is not my original novella.

Mister Kafka.
A rhinoceros is not in the novel.
In love. A blind rhinoceros.
No, no.
Audiences love a tale of love.
I asked Max to burn everything.
So you agree to the rhinoceros.
No, no.
Mister Kafka.
Nein. Please.
A screeplay, if you will.
No more *spiel*.

Kafka stands up before the faux granite executive desk and pushes his clenched fists down. *Nein*. Gentlemen. I did not write this *schlock*. Never finished any of my novels while I was alive. You cannot insist I finish this work, and you cannot force me to adapt it into a screenplay. Film noir, horseradish, avant-garde. Nothing I ever wrote, I tell you. How absurd. Rhinoceros or not, love or not, I am not the author. I do not even know whether I am the Kafka you say I am, whether biologically engineered from a finger-bone illegally excavated from a grave in Prague or a hologram designed from one of my photographs. My rose-colored, pseudo-memory-bank is assembled from biographies and letters and translations. What sort of absurdity for one who should've been long forgotten, and everything burned—journals, books, letters, diaries, postcards—summoned to complete unfinished work from one's lifetime? Absolutely punitive. Penal. Don't threaten me with attorneys. I'm already one, representing myself, a Doctor of Law from the university in Prague.

Mann No. 1 sniffs the air.
What is that? asks Mann No. 2.
What are you talking about?
That perfume, a gingery scent.
Oh, it's Kafka-san.

Where did you get it?

At the parfumerie near Pico.

What's in it?

A secret.

Sold there, you said.

I designed it myself.

How Kafkaesque of you.

Not at all Kafkaesque.

Kafkesque, indeed.

ENGINE IDLING AS I roll down the window to greet Kafka-san, who furiously pushes the revolving door of the Wilshire tower, I gently ask how he communicates with the film director and film producer, since they do not speak German, Czech, or French, and I know Kafka does not speak much English. How do you converse, may I ask, if my interpreting skills are absent in this situation? Wouldn't one assume I was hired—not only as a local guide, but to serve as an interpreter for your professional interactions?

We just argue.

Then you understand each other.

Not at all, says Kafka.

Do you have an interpreter?

You are my only one.

Machine translation?

If they created me from a hologram, why not.

I am sorry, Mister Kafka.

When parts of the work make no sense, Mann No. 2 inputs those into the machine.

Nonsense.

If I say, *this is not my novel*, Mann No. 1 and Mann No. 2 say, rhinoceros this, rhinoceros that.

What is the title back-translated into German?

Nashorn der liebt.

Rhinoceros who loves.
Why not a rhinoceros in love?

On the drive back to the hotel, Kafka-san sulks, fists balled, unbuttoned cuffs awry. Mister Kafka, I say. Mister Kafka. Finally, he grouses, where is a good bowl of borscht to be found in Los Angeles? Real borscht, he continues, the original borscht, out of the dark root cellar, with a soup bone, a head of cabbage, whole onions, and beet leaves. How does one explain what one expects from a good bowl of borscht, not this watered-down Amerikan beet-broth? What is the essence of borscht, the ruddy hue of root-blood? Not even an adept interpreter like you can translate this into English, graced with a sprig of cilantro, with sour cream and chives, the rich borscht of my childhood for an ever-suffering mother's ills. Yes, give me borscht and not a rhinoceros.

What does a rhinoceros do when it's in love?
Kafka-san shakes his head.

I wonder. Does it snort like a boar, stomp its hooves like a herd of cattle? Horses? Does it wallow in the mud, aflame with infernal fusillades of insect-bites and miserable skin rash, or go for a swim in the shade, under willow trees? Or rub its backside on a paper-bark acacia? How does a rhinoceros tolerate the neap tide of desire, season to season, conceiving in love, abandoning in winter? Or vice versa? Why do we call this love, in any case? Does a rhinoceros even love? Sniffing the rough-seeded grassland, rumbling along on the ground, mumbling with the stones, attentive to the earth in a rugged, brutish way, vigilant, rattling a string of cans pulled by children. I pity the rhinoceros who must live alone in a zoo, shy of its own image in the water trough, without another rhinoceros in sight, flicking its hairless tail to and fro with bristles on the end, the only hair on its tough hide. A stalwart warrior, I imagine, on the savannah. Why not a rhinoceros in love?

In all of Bohemia . . .
Silence.

No *schtick* is this absurd.
No good borscht, sir.

Kafka-san *kvetches. Feh,* my hair. Where is a good barber to be found in Amerika? *Ach,* never mind. Barbers give me the willies, so to speak, all that clipping and shaving and mad scissoring, although I could use a good haircut.

Barbers uses buzzers nowadays.
Buzz, echoes Kafka, is for bumblebees.

And then he remarks, *origami,* I heard children say, *origami,* on the street. *The art of Japanese paper-folding.* And one folds paper for what reason? *For the sake of artistry. Or for ceremonial reasons. Letters. Weddings.* What does one fold? *Origami paper.* Into what? *Boxes, birds, persimmons, lilies.* Rhinoceros? *Yes, it takes nineteen folds.* Why does one do this? *Why does one create art? Ach,* why does one create hunger? *Ask your hunger artist.* Did I write about hungry artists? *Yes, a short story.* Yes, I remember this now. *Hunger artist.* Never a rhinoceros if one existed, see.

THE SILICATE LUNG of Los Angeles caresses its denizens with fly-flecked mannequin dust, parched blue ozone, and a billion industrial tons of jeweled diamond grit, a wry incandescence. On South Figueroa, as we make a left onto Pico, a wisp of hazel wool loosens from Kafka's sweater. With dexterous fingers, and blinking rapidly under a shadow, he tugs. The yarn unravels until it is the length of his arm. *Don't tug,* I say to Kafka-san. *You'll unravel the entire sweater.* A nimbus cloud passes over the sun momentarily, and I glance up. Kafka looks, too. It's a dirigible. Silver with *uber*-lettering for an *uber*-advertisement.

What does it say? asks Kafka.
I squint up. Count Ferdinand von Zeppelin.
Is that all?
Zeppelin.

The blimp vanishes over a hedge of cubical pillars, totemic stones at noon, alive with sky-beams at night, on L.A. Live Way. This avenue used to be called Cherry Street, I say, like clafoutis desserts or blossoming trees. Cherries, *die Kirschen*. As Kafka-san tugs on the loose yarn, the breeze turns chilly in the daylight. Winter is the tiny hazel skein wrapped around Kafka's index finger, a loose end of memory from his childhood, the bullying shadow of his father, maybe, reprimanding him for this very gesture. Kafka folds his arms and looks down at his non-flapper shoes as he walks. The two-toned mortar pavement is uneven. Why doesn't the city of Los Angeles fix these crooked slabs, he muses aloud. Ash-laden in unison, the ghastly Angeleno freeways take on the voice of his father. *Halt! Halt!* shrieking in the chicken-wire tunnel between five-star skyscraper hotels, up the cul-de-sac limousine driveways, beyond the thundering sports arena, over the pasteboard cafés on the first floor of the lodgings serving pekoe tea at eight in the morning and four in the afternoon. *Hör auf mit dem Radau!*

Kafka-san stops. Leans over, ties a knot on the loose end of the yarn, then winds the rest of its length into a tight sphere. Next, with a pair of nail scissors I loaned him, Kafka neatly snips the hazel ball from its leading yarn and drops it inside his trousers pocket. A memento, says Kafka, of my trip to Los Angeles. Perhaps, like this dirigible, the zeppelin that passed overhead, this ball of yarn will grow enough to send a prophetic message over the city. CLEAN UP YOUR ACT. THIS IS AIR-MAGEDDON. Kafka stops mid-stride and chuckles mischievously. On second thought, I would never write that.

Julio Cortázar, I say.
Who?
Argentinian writer.
Would he write this?
More or less.
Why?
Hot-air balloons or zeppelins...
Where is he now?
In my library.

Where does he live?
Buried in Paris.

A RESISTANCE SONG OF ZEPPELINS FOR JULIO

Helium rebels join the global Occupy movement.

On this planet, at this very minute—a thousand men
and women in exile release balloons filled with poems,
or poems are taped to balloons as they float over us.

As the balloons pop, syllables in nebulae of gas

drift over onlookers who read aloud the words
until they sail out of sight.

The balloons take poems wherever they go,

dropping at the mercy of hail or lightening.
The radius of each balloon is lineated in stanzas.

We imagine balloons rising over barricades
as poems flutter out of a foggy Manhattan noon.
Midnight in Paris, a vending machine

sells books for francs. *Le livre à toute heure!*
Baudelaire, Celan, and Valéry have no inkling
their labors are sold by automated vendors.

I covet a book-machine for my living room
and a portable wax museum or diving bell,
variations on an iron-cast balloon.

Ars poetica slams through Avocado Heights,
shouting our cloud-based voxels around the clock
as silver pixels hum *occupy* over the world.

When we open our windows, molecules of air
wander from a fleshy durian
on a floating river market in Bangkok,
        not quite making it to this zone
in time

for balloons.

A summer monsoon carries the odor of durian,
                                        turpentine and onions.
Desiring solitude on a beach at Racha Noi in Phuket,
a woman writes the word, *soledad*, while reading
to fishermen in the Andaman Sea.

The word is *globo*
for balloon.

My name
in the light is

Soledad.

KAFKA-SAN MEETS ME for tea and cakes at three o'clock in the hotel lobby, which serves partly as a café, a lounge, a sky-walk, and a restaurant. He orders a cup of strawberry black tea, and I order green with an acai berry infusion. We do not order cakes. Since Kafka-san asked about Japanese origami earlier, I unwrap a cellophaned envelope of origami paper—in gold-leaf, silver, hand-painted designs of red flowers and solid-colored ones, turquoise, vermilion, and canary—and a booklet—a chapbook, rather, of step-by-step folding instructions. We spread out the squares of origami paper on the table, and Kafka chooses the turquoise one to start. Fold the Japanese crane you described, he says. Please.

Crease the square and open.
Kafka folds the square and opens.
Now crease it the other way.
Kafka folds it the other way.

Now you have an open square with creases going one way, then the other.

Kafka studies the booklet. Which one is point A?
Don't skip ahead.
What next?
Rotate the square like this.
Kafka rotates the square.
Now fold point A to point B.
How does one know which is which?
It doesn't matter in this case.
Kafka folds point A to B.

Well, in this case, you need to fold so the colored side is up.
Kafka opens the triangle and reverse-folds it.
Now unfold the triangle and push up so the edges collapse inward.
Kafka puts the triangle down. How does one get from this to a bird?
We haven't even created the bird-base yet.
What does that look like?
A diamond with hidden folds inside.
An envelope?
Not quite. An elongated diamond with flaps in the center.
Could one send a letter?
Since the flaps do not overlap, it's not an envelope.

Kafka-san puts the origami square face-down, open it along every single crease, and starts pacing the lobby, agitated. Not easy, since the vestible is thronged by conference attendees. What sort of art is this? *You, of all writers, understand why this is art. Perhaps origami is a metaphor for writing absurd short fiction.* That's far-fetched, says Kafka. Sentimental, besides. *Pause.* Where are these strangers coming from? *Those are conference participants. International digital humanities, something or other.* Do I ever recall attending conferences while I was alive? *Perhaps a colloquium or symposium here or there at the university. Or on insurance-related matters. Actuarial policies. You did read your work aloud in various settings, but not too frequently.*

Yes. Now I recall.
Save your origami for November.
Why is that?
Shichi-go-san.

KAFKA ON SHICHI-GO-SAN DAY

Dear Max—
If only I were born a child in J-town!
Seven-five-three
sporting a *haori* or *kimono*
and my hair no longer shaven.
Prime numbers at ages 3, 5, or 7.
Long rods of thousand-year candy
adorned with cranes
for longevity
to bless the flute-boned bird I am.

SHOULDER TO SHOULDER, this is Los Angeles, says Kafka-san.

Stranger to stranger, shoulder to shoulder. As you walk down the street, a loose brown yarn strays in the wind, shoulder to shoulder with ash under a coralline sky, neither sunrise nor dusk, shoulder to shoulder with an invisible wind-tunnel in the daylight. A faded carnation lies on the sidewalk, trodden underfoot by pesticide-shod masses, ash to ash. Shoulder to shoulder with a pick-pocket who, by some unmeditated act of grace, passes over you. Does not pick your pocket. You look him in the eye, a lean ruffian not unlike yourself. The two of you pass over one another, shadow to shadow in broad daylight, a form of grace. Thieves turn away from you. There is nothing in your pockets, after all, except a mentholated lozenge from a dish in the hotel. Neither do you say anything to strangers. Why, then, this act of grace from you to this stranger in Los Angeles, or vice versa? He does not mistake you for a street peddlar, a wealthy one, or an impoverished one. Neither does he mistake you for a bedazzled scribe with a four o-clock shadow, *braun* sweater on, avoiding eye contact with the masses, hoping not to be recognized.

On the contrary, you are Kafka-san. Only the image of the late Kafka. No one recognizes you in Los Angeles. This is the grace you receive out of a divine mystery of the universe. No one tears you to shreds in Los Angeles for strumming the lyre of your surreal allegories. Only your father tore you to shreds in Prague. Yes, except for Mister Mann, Hermann, the father. *Der Vater, der Vater*. In Berlin, no one tore you to shreds, as the Furies did to Orpheus. If only one could call this act of writing a form of prayer, of forgiveness, of blissful divine communion. Playing this earthly psalm unworthy of angelic consideration, you remain anonymous and ever yours, in the devoted hands of the only maestro of the universe, and strangers, genuinely yours, on this solo lute string, Kafka-san.

WHERE ARE THE graveyards? asks Kafka. Underneath the sprawling, petrol-drenched city avenues? Underground necropolis, with sacks of potatoes, beets, and rutabaga? Near wine cellars, or coffins deeper still, miles below fermenting vintages? Inside the hospitals? Only crematoriums? Housed within morgues? Where does one bury the dead in this forsaken valley? Where does one seek and worship God? Where are the synagogues and churches? Where are the mausoleums? All I see on the sidewalks are brassy stars inlaid with mica-flecked granite. Are the dead here? Where are the sanitoriums? Do you bury the dead at sea? Do you scatter the ashes in the fire-hills? Do you keep them together or apart from the sanatoriums? If tuberculosis is eradicated, how many years is the life expectancy? How old is a man before he closes his eyes one last time? How many days can one outlive the fresh-cut bouquets of carnations and alstromeria and double-flowered roses endlessly pouring in and out of sick rooms? Has anyone discovered the *aqua vitae*, water of life?

In this advanced civilization where tuberculosis is forgotten, where the highest mortality rates are from diseases like congenital heart failure, cancer, then vehicular accidents, not kidney stones or bird pneumonia or scarlet fever, what does one do with the gift of longevity? Does one squander the multitudinous hours to finish all the novels one ever started? What does one's labor mean when the bread-job ends and the years of retirement commence? Do the extended years automatically turn golden? Or is there only the vantage of hindsight silvered with age? Is everything on our backs destroyed—irrevocably burned—to the last exhalation, or does incorruptible treasure of our souls persist in the dust, ruined yet salvageable in the dried-blood ash? As the Torah says, *I remember the days of old, I meditate on all Your works; I meditate on the work of Your hands. I spread forth my hands to you. My soul thirsts for you, like a parched land. Selah.*

KAFKA-SAN TURNS ON the tap in the bathroom. *I thirst.*

Where does this running water come from? Origins? Clean but not fresh like good mineral water. A metal tang of chlorine. Rust. Oxidized iron. Cold, but not of a glacial high-altitude spring. The water in Los Angeles is not good. How does one escape the micro-layer of ash over every surface in the city? Why don't the wealthy clean up the smog? When will we invent an automobile without depositing an aerosol garbage heap in the stratosphere? This is like the smoky coal factories of the worst European cities. No, it is worse, black lung disease under the auspices of efficiency, of modern civilization at its most decrepit. One is not buried but rather, cremated alive. Burning desert lung, pulmonary alveolar microlithiasis, you say. Ash to ash with chlorofluorocarbons inhaled on an hourly basis, the irksome microscopic particles of airborne death, the inheritance of your tuberculosis-free civilization.

Mister Kafka, sir.
Nothing I said has moved you?
Always a fresh-air fanatic.
I was, wasn't I?
Angeleno air improved in the last decade.
I wasn't alive.
Underground water, Mister Kafka.
I wouldn't drink it.
Aquifers.
And what if I said they'd well up with your tears?
Not much of a crybaby, Mister Kafka.
Never?
I rarely weep.
How unusual for a female, Miss K.
As a schoolgirl, my inventory results said I was *cerebral.*
Are you saying female logician-philosophers don't weep?
Not a logician-philosopher, sir.

I HOLD UP a souvenir-gift: For you, Mister Kafka.

A Japanese origami crane, two inches by two inches.
He takes it cautiously, turning it around.
Mit Dankbarkeit. With gratitude.

The Last Genuine Cowboy

Katie Carmer

On the only occasion we spoke, Fargo Kesey told me he bet I could throw a rock pretty far, even if I didn't look like it.

I regarded his faded jeans, his western shirt and cracked boots. Later, I remembered him wearing spurs, but upon further reflection I decided I only wished he had. I know with certainty that he wore a Stetson that cast a shadow over his tan, wrinkled face.

I don't know what compelled me to drive three hours south to a jazz festival in a one-stoplight desert town. I don't know what drew Fargo there, either. He was sitting alone in the sparsely populated front row, under the blazing late May sun. I took a seat on his left, leaving one empty chair between us. As I glanced at him out of the corner of my eye, I tried to guess his age. His shirt draped over stooped shoulders, but his mouth was set into a firm, sure line.

As the band on stage finished their set, a train rumbled in from the distance, rattling the coffee mugs and trinkets for sale at the art fair adjacent to the seating area. It was difficult to think through noise like that.

When the train whistle faded to a faraway whine, Fargo turned his head slightly.

"Nice music, ain't it?"

I looked over my shoulder, thinking he must be speaking to someone behind me, but there was no one there.

"Yes, it is."

He finally turned to look straight at me. His brown eyes were cloudy with cataracts.

"I had a boss once who liked jazz. Mean fellow with a sharp tongue. But give him a drink, play him a Coltrane record, and he turned soft as a lamb."

He regarded me silently for a long moment before continuing.

"That boss almost got me killed. Sent me out alone with a head of cattle, even though he knew a storm was coming in. I prayed to God all night. I don't fear God, miss, but I feared that storm."

For a moment, I wondered if I had met this man before, such was the familiarity with which he spoke. But I was sure I would have remembered someone like him.

"When was that storm?" I asked.

"Must have been '53. Back when I was young and good looking, if you believe there ever was such a time."

He turned his head away from me again and launched into the story of that summer. He spoke to the empty space two feet in front of him, keeping his eyes locked on that spot. I leaned in to hear, occasionally interjecting a question. Sometimes, all I could make out was a hoarse mumble, but I pieced together his memories of scorching cattle drives, hard labor, and cantina music.

He seemed happy to talk, happy to sit in the park and remember. I learned that Fargo was now in his late eighties and that he had spent his early adulthood driving cattle on horseback in New Mexico and Texas. He'd weathered storms and broken fingers, he'd eaten heartily and slept deeply, and he'd seen the world change—slowly at first, then rapidly. Did it feel like being chased, or left behind? He didn't know. Both, he supposed.

I looked around, expecting to see a caretaker lingering near him—the person who had brought him here, and would take him away to some nameless, faceless home. But he was alone, this frail man full of stories. The way they poured out of him, I imagined two alternatives: either he repeated the same memories every day, to everyone and no one, or he hadn't told them in years, and he spoke with the fluidity of a man who knows he must put his stories into the world before he leaves it.

When the conversation ended, I had the urge to kiss him on the cheek. I didn't, though. I thanked him, stood up, and wondered what it would have been to live in Fargo's world. I felt a sudden longing to step into a sepia-toned version of the scene in front of me: the old movie theater, advertising a showing of *Casablanca*; the storefronts with their hand painted wood signs; and in the distance, those bare purple mountains rising above the desert floor.

I blinked. The world was still too bright, too loud. I knew my soft brown-and-white fantasy wasn't as dreamy as it seemed. When we romanticize about the past, we forget to include the injustices, the diseases, the backward traditions that would make life at that time more painful than not. I knew this, and yet I sensed that there was some magic in Fargo's past that had nearly faded from the world.

An echo pulled me gently back to the present. I realized Fargo was speaking to me, his parting words:

"Be good, make 'em happy, but don't let 'em tell you what to do."

When I turned around to face the park again, Fargo Kesey was gone.

I WISH FARGO would have just told me what to do—how to live a life as full and large as his—but that wasn't his way. He talked straight, but not in straight lines.

Once in a while, I meet a man in the second half of his life who reminds me of Fargo, who speaks in the same language of stories and subtle jokes. One is my neighbor; another walks his white-faced pit bull in the park. These men share Fargo's values and many of his hardships and pleasures, but they are of a younger generation. They are the sons of cowboys. They are retired mine workers, prison guards, and carpenters; they are midnight poets.

The cowboy philosophy that these men inherited is a progressive one. They are humanists because they have seen suffering and they have suffered. They take you at your word, as they expect you to take them at theirs. And no matter who you are, they believe you deserve what you work for. They'll give you your dollar at the end of the day, and they don't care who you sleep with.

Yes, there is a group of aging men in the west who share this philosophy, and they are the sons of cowboys, but they are not cowboys. They learned from their fathers what it means to live, and they try their best to show their own children how to do it.

Fargo Kesey is a cowboy, and he has no sons or daughters. Perhaps that is why he talked to me.

I COULD TELL you what it was like, seven years ago, to move from my soft midwestern valley to the breathless, empty desert. I could tell you what it was like to drive through the rolling hills of Iowa, the teeming feedlots of Nebraska, the phantom mountains of eastern Colorado. I could describe the way the earth cuts out and the sky swallows you up when you drive down from the plateau you didn't even know you were on. But these stories will do nothing to relate the pit that opened up in my stomach when I realized my new home—my new life—was full of jagged edges and strangers.

It wasn't that Fargo changed my mind, made me adopt a place I had worked so hard to push away. But if a man like Fargo could sit in a railroad park and offer me his earnest and rough religion, I knew I could not turn from him. So I took the cup to my lips, and I drank, and I realized that sweet wine already flowed through my veins. I understand now that it wasn't the land I hated, nor the people, nor their habits. What I hated was the uncertainty and loneliness of a particular season of my life, and in trying to cast those feelings out, I imprinted them onto the red rocks.

Now, when I look out at the Sonoran Desert, I see green. Everyone notices the saguaros, but I see the ocotillo, the cholla, the palo verde. There are secret rivers and pools where you can cool your feet and watch the wild horses drink.

There are other secrets fading fast. When the last genuine cowboy draws his last breath, some of those secrets will blow away forever on a dry wind. His unadorned wisdom, though, lives on, for he has cast its seeds across the earth with a generous hand. Perhaps it will take root in the heart of a toddler with pigtails, a young mother working the night shift, a widower who eats his dinner alone each night.

Perhaps Fargo sensed I needed a piece of that wisdom and passed it to me in the hour we spent talking. Maybe he baptized me, even as he asked the earth and sky for his last rites. Whatever happened that day—whether it was sacred or merely lucky—I don't think it matters. Meaning is ours to make.

I DROVE DOWN to the jazz festival again this spring. I sat in the railroad park next to the trinket vendors and waited for Fargo Kesey to appear next to me. He never did. Hot dogs sizzled on the grill, the jazz band played "Autumn Leaves," and Fargo did not come.

The train approached from the distance—I could see it from a mile away, crawling across the sand. The closer it came, the faster it seemed to go, until it was hurtling through the park like a hurricane. Jewelry and clocks rattled. The crescendo of the whistle—higher, sharper—it cut straight through me. In that moment of stupefying noise, I squinted through watering eyes, straining to glimpse the conductor through the locomotive window. I saw the dark outline of a man wearing a Stetson. He waved to me.

What We Tell Ourselves

Jac Jemc

Her mother had told her not to, but Mari walked to the water anyway. Mari knew better than her mother. The water was beautiful and still. She liked to watch the way even the slightest ripple would echo wide. She had always enjoyed the feeling of salt on her skin, the tackiness it left behind, the way it brought out waves in her otherwise highway-straight hair, the way her cat settled onto her lap and licked her arms when she returned home.

At the edge of the water, she left her clothes in a neat pile. They would be coated in chalk when she arrived home, but what did that matter? In the glare of the sun, no one could be sure what they saw anyway.

IN 1904, THE Alamo Canal that supplied irrigation water to the Imperial Valley crowded with silt and a new intake for the canal from the Colorado River was engineered, inexplicably without headgates, 60-feet wide. In January of 1905 though, the seasonal flooding widened the aperture to 150 feet, and then again to 2700 feet. In other words, *most* of the Colorado River flowed into the Salton Basin for two years. The Sea crept to 15 miles wide by 35 miles long before the Southern Pacific Railroad dropped in enough hoppers of rock and gravel and clay to close the breach.

The flood should have dried up, but runoff from nearby farms continued to keep the sea full.

MARI FELT THE bones and barnacles crack and shift beneath her feet. She was grateful for the calluses she refused to buff away. They meant she could live on the land. She could stand the heat. She would be safe even if more was taken from her.

The sea water felt slippery, not like the grit from the showerhead as she squeaked the soap down her arms at home. She stared out across the sea and idly ran her hands over her body beneath the surface, relearning what she already knew with the glide of the saline. When her mind had fully emptied, she let her feet rise to a float, her body an asterisk in the death that the sea had come to symbolize.

IN THE 1940S the sea became the go-to R&R destination for soldiers on leave from the Salton Sea Naval Base. Whatever could be caught in the Sea of Cortés was trucked the 140 miles overland to the desert for fishing there: tuna and grouper and snapper and lobster and squid.

In the 50s and 60s, resorts sprung up around the water. The Rat Pack flew around on speedboats, too tan, with towels slung around their necks and cigars in their mouths. Developers advertised the Salton Sea as a desert riviera, a blue-collar getaway for veterans who remembered their good times off-base as young men. Land was sold, houses built, but the speed of the municipal infrastructure never caught up. The location was remote, the low desert an inhospitable climate, too expensive and complicated to properly establish and maintain.

AND THEN: A frenzied splashing behind Mari, an arm around her waist, a hand over her mouth. There was no one else for miles that might hear, but sound carried on the playa and this man knew that.

When Mari came to, she looked at the rock walls around her and thought about how she must be far from home. The mountains were something she only ever saw in the distance. For all of her life she'd lived within sight of them, but never ventured to even the edge of one. She lived in the deep valley between two ranges. A valley so deep it was the first to erase itself with water as soon as it rained somewhere else—the rain always somewhere else, always a myth in the low in-between.

Mari was not bound. She was alone. She was naked as she had been in the water. She walked toward the light, the opening of the cave, and saw that there was no way out. All around her was sheer rock wall.

The man always arrived when Mari was asleep. There was no telling how. She imagined him as a bird transformed, alighting into the cave, and then tucking in his wings until he was the shape of a human again. She searched his features for anything beaky or beady, but he appeared to be a man like any other she knew: weathered from the hard desert life. Skin worn and tanned dark. When he visited her, he told her stories of the people who had died in the valley: people who ran out of water and food and drugs and cool, clean air. And when he told her these stories, the pangs of hunger that had fretted at her insides disappeared. She felt her bones emerging from beneath what used to be flesh, but she didn't want to eat.

IN THE 1970S, Hurricane Kathleen caused the sea level to rise. The resort towns flooded and any work to build up a thriving Riviera was abandoned.

In the 1980s, the farmers learned to use the water they were allotted more efficiently and the sea shrank.

The lake began to stink. The quantities of fertilizer in the water rose causing massive algae blooms. The sea became saltier than the ocean. Dead fish littered the shore.

In 1996, botulism infected the dying tilapia, and, in the span of four months 14,000 birds—10,000 of them pelicans—died from eating the fish. For weeks, the carcasses were burnt in incinerators 24 hours a day, in the hopes of stopping the spread of infection.

The shore slunk back and water levels plunged—sometimes as much as 6 inches in a year. The sand imported for the resort era was separated from the water by blocks of a newly formed crust of bones and shells now bleached by the sun, salt soaked, toxic to nearby residents when shattered and kicked up as dust that concealed itself in people's lungs.

MARI ASKED THE man to let her go. She missed her family and she could not keep listening to the tales he told her. She knew she would not survive. The man told her he would release her. Just like that. Like nothing at all. Like she had chosen to be there. The only condition was that she could not tell anyone where she'd been, or she would die. Mari saw no choice. She promised to keep the secret. "Why did you bring me here though?" she asked him. "And why would you make me listen to all these horrible stories?"

"We take what we can get away with," he replied. "And we give what we have."

Back home though, the only thing anyone wanted to know was where Mari had gone. All of the worry and grief they'd felt over her absence had been immediately replaced by anger and frustration that she had returned unharmed and refused to solve the mystery that had consumed them. If she couldn't explain what had been done to her, then she must be to blame. Her friends ignored her because she would not confide in them. Her mother chastised her for running away and making them spend time and energy and heartache on trying to find her. "I didn't run away," Mari said, but this did not satisfy anyone. She stared at the Missing Person posters that had been made and felt the truth of them. That person was still gone. The Mari who had returned was not the Mari in the photo. She taped the flyer to the wall of her bedroom and wished for a way she might be found. This was no way to live. She would need to tell them the truth.

FOR HUNDREDS OF thousands of years the valley had flooded and dried in a cycle. Animals inhabited it for a time and then they died off. This was nothing new.

Before the Salton Sea, Lake Cahuilla, six times the size, waned to nothing by early 1700, named by a white man with an exonym used to refer to the indigenous people who lived there, a misappropriation of the Ivilyuat word kawi'a or "master." For centuries, the Cahuilla had adapted themselves to the lake's variable shorelines and even its absence.

AND SO MARI told them. She told them about floating in the lake. She told them about being knocked out and kidnapped and held in the cave far out of reach. She told them about the way the man knew about everyone who had died in the valley and about the way he had released her and made her promise to keep his secret.

But the people did not believe her. Where was this man? Where was the cave? How did he get there? How did he bring her home? Mari was without answers and the people were now even angrier at her insistence that she was the victim in an impossible story. "Why were you in the lake to begin with?" her mother asked.

THE SEA BECOMES inhospitable to life because it is terminal. It can't stabilize because there is nowhere for it to go. It is a bottom. It is an ending. Without an outlet, the water can escape via evaporation, but everything else that arrives there—the salt and fertilizer and selenium and DDT and arsenic and the people who arrived with hope and autonomy and health—are trapped.

MARI 'S BODY WAS found in the lake, floating in the salt-rich water with the desert pupfish and the Yuma clapper rails. A hawk soared above, hunting. Farther out still, a fireball blazed across the sky.

But with the sun so bright, even meteors are invisible.

~In acknowledgement of the Salton's Sea's location on Cahuilla land and with gratitude for the legend of Tahquitz.

Canada, Maybe Even California, or Other States (Wyoming? Montana?)

Kate Bernheimer

On the way to our next location, I first wanted to stop at the nature preserve. My manager had heard of it or possibly seen it, the last time that I had performed in that state.

He told me it was in a setting like a dream I used to have about a small beach or harbor that was near a place that is hard to describe. The real nature preserve had water, ducks, and birds. I could not decide whether ducks are birds or not, so I asked my official companion. She said, "Of course they are, what a dumb question." My manager had hired her to be sure I had all that I needed. I was surprised to learn quickly that she was not very kind. Another time when I had given her a letter to mail, she had asked if first she could read it. I had said, "No?" She asked why. I said, "Because it is private?" To which she had answered, "Well, I do not trust you."

The whole situation bewildered me, but at the same time I relied on her for a great deal during my tours. I did ask my manager why he had selected a candidate for the position who did not seem to like me at all. He explained how in her application, she had noted how influential an artist I was on a new generation of performers. He shared that in her interview, she had acknowledged that she herself did not care for my "kind of performance." He said that she referred to herself as a stodgy old traditionalist, even though she was a full ten years younger than me. He assured me that she vowed this would not compromise her ability to work with me as a true professional. "We are all Annas here," she had told him. It was true we all went by the name Anna on my tours. That is my name.

MY COMPANION AND I walked toward the preserve. It was a long walk down a dark road lined with pine trees and oaks. The trees were old growth, which surprised me, as loggers had long ago emptied the mountains nearby. The companion warned me to move further away from the road. "That isn't safe!" She really thought I was an idiot, this was apparent. I got a clear sense of her annoyance at every turn. It was remarkable that she had chosen to be responsible for me in between my engagements, to have the total care of someone she deemed so stupid, and yet also acknowledged as very important. I made no claim as to my own importance—it was other people who attested to it, and what choice did I have but to go along with it somehow, even if I chose not to address that directly? It seemed to be part of the territory when one had audiences of millions. I could have argued this publicly, for it goes against my ethics to claim my own importance to others, but what good would that do for the whole operation? My manager told me over and over again that I must tour in order to continue my chosen form of expression—my video tapes. He says I cannot do the latter without doing the former, and who am I to contest this?

My companion knew nothing about the real nature of the work that I did, of course. I was not so important, I knew, and not only due to my ethics. I was the least important person in my position, but at the same time: I was the only one in it. Therein lay the conundrum. Suffice it to say that the whole operation relied on me, and me alone, and at the same time it had nothing to do with me. (It was all for the girl. But on her, I cannot go into detail right now.)

Anna nudged me toward a grassy area alongside the road. I hadn't realized I was in the road, so though it was a constant embarrassment to be corrected by her, I did sometimes have my head in the clouds. It was uphill. We realized we were already at the nature preserve. This was quite a surprise. There was more traffic at the nature preserve than we had expected. The nature preserve both was and was not secluded. To our left we saw a darker area that had some kind of hydraulic device that plummeted into the ground. The ground was contained in a space that was square or rectangular and filled with brown water. This area was something like the city water area, that place where cities keep water. But this wasn't a reservoir or even a well. The area was industrial with a lot of concrete and seemed abandoned. Water flowed into the square area which was made of metal but also concrete.

At the far end of the basin, I found a metal sign that explained a little bit about this preserve, but not a lot about it. The sign mentioned bees. "To make a prairie," I read. "It takes a clover, and one bee." Below this sentence was a black and white illustration of a clover and one bee. The parts of the clover and bee were identified: leaves, flowers, spikes, wings, stinger, eyes, etcetera.

And this brought me to the mother I once lived next door to in a small city that was more of a town. That was long before I had this assignment, but I believe the mother herself, who was also an Anna, had been preparing me for it even back then. And so it would be important to investigate my associations to that mother—associations in my own mind, that is.

I looked back to see if Anna had followed me to the clover and bee sign. She had not. I took the opportunity to follow a dirt path into a small grove of trees, even though this was a risk. She liked to have her eyes on me at all times, not only for my safety (she said) but because, as she had said prior, she did not trust me.

At last, solitude!

I was free to associate, in my own mind. So it went:

That mother had twin girls and a son. I can't remember the twin girls' names. One was Alexandra. She was so natural! The mother. She was so natural! She used to take her little rope bag and walk to the grocery store. No one did that. She'd buy like one onion. She made those wonderful German cakes. Which of course, I never ate. It wasn't allowed, for me to eat much. This was a problem, but I was not allowed to discuss it. There were a lot of rules being set in place, before I knew I would end up being entirely responsible for finding the girl. How could I know? She hadn't even disappeared yet. When this mother went out with her husband on a date, for they did that sometimes, she would wear her hair down and wear a sweet cardigan sweater. She was so old fashioned and made such a nice house for her family that was so simple! The reason I was thinking about her is because she was a beekeeper and she traveled each summer to drive a truck around and move beehives. I envied her greatly even though she tired me out but now thinking back on it, it was I who was tiring. I can still hear her voice yelling for her son, which grated on my nerves then but now I recall with affection: "Eugene! Eugene!" Constant. She was constantly yelling for him. She made him wear *leiderhosen* and she would not cut her twins' hair. Down to their waist—even way past it.

"TEN THOUSAND ACRES, was it?" Anna's voice interrupted my reverie.

I had not realized I was speaking aloud, but I engaged with her, nevertheless. "Oh, no, it was a great deal more acres."

The properties she would drive every summer, gathering hives, spanned Canada, maybe even California, or other states (Wyoming? Montana?). Vivian? Yes, Vivian.

Then just like that, we had to leave the preserve to go to the apartment. The apartment belonged to an old man. Now, when I say old, I mean old. I mean more than ninety, perhaps even one hundred. It was a lovely apartment with very small rooms, each with just-so furniture. The furniture was all from the 1940s. It was so pretty! Just one or two pieces in each room. The nice hue of wood like my grandmother's sideboard I had in my living room, which is parquet. Not the right word! Somehow, due to my reverie, I seemed to have lost lots of words. Perhaps that was the danger Anna tried to protect me from, because I needed my words to perform.

There were others in the apartment with us. They seemed to be officials of some kind. They wore uniforms like the plain clothes detectives in the books I so love. The one I was reading at that time had the peculiar title of *Her Lost Automobile*. The officials were from some sort of operation, but not one like mine.

I kept a low profile in a back room and looked in a drawer at some index cards, with images and words printed on them. One reminded me of my grandfather—it had a drawing like the black-line drawing of his face that's on his so-called "memoir"—it struck me that black-line drawings seemed to be coming back in style (bees, clover, etc). On the other side of the card appeared some handwriting to the effect of "*Saturday at 10:00 a.m., got it?*" The implication was the man who had written those words had given it to a girl, whom he was going to ask out on a date, or something much worse. I feigned that I was only mildly curious in the card, and deftly tucked it into the pocket of my trench coat. Any intrigue to do with a girl was of interest to me, and to my performance.

In the front room, everyone readied to leave. The man whose apartment this was sat in a little cubicle, like a front desk, but it wasn't right in the front, his cubicle. It was to the back of the room where a closet would be, but it was not a closet, it was his office, and it was actually at the back of the room but also in the same location as where the entrance was so in the front of it too. I found myself very bewildered by this strange little space, though at the same time I found it a comfort. Outside of the windows, I could see snow-capped mountains in the far distance. Just under the window, outside, was an enormous pine tree. In its branches was a very small nest, and in the nest were some tiny blue eggs.

The old man was at a tall desk, examining something through his glasses. He said *"Bonjour!"* in my direction. I looked over his shoulder. He had a live bee under a glass dome on his desk. There was also some clover. The bee, remarkably, spoke to the man. Clear as a bell, I could hear her:

"We bees are few."

The man and I quietly wept.

The moment was very short-lived. The others had finished their work. My companion briskly took my arm and began to drag me toward the front door with the detectives. Apparently, they would accompany us to my concert. I had no interest in a performance that night, but the only reason I had traveled to this location was to perform. I would just have to do it.

"There will be a terrific sunset behind you tonight," one of the plainclothes detectives told me in the car as we drove toward the venue.

"That's nice," I murmured.

Beside me, Anna held back a grimace. I swear I could not speak without her doing that. As I began my interior exercises to ready for what I would have to do later, the slow, poisonous realization came over me that *I* did not like *her*. Someone wise in my life had suggested to me that I "like my dislikes," and I struggled to embrace the concept at the same time as I reminded myself I was there to help others with Art.

Salt

Tara Lynn Masih

Her plan was to slip through Utah. She told me this, before leaving our small town in the Rockies. That she was on her way to meet up with an old boyfriend in Lake Tahoe. So she rented a car that would be as indistinguishable as possible, saying, I won't take one of those white SUVs they are always giving me, which scream rental. She insisted on a gray sedan. Gray, the color of dusk, not a color to catch your eye, because the ex told her Utah was dicey in places, so she should be careful. She tried to stay on I-80, avoiding truck and rest stops and any bars with less than a parking lot full of drinkers. She almost made it to the Nevada border unnoticed.

She did stop to take in the Salt Flats. *Miles of chalky white*, she scrawled on a postcard, *the residue of a long-dead body of lake water. Proof that anything can, with a small adjustment of fate and circumstance, become something entirely different from itself, yet still retain its most basic elements.* She'd underlined the last three words three times.

This landscape must have been imprinted on her mind when she finally pulled up to a roadside saloon, into a parking lot jammed with dusty Ford flatbeds and rust-specked Chevys all cater-cornered to each other. He was examining his beer in the bar light, she said, about the man who made her change course. He took her back to his farm, her rental following behind on flat valley dirt roads, his rear lights two beacons that beckoned.

You see, she told me, this man farms the fantastical. He breeds magic and the impossible. His cows produce milk that when spun turns to miles of clear silk. His chickens lay eggs that, when broken open, reveal pearls. Picture this, her voice quickens and is breathy on the phone, us on his front porch, in the evenings, cracking open green shells to remove small luminescent orbs that glow like dozens of tiny moons in his orange Pyrex bowl. Like we used to shell peas, remember?

There is more—horses whose hooves turn to copper as they age, snakes whose venom cures cancer. All this amongst weather-beaten barn boards, tumbleweed, abandoned metal equipment, Queen Anne's lace, whistles and warbles and yellow flashes of pasture meadowlarks.

How could I not stop for this? she asks me. She doesn't even remember where she was going, or why, and I don't remind her. Like those salt flats, her old life just evaporated. She lives with mystery and change every day, sleeps with a man who performs daily miracles. Strands of DNA weave through their conversations like multicolored necklaces, and lab smells mix with their sex smells.

She now knows anything is possible, and nothing should be passed by, ever again.

Somebody Is Going to Have to Pay for This

Benjamin Percy

David works for the city, the water division. He spends his days driving around Pine, Oregon, in a pumpkin-orange Chevy Astrovan. He's done the math: every day, on average, he puts a hundred and fifty miles on the odometer. That's an eight-hour day, five days a week, for the past ten years.

He clocks in at seven each morning. He drives around until ten. Then he selects a hydrant and cranks it open, letting its water rush into the street. This is called hydrant flushing, and it's necessary because rust and sediment settle at the bottom of the pipes that interlace like veins beneath the ground. He does four or five hydrants a day, and each job takes only ten minutes or so. While the water roars—thousands of gallons coming out brown, then yellow, then white, then clear—he waits in the van, reading the newspaper. He reads every page, even the classifieds. When David wrenches off the water, a hush falls over the street. The only sounds are the drip and gurgle of water, the distant blaring of car horns, and the squeak of his shoes as he returns to the van and settles his weight into it. Depending on the time, he may hunt down another hydrant, or take his lunch break, or just drive around some more.

It's a job. And at fifteen dollars an hour, it's a good one, giving him more than enough to cover the rent and pay for the Coors that runs down his throat every night when he sits in front of the TV, watching nature shows where big animals tear apart little animals.

Joe is his supervisor. He's an old guy, closing in on seventy, with a pack-a-day habit and too much weight piled on his small frame. His nose and eyelids are a mess of broken blood vessels and his cheeks permanently carry the beginnings of a white beard. For four years he's been threatening to retire. Instead he sits in his office with the blinds closed. He smokes cigarettes and reads old copies of *Field & Stream* and listens to talk radio.

Today he waves David into the fluorescent buzz of his office. David hesitates a moment, and winces. The last time he went in there was nearly six months ago. It looks much the same. Stacks of newspapers yellow in the corners. A nudie calendar, several years old, hangs from a nail. On a desk in the middle of the room there's an unfinished game of solitaire, a Yosemite snow globe, and an ashtray piled high with cigarettes.

Joe pulls out a rumpled pack of Marlboros. "Smoke?"

David shakes his head, no. He is wearing a Trail Blazers ball cap and he pulls on its brim, bringing a shadow to his face. Then he sits in a chair facing Joe and spreads his hands flat on the tops of his thighs. Out of nervousness—wondering why he is here—he drums out a song with his fingers.

Joe shakes out a cigarette for himself, lights it, and says through a cloud of smoke, "You know Johnny Franklin, right?"

He's talking about the fire chief, a broad-shouldered guy with gray mutton-chop sideburns.

"He's got a son," Joe says. "Just finished a twelve-month deployment with the Army National Guard in Iraq. Now he's back. Johnny asked me to do him a favor. I said I could help."

"You're letting me go?" David's voice comes out as a croak.

"No, no." Joe neatens the cards on the desk and smiles. "I'm giving you a partner."

David leans back in relief, and when he raises his hands their sweat leaves two gray prints on his jeans. He smiles, but the smile fails a little when he realizes that he will have to share his life with another. He feels like an only child whose parents have announced the imminent birth of a brother. "Thing is," he says, "with the work I'm doing, I don't know that I need somebody—"

Joe cuts him off. "I told him to show up at seven-thirty." Smoke tusks from his nostrils. "Should be here any minute. You'll show him the ropes for me, yeah?"

"Sure." David nods his head and mumbles through his lips. "I can do that for you."

"That's good." Joe gets up heavily from his swivel chair and they shake hands.

A BIRTHMARK OBSCURES the right side of David's face. His whole life, when he walks into a room, it seems like everybody swings around at once to give him a long stare, heavy with curiosity and disgust, the way you might look at a broken leg or a homeless man shouting at a cat.

The purple skin is raised and coarse. It looks like blood spilling down his cheek from a gash in his forehead. He walks around with his head ducked, his ball cap pulled low, trying to keep his face hidden. It's a little like being held hostage, riding in the Astrovan with the right side of his face exposed.

The man seated next to him, Stephen, has a boxy jaw and a blackish buzzcut that glistens like a wire brush. His skin is deeply tan, and his shoulders are rounded with muscle.

They've been tooling around Pine, with the radio filling the silence between them. David isn't used to talking. He is used to driving. So he answers most of Stephen's questions in an abrupt barking way, concentrating on the road before him as if this were an unfamiliar city.

"So this is it?" Stephen says, all the vowels stretched out in a Central Oregon drawl, each word a lazy sort of song, clipped off by a hard consonant. "We just drive around? Every now and then flush a hydrant?"

"Pretty much."

"Nice."

David tends to notice the ugly things about people, itemizing them in his head, creating a checklist that brings him some kind of comfort. Now he takes note of Stephen's hands. The palms are yellow and callused, the tops hairy, knotted with veins. They look like hands you might dig up in the desert, long buried.

Stephen studies David too—not so subtly.

"You ever watch any of those Dr. Phil shows?" Stephen says.

David jerks his head to look at Stephen straight on, wondering if this is the lead-up to a joke, but Stephen appears sincere, his forehead puckered with concern. "That's one of the things I missed most. TV. No TV over there. Ever since I got back, I watch everything. I can't get enough of it. Even the Food Network. Can you believe that shit? I don't even cook. The other afternoon, I'm watching that Dr. Phil show and I see somebody had the exact same deal as you. They zapped him with a laser, cleaned him right up."

David feels his hand, like something separate from him, rise to his cheek. He traces his fingers along the birthmark, shielding it partially from view. "Really?" he says in a half whisper.

"Just like that. Clean as can be." Stephen's hand polishes an imaginary spot from the air. "Like they wiped wine off a counter."

David isn't sure how to feel, until he realizes that no one has ever been so direct with him. It puts him at ease, unlike those people who look at him out of the corner of their eye, their mouths pressed into self-conscious frowns. He glances at the road just long enough to say, "Could never afford something like that," and then his eyes shyly meet Stephen's again.

"It's free. The show does it. Can you believe that shit? And hey, hope you don't mind, but you should look into it. You're not an ugly guy, you know. Under all that."

David says, "You think?" but Stephen doesn't hear him. He's talking about some guy named Cody—a first sergeant from Tennessee. "Prettiest man alive. Truly. Looked neat even in his fatigues. Anyway, one day, routine patrol, IED rips his Humvee to shit. Flames everywhere. Humvees look tough, but they burn like crazy. Thirty seconds and you're up in smoke. That's what happened to Cody. Poof. God knows how, but he ends up living. Third-degree burns—or whatever the worst degree is?—first-degree maybe. You know what I mean. The kind of burn where you can't tell muscle from skin. I went to see him in the CSH. Downtown Baghdad. Dude was fucked up. Looked like a skeleton glopped with red paint." He goes quiet for a minute, and when he speaks again, his voice comes out soft, gray-hued. "What I'm trying to say is, you got a birthmark, so fucking what? You know?" Stephen punches David in a desperately friendly way. "You know?"

David feels his mouth curl into a smile, tentatively, and he gives Stephen a tiny nod, the smallest of movements.

THE NEXT FEW weeks, things get better, not all at once, but incrementally, so that the change doesn't really register with David, like the air that slowly cools as September turns into October. He doesn't feel happy, not precisely, but he does feel something new, a sting, a want.

They drive along North Avenue to Seventy-sixth Street, to Kenwood, and up into Pharaoh Butte, where retired Californians live in three-story homes, set back in their own spaces of lawn with wraparound porches and American Beauty rose gardens surrounded by Japanese maples. River-rock pillars flank the front doors. Chandeliers hang in the entryways.

"You ever visit Saddam's palaces?" David says.

"Nah," Stephen says, as if he wishes he had, not wanting to disappoint. "Drove by one once. Real nice place."

"Yeah?"

"A regular Taj Mahal." Stephen nods at the homes sliding past their windows. "So what—lawyers, doctors—what do you think these cocksuckers do?"

"Don't know," David says. "Important stuff, I guess."

They turn around and drive along Grand Avenue to the Parkway, to Mayfair Road. They dip under a rust-stained bridge and zip past the dump, where seagulls and crows circle the pale wash of the sky. In Moccasin Hollow, a collection of trailers hidden among the pine trees, Dobermans, tethered to the ground by chains, bark when they pass. Children in soggy-bottomed diapers throw pinecones as if they were grenades. A three-legged deer leaps awkwardly across the road and they swerve to avoid it.

They know a week in advance what hydrants they will flush, and part of their job is contacting local businesses and residents, letting them know the water pressure will drop, advising them not to do laundry during this time because stirred-up rust can stain clothing. This week they're assigned to the Moccasin Hollow neighborhood. They knock on doors and talk to a bloated woman with five squalling children, a war vet with a mechanical hook attached to a putty-colored stump, an ancient man with hair growing off the end of his nose, and a big Indian who chases them off his porch with a ball-peen hammer.

"Jesus," Stephen says at the end of the day, "I hear Baghdad's nice this time of year."

TIME PASSES, AND like a couple settling into a marriage, they figure out a routine. They flush a hydrant. They stop for coffee at 7-Eleven. They flush a hydrant. In the back of the van they set up a makeshift bed, a pillow and blanket. Stephen takes a nap while David drives, then David naps while Stephen drives. They flush a hydrant. They eat lunch at the Bald Butte Drive-In, where they down Cokes and eat mushroom-and-Swiss burgers and waffle fries, a cold splat of mustard along the edge of their plate. They flush a hydrant. They swing through the ExxonMobil, and when the attendant asks, "What'll it be?" they say, "Fill it with premium," and smile at each other like kids getting away with something. They flush a hydrant. Every now and then, they steal construction barricades and set them up in the rich neighborhoods of Pharaoh Butte, Horse Back Butte, and Paiute Creek, blocking off streets and driveways. In the background, always, music plays—KICC 100 and 95.5 The Oink mostly—making them nod their heads and purse their lips in a whistle, filling the space between their conversations.

These are the kinds of things they talk about:

"Did you know hydrant pressure is indicated by the color it's painted?" David says. Red, yellow, and green, with green being the most powerful, letting loose one hundred pounds of pressure, enough to knock a man down and blast him across the street if he isn't careful.

"No shit?" Stephen says. He brings his hand to his mouth and chews at the callus beneath his forefinger, then peels it away with his teeth and eats it, seeming to pleasure in the salty taste. "Did you know a whale penis is nine feet long? Did you know a pig orgasm lasts ten minutes? Did you know before 1850 golf balls were made of leather and stuffed with feathers?"

"No shit?" David says with laughter in his voice, the laughter cut short when Stephen says, "Did you know I once shot a man in the face?"

His smile is not a smile. His eyes are dark-circled. One long minute passes before he continues. "It was at a traffic checkpoint. Everybody was supposed to stop, but he didn't stop. He kept coming. Even after I shot out his tires, he got out of the car and kept coming. He was yelling something, crazy Arab gibberish. I didn't even realize I did it. Pure reflex. You get to that point. A jet flying overhead sounds like a bomb, a car backfiring sounds like a bomb, a bomb sounds like a bomb. I was jumpy. So I shot him. His head jerked back and his hands went up to it and came away red. His jaw wasn't exactly gone—but basically. I could see all his teeth and into his throat, and he kept coming toward me, going nuuuh, nuuuh, nuuuh."

Behind them a truck honks. David sees that he is going only ten miles per hour. He stomps his foot down on the gas and the van growls back up to speed. "Did he have a bomb strapped to his chest or something?"

"Wouldn't you think that?" Stephen massages the bridge of his nose, sorting through the memory. "No. He didn't."

David says nothing. He thinks the conversation is over. But Stephen says, "I guess he was just mad," and his hand falls from his face and turns up the volume on the radio.

THE SLANTED LIGHT of early evening is coming in the windows, and on the television a lion gnaws on a gazelle while hyenas slink about, waiting for their turn at the corpse. David squeezes an empty beer can. It crumples grudgingly, the metal splitting open in places, slicing the skin beneath his thumb. He places the can on the floor, among four others, similarly deformed, and then brings his hand to his mouth, sucking the blood absently while watching the screen.

He punches the remote until he lands on a triple-digit network airing a Dr. Phil repeat. He has never seen the show before and he listens now as the doctor—a big bald man with a heavy Texas twang—yaks it up with a young couple experiencing sexual problems. At first he makes small talk with them, joking around, hoping to make them forget about the cameras so they'll trust him, so they'll open up and he can get down to business and solve their problems by offering advice in a loud no-nonsense voice. "What you need to do is," he says, "you need to move away from where you've been and toward a new beginning." He likes this advice so much he repeats it, motioning from left to right with his hands: "Away from where you've been and toward a new beginning."

The audience applauds and Dr. Phil says to the camera, "Don't you go nowhere, you hear? Be back before you know it." The screen goes blue with white lettering—listing a Web site and a California studio address—while a baritone announcer's voice says, "Would you like Dr. Phil to solve your problems? Send an e-mail or letter to the listed address for the opportunity to be on our show."

David gets up, dodging through the beer cans and dumbbells, and goes to his bookshelves, where he pulls down the phone book and flips through the white pages until he arrives at F. His finger runs down the names, pausing and tapping Franklin, Stephen. David writes the address on the back of his hand, where the ink looks a lot like stitching.

The drive takes ten minutes. He has trouble, with the beers in him, focusing on the numbers hanging above doorways, and he circles the block several times before spotting the ranch house with the chain-link fence around it. He parks a hundred yards away, on a side street. When he gets out of his truck and walks steadily toward the house, his snow hat, pulled down low over his face, makes him feel invisible. The houses all around him appear scorched in their darkness.

The living room window is an orange square of light. Inside it Stephen sits in a green recliner, drinking a beer, watching Fox News. The screen flashes between Bill O'Reilly speaking forcefully into the camera and insurgents who shake their fists and throw stones at soldiers and fire rifles into the sky.

David creeps up the porch for a better view. A few minutes pass, and a woman appears next to Stephen, her blond hair in a ponytail. She wears gray cotton shorts and a tie-dyed tank top and she spreads her feet and puts her hands on her hips in a Wonder Woman pose. This is Stacy. David knows because Stephen talks about her nearly every day, sometimes saying things like, "She's got this peach of an ass. I just want to shove my dick in there and break it off," and at other times saying things like, "Swear to God, she never stops nagging. I thought I was done with taking orders. But look at me, saying I'm sorry about drying shit of hers that shouldn't get dried, getting my pubic hair all over the bathroom floor. I mean, Jesus."

They met a few months before his battalion was activated, and when he asked her to marry him she surprised him by saying yes. When he came back alive, she was the one surprised. Now she says something that makes Stephen stand up so forcefully the recliner nearly tips over. They yell at each other and make stabbing motions with their hands until Stephen throws his beer bottle against the wall. It explodes in a star of foam and glass that quickly loses its shape, trailing to the floor.

From where he stands David can barely see the flattening of her lips as she says, "Fuck you," and stamps her foot down, grinding it into the carpet as if crushing out a cigarette. Then she leaves him, disappearing down a darkened hallway. Stephen stares after her for a time before settling into the recliner again. He brings his hand to his mouth and begins to gnaw at its calluses, spitting shreds of skin onto the floor.

A moth bangs against the window before fluttering off into the night. The noise draws Stephen from his recliner, his black silhouette filling the window. David crouches down and stays perfectly still, so close he could punch his hand through the glass and grab Stephen by the wrist.

THE NEXT MORNING Stephen comes to work a paler color.

"Something wrong?" David says after they snap their seat belts into place.

Stephen regards him with eyes that are only partially lit. "Rough night is all. Didn't get much sleep." He gives a smile that appears to ache from the effort of making it happen. "Mind if I smoke?"

"I didn't know you did," David says. "Smoke."

"What do you know about me? I'm not asking that. I'm asking if you mind."

"Be my guest."

David turns up the heat and puts the car in gear and drives through the back lot. Gravel pops beneath his tires when he crawls past the postal jeeps and school buses and orange construction vans and trucks parked there. He pulls onto the highway and clears his throat. "It's your girl, isn't it?"

"The fuck do you know?" Stephen's mouth curves into the shape of a scythe.

"Sorry."

"I said it's nothing and it's nothing. Mind your own business." Stephen stares at him very closely, hardly moving, with a look of obvious disgust on his face. David feels a familiar panic grip him, hating to see someone seeing him that way.

"Sorry," David says and pulls his hat a little lower on his head. "I was just—sorry."

For the next hour, Stephen stares out the window while David drives, stealing glances at him. Then, all of a sudden, Stephen brings his fist down on the dashboard and says, "Bitch."

David darts his eyes between the road and Stephen, not knowing whether to say anything.

"Yeah," Stephen says, as if they have come to some sort of agreement. His face brightens. "You know what? Fuck her."

He playfully punches David a few times in the shoulder, saying, "Fuck her," with every punch. The touch of his hand sends a charge through David that burns inside him and makes him say, "You know, if you ever need a place to crash, you can always crash with me."

"Yeah?"

"Yeah. Whatever. I mean, I've got plenty of room."

"We'll see," Stephen says, but he sounds contented.

In the middle of Pine, there is a cinder cone, Bald Butte, dotted with sagebrush and rabbitbrush and the occasional stunted juniper tree. A poorly paved road swirls around and around it, all the way to its summit, where teenagers park at night and tourists snap photos during the day and the city fires off fireworks on the Fourth. This morning David drives there and pulls out of the glovebox a half-empty bottle of Jack Daniels.

"Breakfast," he says, and they each throw back a mouthful of the dark liquor. It tastes like gasoline, but it seems right to drink, as if they are celebrating something, or mourning something. They get out of the van and climb onto its roof and watch the town redden under the sun, the shadows dissolving, while they pass the bottle back and forth for half an hour.

"You must be pretty bored," David finally says. "After all you've been through—over there—this job must bore the hell out of you."

They sit there, comfortably silent for a long time, before Stephen says, "Actually, that's not the case at all. It's kind of familiar. The driving. Feels like that's all I did over there. Drive. And wait. Wait for somebody to shoot at me, wait for an IED to go off, wait for my commanding officer to tell me some bullshit." His voice has that sincere wistful quality men normally reserve for taverns and locker rooms. "Being over there, it's just a job—with bullets, of course—but still, it's just a bunch of sitting around, trying to figure out what's next, what the fuck's the point."

WEEKS PASS. FALL deepens. The birch trees go gold, and in the failing light the world seems to take on sharper angles. In early November a water main breaks. Joe comes on the CB and sends them over to help. It is one of those new neighborhoods where all the houses look like they came from the same box and BMWs crawl the freshly paved roads.

When they park at the end of the block, a guy wearing a yellow polo shirt tucked into his khakis bangs open his front door and starts down the driveway. He moves with a prowling intensity that betrays his anger before he starts yelling. They can hear him from where they stand across the street as if he were right next to them. "I called two hours ago," he says.

He spells it out for them: a) he tried to take a shower and now he smells like somebody else's shit; b) he started up the dishwasher and now his plates and glasses are streaked with mud; c) he just put sod in and now his front lawn is a fucking swamp.

He is wearing boat shoes—no socks—and he brings down his right foot for emphasis. A crown of water splats up around it. "Somebody is going to have to pay for this," he says.

David could probably break the man over his knee if he wanted, but he presses his mouth into an apologetic frown and casts his eyes downward, toeing through the grass until he finds the cap to the water valve. He flips it open and goes to the van to retrieve the key, a long metal rod that reaches deep into the earth. He fits it into place and spins it, and with a rusty creak, the water ceases to flow.

A truck full of Mexicans arrives. They wear jeans and orange reflective vests spotted with flecks of tar. One of them sets to work with the jackhammer while the others huddle around and watch it bite through the asphalt. Then a semi pulls up with a backhoe resting on its trailer bed. One of the Mexicans climbs into its cab, and it growls to life with a clattering of metal and diesel. It rolls down the ramp, and its shovel peels away the blacktop, the gravel, and the dirt just a few inches at a time, taking care not to strike a gas line. "It's guesswork," David explains to Stephen, his voice nearly lost under all the noise. "Nobody really knows what's underneath us."

Once the shovel strikes metal—with a cling—the backhoe quits digging and scoops up a ten-by-ten steel brace to lower into the soggy square hole it has fashioned. This is to keep the walls from caving in on David and Stephen and the rest of the men when they climb down and set to work with their shovels, exposing the main so they can apply a clamp over the crack.

David digs deep with his shovel, dragging the blade through the mud, tossing it over his shoulder, enjoying the damp smells of the earth. In the cool November air his breath puffs out of him in short-lived clouds, and his sweat gives him a chill. The effort feels good, the blood burning through his body. It feels substantial, like his job is a real job.

While they work, the polo guy paces back and forth, smoking his way through more than a few cigarettes—menthol, by the smell of them. When David and Stephen climb out of the pit for a water break, he says, "Done? I hope so. For your sake."

He flicks his cigarette in their direction. It arcs through the air and lands on David, on his forearm, just long enough to burn him. He brushes it away hurriedly and says, "What's wrong with you?" his voice coming out genuinely hurt.

"What's wrong with your face?"

David looks at him uncertainly for a second, and then at Stephen, who does not return his gaze but squints across the expanse of mud at the man as if at a target.

Then Stephen leaves them standing there and climbs into the backhoe. He keys the engine and fiddles with the levers, not so different from the levers of a tank. With a roar, the backhoe comes alive. It crushes a path across the sidewalk, the driveway, the lawn, eating up with its tread the grass and mud. When the man tries to intervene, waving his arms in a fury, the backhoe swings around like a scorpion, its shovel knocking him down. An accident, everyone agrees.

THE FIRST DAY of deer hunting season in the fall is an unofficial holiday in Deschutes County. Stephen invites David to hunt on his father's property, out near Sisters, twenty acres of big pines that run up against the Black Butte wilderness area. They set off early in the afternoon, wearing jeans and blaze-orange jackets. The sky is a copper color, and the air is sharp enough to make their breath ghost from their mouths.

The forest swallows them, whispering and snapping, before disgorging them in a clearing of fireweed and browned strawberry beds. They head toward a cluster of thick-waisted junipers that surrounds what looks like a clubhouse on stilts. Ten or so feet off the ground, it has a slanted steel roof and a camouflage paint job. This is a high seat, the penthouse of tree stands. Beneath it is a trough, baited with salt licks, rotten apples, corn.

They climb a ladder and push through a trapdoor. Inside there are army cots, a cooler filled with Coors, a wood bin, a wood stove, and aluminum chairs set before sliding-glass windows. On the wall is a poster of a big-breasted woman in a bikini bent over the hood of a Camaro, both the woman and the car oozing with soap suds. And next to the poster, the charred corpse of an animal is nailed to the wall. It is the size of a small child, its legs curled up against its torso and its teeth visible in a small snarl. When he was eleven or twelve, Stephen explains, he baited a steel-mesh cage with jerky and trapped a raccoon that had been getting into their garbage. He released it, but only after dousing it with gasoline and sparking a match. There was a foomp sound, and the coon took off like a comet, zigzagging through a dry field of crabgrass, setting it aflame in strange orange designs Stephen stomped out with his foot.

When his father discovered what he had done, he nailed the coon to the wall of the high seat as a reminder. "That way maybe you'll think twice before you pull the trigger." Never firing off a round out of boredom—at a jaybird, a jackrabbit, a doe—hungry to kill something, anything, as boys often are.

"Jesus," David says.

Stephen breaks the silence by kicking a folding chair. "Best seat in the house," he says. The chair faces a window that opens up into the forest. "All yours. Just keep your eyes on that game trail." He winks. "Fish in a barrel."

They take their chairs and cradle their rifles in their laps. They don't speak for a while, their silence deepening with the shadows in the woods. Then Stephen gets up to pull a beer from the cooler and offers one to David, who pops the tab and, after slurping at the foam that comes boiling out of it, says, "Hey, did you know a whale penis is nine feet long?"

Stephen gives him a blank look. "I'm the one who told you that, man."

"Are you?"

"Yeah."

"Oh. Sorry." David feels his grip tighten around his beer, the metal giving way. "Things any better with Stacy?"

Stephen returns to his window and looks out it. "So-so."

"Just so-so?"

"Let's put it this way," he says, keeping his voice at a low volume. "Are you still good on that offer? If I needed to, I could crash at your place?"

"Sure." David tries hard to control his voice. If there is too much excitement in it, he can't tell.

"Just in case," Stephen says.

"You're always welcome. Stay as long as you like. There's plenty of room."

Stephen twists the tab on his can until it snaps off. "Good to know."

They fall silent again. David finds it difficult to concentrate on the woods and throws a glance over his shoulder every few minutes to check on Stephen. It feels different, sitting here with him and not moving, not listening to the engine hum, not watching the world slide by. It feels good—permanent.

Time passes and his vision blurs and the forest falls away as he imagines the two of them as young boys, dirt under their fingernails, carrying in their hands slingshots and BB guns, darting through the trees, headed toward where they heard a chipmunk chattering minutes ago. The false memory makes him feel so close to Stephen, his friend, he wants to reach out and touch him.

He glances over his shoulder then, just in time to see Stephen snap off the safety and bring the 30.06 to his shoulder. He rises from his chair, slowly, the metal complaining only a little. David follows the line of Stephen's rifle. There, at the edge of the meadow, less than thirty yards away, a buck untangles its antlers from the forest and moves cautiously toward the trough.

Halfway there it pauses. It swishes its tail. It raises a hoof and puts it down again. Maybe it smells them, or maybe it smells the blood in the grass. David holds his breath, anticipating the shot. When it doesn't come, he says, "What are you waiting for?"

"I don't know," Stephen says.

David gently pushes him aside and nestles the stock against his cheek and sights the buck through the scope. Right then it raises its head and looks at him. The blood in his ears buzzes, like a wasp loose in his skull. The rifle kicks against his shoulder. The gunshot fills the world.

The buck jerks its head around in a half circle, as if curious where the shot came from, and then it collapses and a flock of swallows swirls from the forest, over the meadow, dappling it with shadows.

A few minutes later, they stand over the body. When David nudges it with his boot, its hind leg quivers, then goes still. Since the gunshot, the air has gone quiet except for the rhythmic knocking of a woodpecker's beak against some distant tree. The woods are softly colored with the gloom that comes with twilight. The hole David has blown in the deer's side is big enough to put his hand in, and he does. Hot, moist. It reminds him, with a sick kind of pleasure, of a woman. When he withdraws his hand, gloved in blood, it steams a little. He smears its redness against his left cheek and says, "There. Now I match."

Stephen laughs as if he is trying not to. "I'm glad you took the shot," he says, his smile fading. "I don't know what's wrong with me."

"Nothing's wrong with you."

Some blood oozes into David's mouth and he spits it back out. It occurs to him then—with blood on his lips and the woods darkening all around them—that he has never been happier.

THE NEXT MONDAY morning, David arrives at work fifteen minutes early and waits for Stephen on the loading dock, an elevated concrete platform with a steel ramp leading up it. Nearby, a poplar, stripped of its leaves, shakes against the wind that comes howling down from the Cascades. A rime of frost coats its branches. With the sun still low in a sky full of torn clouds, the air has a gray quality that carries little warmth. David paces back and forth and stamps his feet, trying to keep the cold out of them.

Eventually Stephen pulls up in a Chevy Cavalier with an Army National Guard sticker on its bumper. Rather than park along the chain-link fence, next to David's truck, he kills the engine at the bottom of the ramp and hops out.

"Hey, Stephen," David says, and Stephen says, "Hey." He steps onto the ramp and pauses there with David hanging over him, obscuring him with his shadow and a big breath of mist.

"Something wrong?" David says.

Stephen brings his hand to his mouth and chews hungrily on it. "Maybe." He sighs deeply, and in a halting voice that seems bothered—by nervousness or excitement—explains that he has been asked to be part of a task force. He and fifteen other soldiers will work as an embedded training team to mentor the Iraqi Army.

"What do you mean?" David says.

"I mean I'm not working here anymore," Stephen says. "I'm going back." He examines his palm. Blood and saliva dampen it. He wipes it on the handrail. "Next week, I'm on active duty. I just came to say my goodbyes and pick up my paycheck." He studies David a moment and irritation creeps into his voice. "Well, aren't you going to say anything?"

David doesn't know what to say, so he says, "What about Stacy?"

"What about her?"

"You can't just leave her again, can you?"

"What do you care?"

"I don't know." His voice has a fine crack in it. There is a pain in his forehead. It makes him think of insects eating away at the space between his eyes. He squeezes the bridge of his nose.

"I better go talk to Joe," says Stephen. He moves up the ramp another two steps, and from here David can see the redness in his teeth, the blood from his chewing.

"I'm in your way, aren't I?" David says and steps aside and makes a motion with his hands, ushering Stephen onto the dock. "Sorry."

Stephen doesn't say anything else, but just before he pushes through the double doors, David yells after him to wait a minute. Stephen pauses, half inside, half out, as David takes a few lumbering steps toward him and offers his hand. It hangs there a second, then Stephen shows off the blood on his hand like an apology before disappearing inside.

WITHOUT STEPHEN, DRIVING feels different, the roads as routine as an old network of veins that has pumped the same blood along the same path too long. David yearns for conversation but there is only the grumble of the engine, the hiss of the tires spinning over the blacktop, the voice of Hank Williams yodeling through the radio.

He swings by Stephen's house once, and then again, looking for a car in the driveway, a light in the window. The third time, when he passes the house at a crawl, he catches sight of his reflection in the living-room window—the Astrovan and his dark shape inside it. Without really thinking about it he raises his hand, and it is as if his hand and the hand in the window are trying to reach across those many feet of space to touch.

At the end of the block, he doesn't turn around to drive through the neighborhood again but instead continues through town until he merges onto Route 20 and drives toward Sisters, then past it, to the plot of land where they went hunting.

He parks the van on a logging road and hikes through the forest to the meadow. His hands are shoved deep in his pockets, the smell of pine drifting all around him. The low rays of sunlight pick out a little red in the soil, the place where they gutted the deer. He kneels there, and though the ground is hard with frost he manages to finger his way into it and pull away a handful of dirt, still the reddish color of blood. He puts it in his pocket, and later in a Ziploc bag, to keep.

The Wind's Last Breath

Jos Burns

It was the end of days, and the Wind had one breath left. It surveyed the situation, the dwindling biosphere on planet Earth, deciding whether to sweep the Mojave glistening clean, as a tribute to its exemplary tradition of vastness, or simply to sabotage the Lieutenant's smoking habit. It was leaning toward the latter. The Lieutenant had wronged the Wind, had scoffed at the Wind's noble ability to whistle through tight spaces, and the Wind found it equitable to ruin the Lieutenant's smoking for all eternity. However long eternity endured, that is. The span of eternity shriveled day-by-day.

For his part, the Lieutenant wasn't a lieutenant at all, but merely a shopping cart rolled far out into the Mojave and settled to rust at an abandoned military outpost. Whether the Lieutenant had arrived a year ago, or a decade earlier, no one could recall. The outpost understood that war would unfold eventually, and had welcomed the Lieutenant as an ally. In the interest of heeding regulations regarding visitors, the outpost had assigned the cart the honorary title of Lieutenant. This in turn had so puffed up the shopping cart with pride that he had taken up smoking, in order to better resemble lieutenantkind.

The outpost and its lieutenant stood ready in the seething desert, but war failed to materialize. Occasionally, a jealous vulture would swoop by the outpost and deride it, calling it sissy names for maintaining a shopping cart as a lieutenant, suggesting that anything—a vulture, for example—would make a more dignified and effective guard. At these times, the Lieutenant would gear himself up for a good rattle, dancing a jig at the gate that could be heard for miles, and the vulture, involuntarily spooked by the noise, would have to fly away.

The Lieutenant had only one friend, a kangaroo rat who would come and scan the horizon with him, alert as only small rodents can be, fidgety and pompous in his smallness. The kangaroo rat liked the Lieutenant because his basket still smelled like food, a remnant from his days that he referred to as enlisted service at the supermarket. Sometimes, the kangaroo rat would hop into the Lieutenant's chrome basket and root around in the cracks and corners, exhilarated by the scent of old parsley and dried chicken blood. For everyone concerned, it was a satisfying way to spend the last days of the world.

On patrol and happily savoring a hoarded cigarette, the Lieutenant figured he had it made: he was an officer—the only one—at a desert outpost, he had beaten out a vulture in qualifying to emulate a man, and the Wind had hardly blown for weeks. He expected the Wind had forgotten its grudge, perhaps even absolved him of their little quarrel. In any case, when the Wind finally died, the Lieutenant planned to spend the rest of his days smoking in peace.

The Wind by now had circled the globe evaluating projects to spend its last breath on. Finding only that vultures were still cursed to be vultures, and that humans had petered out with rather less fanfare than anticipated, it had returned to consider harvesting a final vengeance against the Lieutenant.

The Wind sallied back and forth, looking for the right opportunity. The Lieutenant was brazenly smoking the stub of his cigarette, flaunting his presumed freedom. The Wind found the Lieutenant's confidence irksome. A respectful citizen of the earth would fear the Wind's vengeance until the very end, even if the Wind could no longer blow. The proper thing would be to give up smoking, for health reasons, or fumble with the match and drop it, avoiding the disappointing moment when the Wind would have extinguished the flame. Yes sir, the Wind thought, it's time to teach this Lieutenant a lesson.

The Wind waited until the Lieutenant was absorbed in watching the patterns of smoke swirling around his basket. The Lieutenant's attention on the smoldering butt had relaxed, and with a force worthy of its younger days, the Wind gusted heroically, flipping the cigarette out of the Lieutenant's grasp and scuttling it under the door to the supply room. The Lieutenant started, and cried out, and grappled with his ring of keys, but by the time he got the door open, it was too late. The Lieutenant's precious last box of matches, and nearby cartons of cigarettes, were already on fire. He pushed the boxes around in the dirt and tried to stamp it out, but his tiny wheels had little effect, and the boxes burned quickly in the dry desert air. Soon the boxes were reduced to ashes and the Lieutenant could only stand there, creaking mournfully, thinking of what might have been.

The Wind died, and the world was quiet. The kangaroo rat tried to console the Lieutenant for his loss, but the Lieutenant turned angry and wouldn't listen. Eventually the rat didn't bother coming around anymore. The Lieutenant collapsed beneath the weight of his own bitterness. When the vulture arrived to pick at his bones, he recalled that the Lieutenant was only a shopping cart, and not the fleshy creature the vulture had remembered, one elevated to manhood through love of cigarettes and pride in a dead-end job.

Pyrosome

Kathleen McNamara

I never saw an otter in Otter Creek. Dad said there used to be thousands of them, a hundred years ago, or maybe earlier: before Arizona was a state. Our house stood at a bend in the water, facing a yellow sandstone wall, where stripes of purple rock stuck out like ribs.

"Imagine big giggling packs echoing through the canyon. Then the pioneers killed them all for meat and pelts. Now there's none left." Dad leaned over the edge of the deck, scooting forward on his chest, one hand on the power drill. "Missy—bring me the longest bit." He nodded at his tool box. I went slowly, listening to the porch heave under our weight. Trying not to be afraid of how it wobbled since the last storm. Believing him when he said it wouldn't break.

Below us, Cody balanced a wooden plank over his head as he stood on the lichened stone that banked our house. We'd had a wild monsoon season, and the whole place shivered now when the wind howled through. Dad hired Cody to help him cut new stilts—sand them, paint them, drill them to the bones of our house. Cody shot up six inches that summer and suddenly became useful. He lived downriver, in an A-frame with peeling orange trim, overlooking the spot we called The Lovers, because two cottonwoods crossed from either side of the creek and grew around each other, limbs intertwining.

"Don't let it drag," said Dad. I could hear Cody cursing down there about water seeping into his boots. He held a stilt in place while Dad drilled.

"Blame pioneers if you want—that's not the whole story," said Cody. Cody talked with swagger. The glue of arrogance kept him in one piece. "I heard a shark-snake or an octopus or something ate all the otters."

Dad nodded at the pile: "Hand me another one." It was mid-September then, and hot. The screen door banged and Mom emerged from the house with pink lemonade she mixed from powder. In the other hand she held a plate of hot dogs, skins blistered from the pan.

Cody talked as he pulled another plank over his back. "Every year, when the wildflowers bloom, a litter of otters is born at the headwaters. That shark-snake-octopus comes out in broad daylight, no shame, and eats those pups alive, like he's popping potato chips. And if it weren't for the otters, he'd invade our houses and eat our babies instead."

"Since when do you have any babies?" Dad laughed. "Don't hold it that way—turn it." He reached down to rotate the wood in Cody's arms. "And anyway, what liar told you that?"

"You calling my mother a liar?" The hurt in his voice sounded knife-sharp. Cody's mother, Diane, was sent to prison that July. After Diane got arrested, Cody's little sisters went to live with their aunt up in Flagstaff. Cody's dad couldn't take them because he drove a cattle hauler back and forth across the country on Interstate-40. When he came back to Otter Creek, he posted up in a trailer on the mesa in a clearing called Cowboy Camp. Sometimes Cody didn't know his dad had returned until he'd already left again.

"No one's calling your mother anything." The stairs pinched under Mom's weight as she climbed down to the water. "You're just hungry." She brought a hot dog to where Cody stood on a boulder. "Eat."

Cody lived alone with his grandpa now. Mr. Weaver wandered the A-frame's junkyard driveway with a chainsaw, cutting pieces of clutter into smaller and smaller halves: used tires; couch cushions; the glitter-tasseled handlebar of a rusted bike. Mom said he had a series of strokes after his daughter was convicted. Now he walked around the cabin short-circuiting, agitated but dazed, muttering in what sounded like his own language.

"Well, is it an octopus or a shark or a snake?" I asked. I didn't mind Cody's stories. When half of Elly Franklin's goat herd turned up dead, Cody swore from the bite marks that Mexican chupacabras had devoured them, even though we all knew it was coyotes. Another time, he said he shot a jackalope near Cowboy Camp, and when I asked him to prove it, he showed me a pair of deer antlers. That was all he had, he said, because his mom made stew with its' giant rabbit body. When I asked him how jackalope tasted, all he said was "gamey."

"All three," said Cody. "It's part-octopus, part-shark, part-snake. Part-man, too."

"You're saying it's a deformed mermaid with fangs?" Dad shook his head as he switched drill-bits again. He wasn't one for make-believe. We didn't bother with Santa Claus or Easter Bunnies or Tooth Fairies. We didn't go to Otter Creek Baptist on Sundays. Good things came from his own back-crushing work, he said, and he didn't want leprechauns or elves or invisible men in the sky getting credit for it.

"If the mermaid monster eats all the pups," I asked, "how come every spring, a mother otter shows up and has more? Where'd she come from if they're all dead?"

Dad pointed at me, winking. Made a sign with his hand that meant I was a sharp-shooter.

Cody shrugged, swallowing half a hot dog at once. "Black magic," he said, wiping ketchup from his chin.

THAT'S ONE THING about Cody's mom: she thought she was in a coven. I used to see her with a group of women, all in black hoods, standing in the creek below the intertwined Lovers. They held hands in a circle, and each of them chanted a different part of a song that together made me feel like I was dreaming. Through my bedroom window at dawn, the sound of them sometimes hypnotized me, had my legs up and walking out the door and toward the river before I could even call myself awake. She seemed beautiful then. But when you pissed her off, she said she was going to hex you. Cody's dad was the one who usually got hexed.

"That's not magic," said Mom, "that's meth." Still, I wondered.

Diane got arrested after an incident up at Cowboy Camp. Left Cody's baby sisters in the car while it was running. It was winter then, and Diane said she didn't want the girls to get cold. So, I don't know if it's fair that she got the child abuse charge on top of it all, but she got it anyway. Diane busted into her ex-husband's trailer and tried to beat him unconscious. Screaming nonsense, calling it a spell. Cops found a needle in the cupholder next to the three-year-old. Open bottle of whiskey by the car seat. When Cody sped through our street on his dirt bike, pushing fifty, no helmet, trying to jump hills like men did on TV, my dad rocked on the front patio and let out a mournful whistle.

"That kid's going to get himself killed. Or worse."

"What's worse than killed?" I asked.

"Trust me—there's worse."

Sometimes, on a lap through the neighborhood, Cody stopped at our front door and asked for me.

"Missy's not riding around on that thing, if that's what you're after," said Dad. Cody spat on the ground and sped off again. Then he'd come back on Friday, when we didn't have school. I was alone in the house.

"Ride with me." Cody revved the engine.

"No thanks. I'd rather stay alive."

But he waited in the driveway looking hurt and pissed. "Why not?"

"I just said why not."

"Life's not worth living unless you take some risks." Then he dropped his bike and followed me into the house. In that moment, I felt cornered—afraid of the coyote look in his eyes, of heat he carried on him like a stench. But he just raided the fridge, then plopped in front of the TV with a cup brimming over with lemonade. We sat silently on either end of the couch, watching people we didn't know and would never meet, as they got drunk at a beach house on the other side of the country.

"I bet they're fucking," said Cody, when two people closed a bedroom door and left the cameraman in the hallway. All you could hear was heavy breathing on the microphones—muffled figures rustling under blankets—until those whispers cut to commercial. "You know what fucking is, right?" Cody stretched his legs out on the couch.

ONLY A WEEK after monsoon season officially ended, a woman I'd never seen before rang our doorbell. She had short hair, a deep line between her brows, and talked to me like I was younger than I was.

"My name's Melinda. Are your parents home?" I pulled on my mud boots and walked her around to the porch. Dad's legs hung over the creek while he drilled screws into the new railing. It was almost finished.

"Sir," said Melinda. His hat shadowed his eyes. He barely turned. "I'm a local FEMA representative." She pointed at the letters on her windbreaker. "National Weather Service is tracking a hurricane hurling up from Baja right now. Set to make landfall in three days. We're hoping you'll consider buying flood insurance today. This storm is supposed to be unprecedented. And Otter Creek's been known to climb out of that wash." She gestured at the flow of water below us, as though she wasn't sure we knew where we lived.

Dad stood, pushing up the brim of his hat so she could see his face. "Where'd you say you were from?" He was still holding that power drill, pressing the button now and then so that it whirred at the sky.

"The Federal Emergency Management Agency. We're working with the Arizona Red Cross to help vulnerable communities prepare for the storm."

"I'll stop you at federal," said Dad. I could see Melinda trying not to roll her eyes. Dad liked to say that the purpose of government was to figure out creative ways to steal your money. Mom had embroidered a pillow for him that said I LOVE MY COUNTRY BUT I FEAR MY GOVERNMENT, with stars and stripes around the edges, and he propped it on the fireplace mantle like some kind of trophy.

Melinda kept trying. "Global warming is making these storms unpredictable. Some places are getting what are supposed to be thousand-year weather events every year. It's either climate change or a thousand years doesn't last as long as it used to."

"We've never had a problem." Dad walked to the other side of the porch, tightening screws he'd already tightened. We couldn't just stand there forever, so I led Melinda back out to the road.

"That hurricane's coming," she said. "Pride won't save your house." She climbed into her truck, handing me a card with her number. "In case your dad changes his mind."

"He won't."

"Think I'll have better luck at your neighbor's?" She pointed up the road to the A-frame.

"Definitely not." When she smiled, the line between her brows disappeared. I realized I liked her, even if she was supposedly trying to steal our money.

"Stay safe," she said, "and dry." She looked to the sky, blue only minutes ago, but which already seemed to sizzle gray with electricity.

Then she started the Jeep and I watched it putter around the corner, pulling into Cody's grandpa's long mess of a driveway—everything cut to pieces you could only see if you looked very closely: tiny glints of spoon; cotton confetti that used to be sheets; a once-kitchen-table now scattered throughout the sycamore grove. The old man spent most of his time under those thick branches, roaring thirty years' worth of domestic debris through his table saw. When I asked Dad if Mr. Weaver should be allowed to handle a tool like that in his condition, Dad just shrugged: "Who gets to decide when a man isn't allowed to be who he is anymore, and at his own house?" But just the whir of that saw, the down-canyon sound of its spinning, made me shiver.

"Hello?" called Melinda, following the echo of the blade.

I FOUND DAD in the kitchen. "Help me," he said.

We loaded shovels into the truck. He drove us up the mesa, past Cowboy Camp, onto wilderness land. Spent the rest of the afternoon filling industrial-strength bags with sand. When I got tired and my hands turned raw and blistery, Dad told me to be lookout, but I was watching two ravens peck at each other when a Forest Service Jeep pulled up the road. A man in a khaki-green uniform stepped out.

"Sir, you can't do that here," said the man, looking at the thick white bags stacked in the truck. He pulled at his bushy red mustache. "This is a National Monument."

Dad didn't stop shoveling. "Am I a hostage in my own neighborhood?"

"There's fines," said the man. "This place is protected. For all I know, you might have arrowheads or native pottery sherds in those bags. All goes back to the Antiquities Act of 1906. They'll fine you twenty-five hundred per piece."

"Who will?" I could see Dad smiling as he worked. That same no-chance-in-hell smile he gave me whenever I asked for something I knew was a longshot.

"The federal government will."

"Is that you?" Dad zip-tied another bag and heaved it into the truck.

We'd already piled the bed full. He motioned for me to get in. "It's just dirt."

"There's treasure in 'just dirt.' You can't take it." The man reached for his radio, but Dad had already started the truck, and we barreled down the old road, whirling red dust behind us, so thick I could barely see the ranger as he got smaller in the mirror.

"These'll work better than insurance," said Dad.

At home, Cody and I helped Dad stack the bags on the slope below our porch, then around the A-frame like speedbumps. Three days later, when that hurricane roared through, when on TV they showed cars floating off the highway like unanchored boats, I watched Otter Creek storm against our fortress of sandbags, praying to I-don't-know-what-god that the foundation holding it all in place wouldn't turn to mud. And when the clouds scattered, nothing here seemed broken. Dad was right: they worked.

IT WAS DOCUMENTED fact that creatures lived near the headwaters of Otter Creek that didn't exist anywhere else on earth. That's why they made it a National Monument. A corridor of land so rich, humans had lived here continuously since the moment they'd laid eyes on it. They'd found evidence of human habitation in this valley going back thirteen-thousand years. Our corner of it was called Aztec Well—a name given by mistake. Aztecs never came through here.

In November, all sixteen of us eighth graders visited the Well for a field trip. Normally, we spent every day with Ms. Helms. She taught every subject. This was our biology lesson for the week, she said. She stared at herself in a hand mirror on the bus ride over, teasing volume into her hair, using a long wand to dab lip-gloss into the shape of the mouth she wished she had.

Cody didn't bother with me at school. He had other friends. Penis friends. I called them that because the three of them were always figuring out new places to draw a penis: on the pleather upholstery; on blonde Nevaeh's red backpack; in the hot breath they blew onto window-glass.

I'd been feeling funny all day—cramps in my stomach that made my head swimmy—so I almost didn't recognize at first the bushy red mustache of the forest ranger who waited for us in the parking lot.

"Welcome, Junior Rangers."

"Class," said Ms. Helms, "this is Ranger Brown."

"His nametag says Charles Brown," laughed Cody, and this made everyone clamber to read the plastic on his shirt. Two years ago, we'd all had a substitute for most of sixth grade, and that substitute played us old cartoons on Wednesday afternoons. We had a lot of material for Ranger Charlie Brown. Nevaeh kept saying "good grief" and asking if he had a Snoopy. Cody and his penis friends hummed the *Peanuts* theme song. Maybe I would have laughed too, except I was afraid Charlie Brown would arrest me for stealing dirt. Plus, the pain between my hips felt like I had eaten something that had squirmed back alive. Just standing was hard enough.

"Alright, alright." Charlie Brown and Ms. Helms waved for us to be quiet as they led us up a limestone hill.

"There's blood on your pants," Nevaeh said to me, too loudly, before she skipped ahead on the trail toward the Well. And when I reached down between my legs, I felt dampness there, dampness that explained this sensation of being crushed under a heavy weight, as though all the air had turned to quicksand. I felt hot with panic. I tied my sweatshirt around my waist.

"The Well's not a well at all," said Charlie Brown.

"Cody Weaver, that's enough," said Ms. Helms, but he was still humming the *Peanuts* song out of earshot. I watched as Nevaeh started a telephone of whispers.

Ranger Charlie Brown cleared his throat. "It's a cave that has collapsed to expose its water source. That water pours from the limestone at a rate of two million gallons per day. It's been that way since the Holocene. You know how long that is?" We didn't. "That means for at least the last ten thousand years. Even in drought. And you see those rock walls there?" He pointed to a dwelling, nestled in an alcove that overlooked the gurgling water. It seemed impossible to access, tucked below the ridge where we stood, like the only option was to fall into it from the overhanging rock. "That's an ancient granary. The larger artifacts excavated out of there are on view at the Visitor's Center. But small pieces have been left for posterity's sake. So take only photos, and leave only footprints." Charlie Brown looked around at us, made a show like he wanted us to empty our pockets, then laughed. I remembered what he said to Dad: twenty-five hundred per pottery sherd if you stole one. My stomach clenched again and I looked up at the sky. Clouds covered the sun. Steam hissed off the dark pool. I shivered enough that my teeth started to clatter like a skeleton's at a joke shop. Still, I kept my sweatshirt tied around my waist.

"It just looks like a pond to me," said Nevaeh.

"It's not a normal pond," said Charlie Brown. "First of all, the water's carbonated, and full of arsenic. The water comes from deep inside the planet, and it's always seventy-eight degrees. We've sent scuba divers and robots down there and there's no bottom to it. Just endless geysers. Ancient people thought the first humans emerged here—shot from the innards of the planet into this water. It's a very unique ecosystem. There's a nocturnal leech that's got suckers on both ends of its body, a water scorpion, a microalgae called a diatom, a blue-green amphipod," said Charlie Brown, saying words I'd never heard before, "and recently, we spotted what we believe to be a new species of pyrosome."

"Does anyone know what a pyrosome is?" Ms. Helms asked us.

"Do you know what it is?" asked Cody, but Ms. Helms didn't have to answer because Charlie Brown answered for her.

"It's a bioluminescent worm. It's actually not one organism, but a colony of hundreds of thousands of organisms, all working together as one. It's supposed to live in the ocean. Extremely rare to get one inland. We've only seen it a few times, and it keeps getting bigger. Seems to be mostly feeding on the amphipods. It's about seven feet long right now. I'll show you," said Ranger Brown, rifling through his old leather bag. I could see from the circle of faces looking at me that word had spread. I tightened that sweatshirt around my waist, twisting to check that I hadn't bled through that too. It felt like forever before Charlie Brown held up an enlarged photograph of two white humps emerging from the inky surface of the well. This was the middle of the creature's body, he said. Sharp toothy nodes poked out of its spine. "Took this one myself.

Truth be told, we're not really sure what it is. Or how it got here. Wondering if it was carried here by a bird when it was microscopic, and then it multiplied and grew. Seems like it looks different every time it surfaces. Another ranger said he saw it eat a duck. But that would be very unusual pyrosome behavior. Unheard of, really."

At that, Cody lit up. He whispered to me: "Told you there was a monster here," and as he said it, I felt the sweatshirt loosen around my waist, and I heard him snicker, gleefully, as his penis friends shrieked with laughter. Shame rose like a hot wave up my chest, closing my throat.

"Do you kids want to see where this pours into Otter Creek?"

Ms. Helms shushed the boys. I tightened the sleeves around my waist again. Silence felt like a crater. Charlie Brown read this silence as yes. He guided us down the cliffside. From below, Aztec Well looked like a giant bowl carved from rock. "Here," said Charlie Brown, bringing us to a hole in the ground. Foamy water gurgled out of it, then down a narrow canal that cut through cottonwoods. "This canal's been used since antiquity. Otter Spring's only a few hundred feet up-canyon," he said, pointing north. "Some of what's in the Well comes out in your faucets. Of course, it gets treated first. If you drink this water directly, it'll poison you." He dipped his chapped fingers in the water. "You'll get all sorts of nasty symptoms. Any questions?"

"Could that pyrosome eat an otter?" blurted Cody.

"Pardon?" said Charlie Brown, and Cody asked again.

MOM WORKED AT Otter Creek Family Health Center, a one-room clinic in between the dollar store and the gas station. On Fridays, because there wasn't enough money in the county budget to keep us in school, I sometimes went with her, and sat in the corner by the cash register reading the disintegrating paperbacks they sold outside Otter Creek Library for a dime each: Judy Blume, Stephen King, *Island of the Blue Dolphins*, and *The Outsiders*. I liked any story about someone who lived somewhere other than a place like this. Locals wandered into the Clinic and I watched Mom give flu shots or help old folks check their blood glucose. One day in December, two women I'd seen with Cody's mom pushed through the glass doors, walking slow, looking spooked. One was tall and thin. Had a face like a crow. The other was rounder, softer, older. They both wore hooded jackets and lace gloves. The tall, birdy woman asked Mom if she was a doctor.

"I'm a Certified Nursing Assistant, and today, I'm running this place. How can I help you?" The women rolled up their sleeves. Their gloves reached their elbows. They removed them delicately, wincing. Then held up their palms for us to see. Bone-colored growths popped from their hands like molars. I could tell Mom was doing her best not to look alarmed.

"We've been hexed," said the tall woman. "It's Diane Weaver. I know it's because we haven't visited her since she was convicted."

"You're in the coven!" I said, and the two women looked at me as though I too were an agent of Cody's mom, like they had expected me to guess right.

"It's on our feet, too," said the older woman, as she eased into a chair.

THE NEXT DAY, when Cody rode up our driveway on his dirt bike, I broke the silent treatment I'd been giving him to tell him about the women—the tall one, I learned, was Tarra, and the older one, Betty. Mom said they needed a real doctor: a dermatologist, or maybe an internist, or maybe an allergist, or maybe an infectious disease specialist, and that if it were her, she'd drive down to Phoenix right this instant. She knew they weren't about to do that, so instead, she suggested Benadryl. Told them to reassess tomorrow. Mom didn't believe in hexes, but Cody did. He wasn't surprised.

"Don't cross my mother," said Cody. "I learned that the hard way."

"What does that mean?" I asked, but he just revved his engine, cutting a figure-eight in the gravel. "Have you visited her in prison?"

"Ride with me," said Cody. And I don't know if it was the look in his eyes, usually all mischief and rage, but on that day, I read as sorrow. Or if it was the reminder that he was a partial-orphan, that his witchy mother lived behind bars in some dusty cell outside of Phoenix. Or if it was because I'd finished all the paperbacks I had in the house, and thought maybe he would take me down to the library for something new to read. Whatever it was, I pulled my bike helmet out of the shed and climbed onto the seat behind him. I wrapped my arms around his waist—the mildew t-shirt, the trail of gasoline-stink. We took off too fast, angling around each bend, cutting narrow corners on the wrong side of the road.

"Where to?" yelled Cody, straining to be heard in the wind. His shirt billowed up to his neck. I'd never been so close to him. For the first time, I saw scars like caterpillars pushing through the skin between his shoulder blades. Is this what he meant when he said he learned the hard way?

DAYS WERE SHORT then. By late afternoon, the sky turned the color of a bruised peach. Cody and I rode around town for hours. We ended up hiding behind junipers as Charlie Brown locked the gate to the Well. We waited to hop the fence.

"Think the monster's hungry?" asked Cody. At the gas mart, we'd bought potato chips, and now Cody threw a handful toward the water, trying to lure the pyrosome from the depths. But as soon as the chips hit the surface, they dissolved into nothing, like whatever filled that sinkhole had grown so potent that "water" wasn't even the right word anymore.

We heard footsteps on the trail behind us. Then notes of a hypnotic song.

"Fuck, fuck, fuck!" he whispered. We hurried down the twilit limestone, looking for cover. He jerked my wrist and I followed him, scrambling to the edge of the cliff. Then we jumped down, into that prehistoric granary. Crawled through the dark rooms that overlooked the arsenic liquid below. On my hands and knees, I could feel scraps of something brittle and disintegrating. A shredded rug or a dried-out cob of maize. Artifacts desiccating there for eight hundred years. And here we were, unable to prevent ourselves stomping all over it.

"Makes you feel like a grave-robber," whispered Cody, pulling me into the next room. The last of the daylight glowed through a square window.

"Help me look for arrowheads," he said, holding triangles of flinty rock up to the dwindling light.

That hypnotic song got louder, and the air in that room made me dizzy. I didn't believe in ghosts, but I could feel them anyway. Could feel the way the breath of the dead seemed trapped here. I stuck my head out the window and watched as the women arrived. They wore black hoods and long lace gloves. It was the coven, and we peered from behind the ancient wall, listening to them chant their dream song. Long-limbed Tarra climbed toward the water. She steadied herself on a lip of rock, dropped down, huddled in the shadows of the cliff wall. She removed her glove, then pulled a long-stemmed wine glass from her coat, and dipped a raw, scabby hand under the Well's inky surface, filling the cup. One by one, each of them drank.

"That rash isn't a hex," I mouthed at Cody, raising my own hands. "It's arsenic poisoning."

But he just pointed, transfixed. The orange sunset reflected on the water's surface in the center of the Well. But at a darker edge, we watched new movement ripple, grow long, a geometric undulation. It surged into the amber-lighted middle. We saw it, then: a toothy, bone-white spine, breaking through that liquid gold mirror. It snaked toward the women, visible and then gone, visible and then gone again.

"What is it?" I whispered. A reflex, because I already knew.

"What do you think it is?" said Cody, too loudly.

I touched the ancient stone wall, the caked mortar that had held it upright for the last thousand years. Felt dizzy again when I breathed in deep. "An invasive species."

"Check this out." Cody held a sliver of rock to the last of the light. Held my hand, brought my finger to its point, pressed down.

"Hey!" I pulled back, nursed my finger in my mouth, tasting the penny-taste of blood. "That hurt."

"Found an arrowhead." Cody slid it in his pocket. Then I froze, noticing the singing had stopped.

A melodic voice called out to us: "Is someone there?"

SINCE WE WERE all breaking the law, sneaking into a National Monument after-hours, the coven agreed they wouldn't tattle on us so long as we kept the secret for them. They recognized Cody; said they owed Diane Weaver that much. And for a while, I forgot about it—that witchy song and the goosebumps I felt shivering up my neck in that granary and the fact that Cody had violated the Antiquities Act of 1906 by pocketing that arrowhead. For a while I forgot about that bone-white pyrosome, which had looked to me like some kind of devil that had crawled into the bottomless Well from below the earth's crust. But when I remembered, it was Ranger Charlie Brown's voice that came to me: "We don't know how it got here."

That was the year Otter Creek had the coldest winter in a century. Every morning for months, a thick rind of ice covered the only bridge out of town. Christmas brought snow, and then we hunkered down on New Year's Eve as another nine inches piled up outside.

"So much for Federal Melinda and her global warming," said Dad.

"It's real," I promised. I never had the courage to tell him that I met the ranger who tried to stop us filling sandbags. Part of me still expected Charlie Brown to show up one day with an arrest warrant or a stack of fines and take back all the dirt piled under our house. But I suppose Charlie Brown wasn't paid enough for that, or hadn't figured out where we lived, or was too busy being in love with Ms. Helms. After the field trip, he stopped by our classroom every Tuesday, on his day off, to impress her and show us artifacts he'd collected—a trilobite, a hummingbird egg, a diamondback skin. Charlie Brown said that the extreme cold was a symptom of climate change.

"I heard thousands of species are vanishing right in front of us all the time, and we barely even notice," I said. Mom wasn't looking so I poured myself some of her champagne.

"That's always been happening," said Dad. "Just take the otters. Gone long before anyone said 'climate change.'" I didn't feel like arguing with him. I went to my bedroom and waited for the New Year alone, feeling all floaty from the alcohol.

Mom went to bed early. Dad started snoring in front of the flickering TV screen, empty beer bottle between his legs. From my window,

I could see lights glowing downriver in the A-frame. Maybe it was the champagne, or the fact that I'd never seen Otter Creek so covered in snow, but I pulled on my boots and stomped through that fluffy moonlit powder over to Cody's. It was the first time I'd ever seen their yard look pretty—all of his grandpa's junk sat invisible under a thick white blanket. Then I heard a cry. Thought it was a raven at first, and followed the sound. Found the man standing there in his underwear, leaning against one of The Lovers, almost blue.

"Mr. Weaver?"

He looked up at me. "Diane? Thank God you're here."

That shattered look in his eye, snow up to his bare knees—I didn't have the heart to remind him that the real Diane was in prison. I could be his daughter for a few minutes. "What are you doing out here, Dad?" A small lie.

"I can't find it," he said, looking around his buried junkyard. I hadn't seen him up close in a while and his eyes were bulgy, bloodshot. His whole body trembled.

"You can't find what?"

"My saw. Or nothing else." He looked around again, absorbing the shock of this imagined loss. He couldn't recognize his own place buried in this snow. "It's all gone." He leaned back against The Lover, starting to weep again.

"Let's just go home now." I took his elbow in my hand. Felt that thin, crêpey skin, ice-cold in my fingers. "In a few days, when the snow's gone, everything will come back," I led him back toward the A-frame. "I promise."

Mr. Weaver clutched my hands. "You always know, Diane." He squeezed my fingers, leaned against me. I felt him shivering. "Before something happens, you always know." We reached the A-frame. The door was unlocked and I pushed it open. Inside, sprawled across the aging orange carpet, we found Cody, his friends, all drunk and roaring with laughter. On the couch lay Neveah, passed out, the buttons of her shirt disarranged, vomit like glue in her hair.

"Holy shit." Cody jumped up.

"Your grandpa's almost got frostbite," I said.

"You're supposed to be in bed, Pops."

One of his friends, the one with bleached hair, looked me up and down. "Come to see us, Missy?" The way he said it made me feel like I'd swallowed a rock. "I know you missed me."

Cody led Mr. Weaver toward the bedroom, both of them stumbling. Without saying more, I ran back home through the snow, shaking from the cold, or from the stench of that cabin, or from the feeling like something had been done to Neveah that I didn't yet know how to name.

"Whose footprints are these?" asked Dad, when in the morning sun it became clear I had cut a path through the yard. I shrugged. He didn't bother asking again.

UNDER THE WEIGHT of that snow, all the buried cacti peppered in the brush around town went limp. Soon, most of them turned yellow with rot—spiky paddles of bunny-ear and prickly-pear and beavertail that fell to the ground—staples of the desert laid down in surrender.

That first storm set off a cascade of them. All that winter, more snow than had ever been recorded piled up in the shadows of town. As soon as it melted, more fell. The only place that never froze was Aztec Well, because the water inside stayed seventy-eight degrees.

The last blizzard of the season whirled down from the Rockies in February, and it was so historic it made national headlines. Up-canyon, on the pine-and-aspen rim that was the lowest steppe of the Colorado Plateau, they got three feet in twenty-four hours. Ms. Helms called to say school was canceled. The state shut down the highway into Flagstaff for days. Thick sleeves of powder hung in the tree branches. When I looked out the window, I saw a long stretch of desert hidden by millions of ice crystals. It felt like I had woken up somewhere else entirely—a place I had invented, or another planet. Staring at this transformed earth, I thought about what Charlie Brown said—that every day, human action and inaction pushed us closer to the edge of danger, to what he said was a point of no return.

A week later, all of it thawed at once. The first yellow bursts of wildflowers bloomed. I'd been avoiding Cody since New Year's, but he came around on a rainy afternoon saying he intended to visit the headwaters that night, to look for his shark-snake-octopus-mermaid. The monster that would devour the last living otter pups, born just for the purpose of this sacrifice.

"I'll come get you at nine," he said.

"No thanks," I said, tracking the look in his eyes. Nine came and went. I fell asleep listening to rain hammer the roof.

WE WOKE AFTER midnight. Melinda in her FEMA jacket pounded at the door. Behind her stood the local Red Cross in 4x4 Jeeps, wading through a foot of surging muddy water. The snowmelt all came down at once, barreling through the canyon with the rain like pent-up rage. It jumped the bed. It filled the street. It seemed our house might pick up and swim downriver.

"These are mandatory evacuations," yelled Melinda, over the roar, a rope harness tying her to the next person. "Governor declared a state of emergency." Already Otter Creek poured into our house. Already the carpet squished under my feet. Mom wrapped me in a jacket. Dad grabbed our hands. Together, we fought against the current, dodging high-speed patio furniture and a floating washing machine and all those white sandbags that now whipped around us like hurled bricks. The Red Cross volunteers pulled us into the rescue truck.

We watched six-foot waves crash against the A-frame. Then heard a sharp crack—the trunk of a Lover cottonwood collapsing into the water.

"The neighbors," said Mom, as a window shattered.

Melinda and the Red Cross brought us to Otter Creek Baptist. We waited all night for Cody and his grandpa to arrive, but truck after truck of neighbors showed, and the Weavers weren't among them.

IT'S HARD TO say how many days passed before the creek settled. Time passed in that church like a movie or a dream: mothy sleeping bags; scratchy hand-me-downs; canned chili I spilled between the pews. When we did return home to survey the damage, every house on our street looked like it had been pulled inside out. Hundred-year-old trees had snapped in half. Someone's basketball hoop was smashed into our front door. Inside our kitchen sat four inches of stinking mud.

"Let's be grateful we're safe," said Mom, trying to steady her voice. She turned her face so I wouldn't see her cry. Our porch had collapsed into the water; those shiny new stilts bent like twigs.

Dad gutted our house of carpet and drywall. One thing that wasn't ruined was his stupid, embroidered I-FEAR-MY-GOVERNMENT pillow, sitting high and dry on the mantel, untouched, until one day I came home and found it no longer on display.

What I remember most about that day is finding Cody standing in the ruins of the A-frame, where the Lover cottonwoods had disappeared. I expected him to explode with anger, to try to destroy what was already destroyed. But when I touched his shoulder, and he turned around, he looked calm.

"I spent that night at the headwaters," he said. "Couldn't find the otters." Then he gestured at all this destruction before us, as if to say, "that's why this happened."

"I'm sorry about your grandpa," I told him. Authorities found Mr. Weaver not far from the broken blade of his table saw, its motor mucked with creek sludge. His body had bloated with river water for days before they found it. When I heard, I was glad I'd let the old man think I was his daughter for a night. He'd given me something, too—given me the thought that I might have some of Diane's magic. Who she'd been before she met Cody's dad, before children, before meth. She'd been like me—a girl in Otter Creek, living at a bend in the river, where the past and the future seemed to collide. It was easy to get pulled into the current, the water indifferent to where it carried you.

I didn't know his grandpa well, but I knew Cody. Knew that he was growing up learning to hate the world right back and that every new tragedy pushed him further over that edge. Cody's Dad wasn't going to take him. "I'm going to have to move to Flagstaff to live with my aunt," he said.

I squeezed his hand. "We'll still see you." But we both knew it probably wasn't true.

That last night Cody lived in Otter Creek, he roared around town on his dirt bike. I woke to tapping at my window, to his raccoon eyes glaring out at me from the dark. I pulled on my boots, unsealed our duct-tape front door, and joined him on the banks of the creek, all of its familiar curves now rearranged.

"Look," he said.

And in the moonlight glow over the water, I saw them: bioluminescent spines worming in the current. An invasive species, on pilgrimage downriver, unleashed by the flood. Hundreds of organisms, that were one, or many, that had a brain like an aspen grove, every trunk connected at the root.

Cody pulled his stolen arrowhead from his pocket, held it up to the moonlight as though it were a talisman protecting us from harm. "The monsters are here," he whispered.

I held my breath, waiting.

Variation on a Legend // Variation on a Myth

Jaydn DeWald

VARIATION ON A LEGEND

"Our most illustrious gardens, cathedrals, waterfalls, stone angels and so forth," said the cabbie, leading us through the dark streets of the Tenderloin. I saw a man relieving himself under the caged light of a tenement building, and I gripped the sides of Stewart's little copper urn, seeing as I couldn't grip his hand. "Champagne, madam?" said the cabbie, raising a bottle. "No, thank you," I said, "—I'm in mourning." He steered with his knee, poured champagne into a flute, then handed it back to me. I saw a woman lean out of a high window, flapping a white sheet, and I drank instinctively. "Ahh, the scent of roast duck after a rainstorm," said the cabbie. He sniffed the air through the cracked-open driver's side window, and I stroked Stewart's urn in my lap, as though I was stroking back his hair, soothing him, as I used to, after a nightmare. I could feel the faintest mist settling around my ankles, the red light leaning into my eyes. "How much farther to the Embassy Hotel?" I asked. "Just over the drawbridge, madam," said the cabbie. The light turned green. The cab moved on. I saw a prostitute ethereally smoking under a neon-lit marquee, his brown skin flickering. When we pulled to the curb, it took me a moment to even see the place, so dark it was, so utterly black against the night sky. "I'm supposed to scatter my husband's ashes in there, in a fountain," I said. "I assumed as much, madam," he said and opened the door for me. "Thank you for the champagne," I said. "Please—it is our job to help you through this difficult time," he said. Out of the darkness behind me, I heard a distant scream, then an awful retching—like a bucket sloshing up a well—and I clutched Stew's urn to my chest. "I'm afraid of the dark," I said. "Well, I might suggest you lift your veil, then, madam," he said, reaching toward me. He lifted the veil, the darkness, from my face. I saw the sun breaking over the Embassy Hotel, a celestial outpouring over the picture windows, over the white façade, and I stepped out of the cab.

My mule stood waiting. Golden mule in the white sunlight. The cabbie hoisted me up. "To the fountain on a path of violet petals," he said, patting the animal's rump. "You've been very kind," I said. "Madam, your husband would be proud." He bowed. The mule shifted beneath me. I spent a moment balancing Stewart's urn up against the horn of the saddle, figuring we might as well enjoy this view together. Then I said, "Goodbye," and disappeared at a brisk trot.

In memoriam B.D., 1921-2011

VARIATION ON A MYTH

1. MANY YEARS ago, on his parents' back porch, listening to *The Marriage of Figaro* over Bloody Marys, J's mother (deep in the shade, languishingly drunk, wearing a broad-brimmed hat and rhinestone shades) suggested that he write a vampire novel. Ignoring his sudden, heavy-browed glare—J wrote detective novels and found the suggestion insulting—she craned her neck to better hear the Count's deep-voiced arrival, that famous scene in which Cherubino cowers behind Susanna's gilded chair, and it was then that he noticed, in the curve of his mother's long pale throat, the tiniest pair of teeth-marks. He set his Bloody Mary on the rattan patio table. *My father's body,* he thought, *isn't even underground—*. J stood, hollered over the music, "See you tomorrow, Ma!" and headed inside to fetch from the kitchen one of her many decorative garlands of garlic bulbs. His mother, head lolling, munching a celery stalk, raised one drunken arm, then fluttered her fingers at him. He ambled down the hall and, leiing himself with the garland, stepped into his parents' bedroom.

2. NOW, AT his writing desk with a mug of coffee in the almost-pink dawn, his marriage failing, his mother and father three and seven years (respectively) gone, J remembers stepping into their bedroom. Quiet. Just muffled opera sounds. Remembers thinking: *Where shall I hide till evening?* In the far corner, under a mound of clothes, sat a purple velvet claw-footed chair, and he at once spotted, on the floor behind it, two faded black sockfeet peeping out. "I'm armed!" he had shouted. A lot of sudden breathing and squirming from behind the chair. Then, very slowly, his father rose up—face powdered white, hair pomaded back, wearing a black-and-red silk cape. J remembers he didn't have to say anything at all: his father simply lowered his white-gloved hands and began to talk. The whole stunt, he'd said, was for J's mother. Their marriage had grown miserable, well-nigh irreparable, from over a decade of neglect and nonpassion: if he struck up a conversation, she'd wander into a distant room; if he touched her, she'd snort and writhe and shoo him away. And at night, worst of all, he'd said, she would crawl into bed and turn her back to him and float away on a dream. J's father

said he had to take drastic measures, life-or-death measures, you know, son? He said he knew she would miss him—and he was right, he added, raising a gloved forefinger—after he was dead.

3. J BLOWS the dust from the album, places it on the turntable, and lowers the needle into the groove. His wife, who also loves opera, first bonded with his mother over cheap sherry and a compilation of soprano arias, so when the overture (after a series of fizzles and pops, like warm RC Cola poured over ice) begins, J is in three places at the same time: in his parents' bedroom, in his current study, and on a rocking chair before the hideous lime-green sofa of his former duplex—kitty-corner from Sacramento's B Street Theatre—where his mother and soon-to-be wife sat gabbing for the first time. He gazes down into his coffee (rippled surface, already cold) and wonders how, after watching the twin mascara-black tears runnel down his father's cheeks, after hiding the old "vampire" at his duplex for a few weeks—he'd later reinstall himself in the home—so he could lope across town in the middle of the night and slink through his mother's bedroom window and whip his cape over them, the two never happier, never (paradoxically) more alive—after all of that, J wonders, how can his own marriage, for almost precisely the same reasons, fall apart? But no: not precisely the same reasons; it's too neat. As a detective novelist, he should know better. He should know that his own marriage is nothing at all like his parents' marriage, that his wife, who dislikes children, who curses Tom Brokaw every weeknight, who still wears army-green Doc Martens and reminisces about the "hot girls" she slept with in college, so that at times his own sex feels vaguely incongruous, humiliating. He should know in his bones that his wife, despite her occasional maternal protectiveness of him—she once threw a fork at an agent in an uppity New York bistro for criticizing his first novel—is nothing at all like his mother. Just then, the first act begins: Figaro on his hands and knees measuring the space for a bridal bed. *My wife is sleeping,* J thinks, *in our own bridal bed—*. He slurps his coffee, remembers the night she trimmed his beard on the porch, grasping his entire head in her hands, checking for evenness. Remembers the afternoon they necked like nocturnal animals in the back of the grainily dark Tower Theatre showing (of all films) *Nosferatu*.

4. J STARES into their bathroom mirror. An assortment of makeup strewn across the counter. A black fur-lined cape curled catlike on the lino at his feet. He presses a little brush into a dish of talc powder and taps it with his ring finger, the way his mother used to ash her Virginia Slims. Then he leans toward the mirror, squinting at himself, and begins to dab his face.

The Run

Willy Vlautin

On Saturday Bill Casey left the Sutro Motel and packed his truck with his belongings and drove two miles to a nineteen forties one-bedroom duplex off Wells Avenue, in a section of Reno his mother called "Little Tijuana."

The house was white with green trim. A small grass yard sat in front and next to that, a gravel space where he parked. He had bought a twin mattress from a furniture store that morning and set it in the bedroom, near the window, and put his sleeping bag and pillow on it. His pants and t-shirts he put in a row on the carpeted floor. He hung his long sleeved shirts and his two canvas coats in the closet, and in a plastic milk crate he put his underwear and socks. He lined his books so he could read the spines and grab them from bed. On a shelf in the kitchen pantry he put a gutted out black and white TV where inside the body he kept his extra money, the title to his truck, his social security card, a picture of his sister, and his birth certificate. He had just turned twenty-one years old.

The run started, he guessed, with the duplex. Two days before he had taken a wrong turn on Vassar and then went left on Wilson Street to turn around and saw the for rent sign. He liked the old cottonwood tree in the front yard of the duplex so he pulled over and called the number. A woman from a property management company answered, they met that afternoon, and once his credit came through clean, he wrote her a check, and received the keys.

The following day was Friday, but when he got off work he was too tired to move so he just showered at the Sutro, put on clean clothes, and walked downtown to get dinner. Along the way he stopped at Louis' Basque Corner for a beer and when he opened the door to go in he heard the old Basque bartender yell out, "Harry's buying a round of Picons for the house."

Luck.

He drank the drink and left for the Turf Club where he bought a Daily Racing Form. After that he went to the Cal Neva to cash his paycheck. There were three women who worked in the main money cage. He hoped to get the woman in the middle, Barb, because she liked that he worked concrete and gave him the most free drink tokes for cashing his check. But as the line moved forward it didn't look like he'd get her, and then suddenly the old man in front of him walked away. So he did get her. She was tall, middle-aged, with bottle blonde hair, and dried and cracked red lipstick.

"I was worried you'd quit," Bill said. "I haven't seen you in a long time."

"Hip replacement," Barb said and looked at the logo on Bill's canvas coat, *Lucky Concrete*.

"Did it hurt bad?"

"Worse than they said it would."

He handed her his signed paycheck and ID.

"How about you?" she asked. "Hard week?"

Bill shrugged and she winked at him and said the same thing she always said, "My uncle did concrete. He was the toughest man I ever met and my favorite uncle. I know how hard you work." She gave him the four hundred and forty-six dollars for his check and said, "Take these three free breakfast vouchers and here's a dozen drink tokes. But don't tell anyone I gave you so many, okay?"

"Okay," he said and thanked her.

"And remember to take care of your back."

"I will."

BILL WENT TO the second floor and drank three beers at the sports book and then went to dinner at the Top Deck restaurant. He ordered food and filled out his five Keno numbers and bet three games. He ate during the first two and was getting up to leave when the third game numbers came up and those numbers hit. All of them hit. He won $380.

He left the casino and bought a pint of Haagen-Dazs Vanilla Swiss Almond from a mini-mart and made the walk back to the motel. When he got to his room, he undressed, found the spoon he kept on the dresser, and got in bed. He turned on the TV to find his third favorite movie of all time, *Butch Cassidy and the Sundance Kid*, just beginning.

THE NEXT MORNING, Saturday, he moved into the duplex. It wasn't even eleven a.m. when he had his things in place and was heading on foot downtown. He had made it three blocks when he came to a moving van parked in front of a small yellow house. Two men were taking furniture from it and staging it on the lawn: a wooden dresser, a black vinyl couch, a matching black vinyl reclining chair, and two lamps. Each lamp base was a golden statue of a lion. Bill stopped on the sidewalk and looked at the things spread out across the frozen grass.

"You want any of it?" One of the movers, an older fat man, asked as he set down a box.

"You're selling this stuff?" Bill asked.

"Nah," the other mover said. He was taller and they both wore flannel coats. "We're taking it to the Salvation Army."

"You're giving it away?"

"We got hired to move all this shit out," the fat man said and lit a cigarette. "What the Salvation Army don't want we have to take to the dump. An old guy died and his daughter didn't want an estate sale and just hired us to clear out everything by the end of the day."

"You guys don't want it?"

"He was a faggot," the fat mover said. "We ain't touching it."

Bill looked over the furniture and told the two men he'd take it all if they'd let him have it. They said he could and he jogged back to the duplex, got his truck and parked it beside the moving van and began loading the furniture off the lawn and into the bed of his truck. As he did the two men kept bringing things out. They gave him a box of plates, one of utensils, one of pots and pans, a small round laminate kitchen table, two kitchen chairs, three black garbage bags full of sheets and blankets and towels, a blender, a mixer, a toaster, and a large color TV with a remote control.

Bill drove back to his place with his truck completely full. He dragged the vinyl couch into the living room and put the glass table in front of it. The TV he set on another glass table and when he plugged it in, it worked. The pots and pans were restaurant quality as were the plates and bowls. There was a set of sharp kitchen knives in a wooden block and a box of quality silverware.

When he left the duplex the second time it was still an hour to post time at Santa Anita. He walked down Wells Avenue and stopped at Taqueria Pocito for lunch. The girl behind the counter, who he'd always had a crush on, smiled at him and her silver tooth shone. She gave him his horchata for free and he could feel her eyes on him as he ate. She even waved as he left and she'd never waved to him before.

THE TURF CLUB was half full and he got there five minutes before Santa Anita's first race. He didn't bet until the third and then he did a twenty dollar exacta that hit and he cashed a $230 ticket. On the fourth race he bet a series of trifectas using the three horse, *Pride n' Powder*, a 17-1 three-year-old from Golden Gate, as his main horse and wheeled three other horses around it. *Pride n' Powder* came in and he cashed a $857 dollar ticket. He lost a hundred on the fifth but on the sixth he won a $150 exacta, and on the ninth race, his final bet, he hit a $75 win. It was the best day handicapping he'd ever had.

THE NEXT MORNING he ate breakfast at the Cal Neva using one of his free breakfast vouchers. He filled out a Keno ticket and put five dollars on his five numbers. His breakfast arrived as the game came up. All five of his numbers appeared on the screen. For the second day in a row he'd won $380. As the Keno lady brought him his money an old couple at the next table congratulated him. The old man was dressed in a burgundy suit and wore a burgundy pork pie hat. The woman had on a gold leopard print dress. When his waitress came by, Bill paid for their food and put a twenty dollar tip on the table.

He realized as he left the restaurant that for the first time since he'd left his mother's house he felt good. He was walking through the casino like a normal person. He was walking through the casino and didn't feel like he was disappearing. He didn't feel like he was drowning at all.

IN THE KING Ranch Grocery parking lot sat an obese man crammed into an aluminum lawn chair in front of an old pickup truck. At his feet was a cardboard box with a handwritten sign behind it. In a black ink scrawl it read, "pupies $20 Obo." Bill walked over to the man and looked in the box and saw four pups.

"What kind are they?" he asked.

The man had a liter of Mountain Dew between his legs and even though it was just forty degrees he wore only a t-shirt, shorts, and flip flops. The skin on his legs looked dark purple and the skin on his toes was flaking off. His toenails were cracked and brown. "The mom is a Border Collie and the dad is a fence jumper," he said.

Bill could tell the man was drunk. His eyes were glassy and he had a pause to him. Like his brain had a slight studder before it could process the things it saw and heard. "I live out in Wadsworth. I ain't positive who the dad is, but I think he's another Border Collie that gets out from a lady down the street. But the mom's my dog and she's in the pickup."

"Can I see her?"

"Sure," he said. "The door ain't locked."

In the cab of a dented white Dodge pickup was a female Border Collie curled in a ball. Bill opened the door, put his hand out, and the dog nervously came to him. He pet her and after a time her tail wagged and she moved closer to him. She was small and black, with four white paws, and a white muzzle that narrowed to black between her brown eyes. He pet her for almost a minute and then shut the passenger side door. He went back to where the obese man sat and kneeled down in front of the box of puppies.

His lease said no pets but the property manager lived in Carson City. She told him that the old lady who lived in the other half of the duplex was half deaf and never left her place. He stared at the pups and thought that maybe with her being so old she wouldn't notice. And if she did complain to the property manager he could always move.

Moving wasn't that big of a deal. His whole life he'd wanted a dog and now there was one in front of him. He'd take it to work. He'd make a bed for it in the truck and when he was on break he would let it out. And when the pup grew, it could become a job site dog, a dog that hung around all day.

"You mind if I look at them?"

"Go ahead," the man said.

Bill went from pup to pup and chose a black and white one with three white feet and a white spot around its right eye. He picked it up and turned it over to see it was a female. He didn't pick up any of the others. He decided to name her Winnie, after the town of Winnemucca, where his great uncle lived.

"I'll get this one," he said and set her back in the cardboard box. He took twenty dollars from his pocket and handed it to the man. "I have to go in the store and buy some things. Will you hold her until I get back?"

"I ain't going anywhere."

"And you won't sell her out from under me?"

"No, you gave me the money. And she's the only female. I'll remember."

Bill nodded and went into the store. He was so nervous that the man would give his dog away that he bought only what he had to have for his work lunches: bread, cheese, lettuce, lunch meat, mustard, and chips. He bought coffee and a quart of milk. He found the pet aisle and got a can of puppy food, a small sack of puppy kibble, and a collar and leash. At the checkout he had the cashier put it all in one bag.

In the parking lot the man was still sitting in front of his pickup drinking off the bottle of Mountain Dew.

"You didn't sell her, did you?"

"Nah," he said. "No one else has come up."

"How old is she?"

"Eight weeks," he said.

"I guess I'll take her now."

The man nodded and didn't say anything more.

Bill set down his bag of groceries and picked her up and held her.

He unzipped his coat and hid her in the warmth of his chest. He kept her like that with his left hand around her, holding her the best he could inside his coat. He picked up the groceries with his right hand and slowly began walking.

AT HOME HE made her a bed in the kitchen of two bath towels and put his groceries away. He looked through the box of dishes and found a bowl and a saucer. He filled the bowl with water, placed a bit of canned food on the saucer, but the pup didn't go to either. She only slept. Bill put the heat up to seventy and turned on the TV. He made a sandwich and ate while staring at her. As night came he picked her up and put a little food on his finger and tried to feed her but she wouldn't eat.

"Don't be nervous, Winnie," he whispered. "We're going to have a lot of fun together."

He set her back on the towel and then moved his mattress to the living room and set it at the entrance of the kitchen so he could be next to her. On the couch he set out his work clothes: a pair of jeans, a pair of wool socks, a white t-shirt, and a flannel shirt and set both of his alarm clocks.

In the middle of the night he woke to the pup whining. He turned on the living room lamp and found her sitting upright staring at him. He picked her up and held her and got her to eat a spoonful of canned food. He then set her on his bed and watched her by the lamp light. She ran to him and chewed on his fingers and crawled on his chest and he played with her for nearly an hour before he set her back on the towels.

When he woke next it was because of the alarm clocks. The first thing he thought of was the pup but when he saw her this time her eyes were swollen and there was diarrhea on the towels. He cleaned up the mess and set her on his sleeping bag and watched her for the next half hour. When six came he called his boss and told him he couldn't come to work until he took her to a doctor.

At eight a.m. he began calling vet hospitals and found one that would take her at eight thirty. He went outside and started the truck and turned the heater to full to warm it. In the pantry he found the cardboard box that the dishes had been put in, he set in a clean towel, and made a bed for her.

He drove her to Truckee Meadows Veterinary Hospital and brought her inside. A woman behind a counter had him sign the needed paperwork and then led him to a small waiting room where an old vet came through a sliding door. Bill set Winnie on the exam table and the vet looked at her. He opened her eyes and took her temperature.

"And she hasn't eaten?" he asked.

"She ate a little bit last night. But when I woke up at five-thirty there was diarrhea all around her and her eyes were swollen."

"Where did you get her?"

"A guy was selling puppies in a parking lot yesterday. There were four of them and I took this one."

The vet shook his head. "You got unlucky. I think she's got Distemper, Parvo maybe." He was dressed in jeans and a western shirt and cowboy boots. He was thin with gray hair and had a scar on his face where it looked like he'd gotten bit.

"Is that bad?"

"We'll have to quarantine her. We'll put her on an IV and get fluids in her and I'll run some tests. But she probably won't make it." Tears welled suddenly in Bill's eyes and the old vet saw it and his voice softened. "But she might. I've seen that, too," he added. "We just don't know. There's no cure so we'll just have to wait it out. You have money? It could cost you if you want to try and save her."

"I have money."

"I'm sorry I don't have better news," the vet said and picked up the pup. "It would be best to get rid of the box and the towels and anything else that came with her. Make sure and wipe down your car and where you kept her at home. Give it all a good once over. You settle up with reception and I'll take her back and get the fluids started. I'll give you a call later today."

BILL ARRIVED AT the jobsite just before ten a.m. They were building the forms for the foundation of a warehouse north of town. His boss wasn't upset with him but even so he worked through lunch and the day was overcast and cold. It was near quitting time when finished unloading lumber off a flatbed truck. He jumped down and when he did a loud pop come from his knee. He fell to the ground and the pain was so severe that he had trouble breathing. He could hear himself screaming. It was like somebody else was screaming. The four other guys on the job circled him but no one said anything. The boss helped him to a truck and drove him to St. Mary's emergency.

They sat in the waiting room for two hours and then Bill was led to an exam room. He was in such pain he could hardly speak. A nurse had him undress. He sat on an exam table in his underwear and the doctor came in, gave him a shot to ease the pain, and looked over his leg. When he left a nurse's assistant came in and put Bill in a wheelchair and took him to be x-rayed. After that she brought him back to the same room. It was another half hour until the doctor came back and told Bill he had what they called *The Unhappy Triad*: a rupture in the anterior cruciate ligament, medial collateral ligament, and meniscus. The doctor gave him a prescription for pain medication and a nurse brought in a removable brace, two pamphlets on icing and caring for his knee, and a pair of crutches. The doctor said he would most likely need surgery and that when the swelling calmed they'd schedule an appointment with a knee specialist.

His boss was still in the waiting room when he got out. He helped Bill fill his prescription at the hospital pharmacy and drove him home. It was nine p.m. when his boss left and Bill ate a cheese sandwich, took two pain pills, and laid down on the couch and watched TV until he fell asleep.

When he woke it was four in the morning and his knee felt like it was on fire. He used the crutches to get to the bathroom. After that he went to the kitchen, ate a piece of bread, took two more pills and lay down and watched TV until he fell asleep again. It was nine-thirty when he woke next and the first thing he did was call the vet. He was placed on hold for a long time but then the old doctor came on and told him the pup had made it through the night, that her temperature was down, that she'd eaten some and was getting hydrated. "Don't get too excited," he said, "But there's more than a decent chance she'll make it."

Bill hung up the phone and fell back into the couch and wept. His nerves were raw and his leg burned with pain. But as he lay there, he thought that maybe *the run* was somehow still going. He got hurt at work so he'd get worker's comp, two-thirds of his pay, and *the run* had given him an extra bankroll. The vet said the pup could be okay. If things held the way he hoped, he would get to be home with the pup every day and get paid for it. He'd get paid to take care of his dog. If the pup made it then *the run* was still going, and if *the run* was still going then his knee was just a part of it. The pup would live and his knee would be okay. He ate another piece of bread, took two more pain pills, made a grocery list, and called a cab.

The Ghosts in the Desert

Day Al-Mohamed

"There was, there was not . . ."

My people have always begun our tales with this phrase because there are always two stories in the world, the story that is and the story that is not. From the time we are children, the stories that are, are repeated over and over, until they take on a life of their own, wrapping themselves around us, breathing and filling the space, molding the world, molding us, until our hearts beat in time with every syllable and we cannot tell what is us and what is the story.

The story that is not, exists in the between spaces, always on the periphery of our vision; existing just beyond the horizon. Like the djinn. They whisper to us in the twilight times and in the darkness of the night when the screams of Man's world fall silent. The story that is not, plays with the coyotes and sings with the nightbirds. It hides in the winds that scatter the dust and in the scent of winters long dead. But it is no less true.

"Once upon a time" belongs to Western fairy tales. Fairy tales wither and die in these rocky sands and unending heat. Fairy tales cannot touch ground nor take root against the scrub brush and spiky cholla pods. They are stories that are told in one way with one purpose and only one truth. The Arizona desert with its arroyos and petroglyphs is a land that is older than the Europeans and their fairies and elves. Just like the deserts and wadis of the Nejd, it is a place of wilder magic and untamed stories. Stories that both are, and that are not.

ACT I – PAST

This was Majid's twelfth tour group into the southern Arizona desert, and it was only May. He crouched close to the edge of the tiny campfire. Even though the night air was already sweltering, he enjoyed the warmth and ignored how the sustained heat would melt the edges of his boots. He swept off his neon boonie hat. It swung from its neck strap, the wide brim flopping against his shoulder blades. He ran a hand over his close-cropped white hair. It was a stark contrast to his dark brown tanned skin. He slowly flexed his fingers. They were still thick and strong, the joints only recently showing the knotted signs of arthritis.

His gaze shifted to the small group of tourists that lounged around the fire: Mrs. Lantower and her two teenage daughters, all huddled together, half-excited and half-fearful but mostly utterly exhausted; the two Finnish grad students whose names he was ashamed to say he couldn't remember nor pronounce; and Bud and Brad, two businessmen from Yuma looking for something new that sounded "extreme" that they could go home and brag to their wives and coworkers about. For some reason, all of them had decided that camping in the wilds of the Sonoran Desert was the answer to all of their desires.

Majid picked up a handful of sand and let it fall through his fingers, gritty misshapen grains with varied colors. He felt them pinch and collect under his fingernails and into the soft skin of his fourth finger where his wedding band used to sit before he gave it to his grand-daughter for her husband. It was so different from the sands of his own desert. He always marveled that their sharp-edged harshness, almost like tiny pebbles. It was not like the smooth ever-shifting fine grains that he grew up with, sand that moved like waves. In many ways the Sonoran Desert was so much more lush than his home. Majid smiled a little bitterly. Home. He had left the Nejd and the oil wars and escaped to the United States as a teenager. He had never been back and yet he still called that other desert home.

"I've spent more than forty years in these deserts . . ." Majid said. He wasn't starting a conversation. That wasn't what tourists wanted around a campfire at night. He'd learned that years ago. No, this was the time for stories. The stories that reminded everyone of their place in the world. And of course, Majid didn't tell these stories for others. He didn't tell them for himself. He told them because they needed to be told. ". . . searching."

He let the word die into the soft hiss and crackle of the fire.

"Searching for what?" whispered one of the Lantower girls.

Majid pursed his lips. He paused, as if deciding whether or not to continue with his tale. He would. He always did.

His voice dropped even lower. "Ghosts."

Seeing the smiles appear on the faces of the businessmen and grad students, Majid raised a warning finger and shook his head. "Ghosts are very serious business. Ghosts seek to be free. Once you find them, that is your duty, your responsibility."

The teenage girls' faces reflected their skepticism. They were too old, too modern, too emmeshed in cell phones, television, and expectations of adulthood to be willing to risk being made fun of for believing in superstition.

Majid smiled, "Well, really this is the story of just one ghost. Did you know Arizona once had herds of wild camels?"

Majid felt the group's interest rise. There was nothing in their faces or body language to indicate a change of mood, just an increasing tension in the air. Like right before one of the great storms that came up from Sonora during monsoon season, dropping hundreds of gallons of water into parched gullies, flooding them in seconds.

He took a deep breath, released it, and began. "There was and there was not, because we cannot swear to the Almighty that we know all truths—though this does have a good mention in Arizona's public record," Majid added with a lilt of humor. "In the 1850s, the US Army came to Egypt, Syria, and Turkey to purchase camels. They thought these animals would allow them to better survey and navigate the broad barren regions that they had bought from Mexico, the Gadsen Purchase, the lands that are today parts of New Mexico and Arizona. Lands where we sit. Right. Now.

"Thirty-three camels and seven Arab camel handlers were brought to this country. Sadly, camels were too different, too unruly, and with the American Civil War, there was less and less interest in this 'Camel Corps'. Slowly, they disappeared; into mines, or to circuses and zoos, or simply set free into the desert.

"But, in 1883, a woman living on a ranch not far from Eagle Creek, was trampled to death when she went to the well for water. Between the screams could be heard the most terrifying sound, a strange moaning and gargling roar."

Majid paused and drew a pair of battered reading glasses from his front shirt pocket. "Let me make sure I get this next part exactly right."

He leaned over to his backpack and after a moment of rummaging pulled out a photocopy of a newspaper article, and pointed to the almost illegible date, 1883.

He read, "It was a 'huge, reddish colored beast... very tall and ridden by a devil.'"

Majid pointed again to the text and then continued, his words picking up speed and intensity, "A few nights later, more than sixty miles way, a couple of prospectors had their campsite torn apart by a vicious red creature that attacked just after sunset. They chased after it, firing shots from their rifles. One shot connected with a dull crack and something toppled from the creature's back. When they arrived at the spot, they realized what had fallen. It was a skull.

"They identified the demon as a camel; a massive red camel and strapped to its back was the rotting flesh and bones of what had once been a man. Sightings of the red ghost continued for more than ten years, until in 1893, when the Mohave County Miner reported that a man named Hastings had shot a frightening beast in his garden, a beast that was then identified to be a camel with scars along its back and sides from where a rider was once strapped.

"That should end the story, yes?" Majid said. "But the question of who was that man is still unanswered. Was he lost in the desert and hoped his camel would take him to water? Was it soldiers from the Camel Corps with a prank gone awry? Was it claim jumpers who had stolen the man's mine, killed him, and strapped him to the camel?"

He tossed a piece of strawgrass into the flames, "Was he one of the Arab men so far from home? A brother from another desert? Is he out here still? His bones scattered amongst the barrel cactus and the prickly pear?"

ACT II – PRESENT

Majid woke everyone up at two o'clock in the morning to see the moonflowers: sacred datura, the morning glory, and several varieties of cereus. He'd even found a spring primrose. Its scent reminded him a little of the jasmine scent his first wife wore on their wedding by the shores of the Red Sea fifty years ago. They'd been so young.

The light-colored flowers seemed to float in the darkness, glowing in the starlight, blooming in the cool early morning hours and gone completely by 8am. As if they'd never existed, leaving behind the dark wooded stems and spiny cactus bodies.

It was a full morning of hiking and they were all tired. There was no trail here. It was all unforgiving terrain, hardpacked sand, and rocky outcroppings. The cactus and scrub thorn with its spines and stickers reached out to grab at legs and arms. And over it all the sun's rays weighed down on them until even Majid could feel his blood pound in his temples from the heat. Majid sipped water from his bottle and pointed out how even in scorched lands that seemed empty of life there were tarantulas, snakes, blue gully monitor lizards, spotted whiptails, rabbits; he'd even stopped their trek to point out a small group of javelina in the distance.

They found the man lying under a small stand of paloverde trees a little before noon. His worn jeans brown with dust and sand. Curled on his side, arms wrapped around himself, body shrunken in. His skin had darkened and turned leathery from the sun and heat—mummified. He wore bright orange sneakers. They looked new.

Majid sighed. This wasn't the first body he'd found. He waved the tourists a little distance away before returning to the sparse clump of trees. Even without touching the corpse, the smell of death fluttered in the thick air and suffused his clothing.

On a map, the southwestern Arizona desert was depicted like a large empty space, the size of Connecticut, a sea of nothing. Majid, pulled out his ballpoint pen and pressed the nib to the worn and stained surface of the paper, adding another red dot to his map. A map of death.

He should have noticed the debris. All around were the signs;

torn and ripped clothing, food wrappers, a backpack, and of course black plastic gallon water jugs. He didn't need to pick them up to know their insides were as dry and dusty as their outsides. Those jugs were sold in Mexico to migrants who hoped to slip across the border. They're told it's better to have black as it won't reflect the sunlight and give away their positions to the Border Patrol.

He sighed again, ignoring the murmurs of the tour group. Mrs. Lantower wanted to go home. The Lantower teenagers were whispering about who would find the next body. The grad students watched silently, their backpacks still on. The two "weekend warrior" businessmen stared at the body from a "safe" distance, munching loudly on protein bars, talking casually about the state of immigration in the country and shaking their heads about the loss of life.

Majid pressed his lips together. More than 300 dead had been found in the desert last year. He'd discovered almost a dozen of them himself—fathers, brothers, mothers, cousins. Escaping natural disasters, poverty, violence. Dead from heat and exhaustion. Dead from desperation. Too many hopes and dreams sucked, like the water, from their flesh. But where do their ghosts go? Do they stay in the desert, walking aimlessly, looking for—what? Are they angry? Or sad?

Majid pulled out his yellow hazard tape, carefully pacing out and marking off the area before he geo-tagged it and radioed in for the authorities. Hopefully, they would come retrieve the body soon before the desert and the animals scattered his remains and consumed his identity just as it consumed his body. But likely they would not bother. One more ghost for the desert.

ACT III – FULL CIRCLE

It was the last night before they returned to the city. Majid always hated last nights. The tourists were all asleep, exhaustion and the stress of the day, demanding deep slumber. The faint sound of snoring from the tent the Finnish students shared made him smile. He was so very tired but he couldn't bring himself to close his eyes. Too soon he would have to trade in the saguaro forest for a forest of concrete, car horns, and burnt coffee from the Starbucks on the corner. A place with nowhere for ghosts to go.

There was a deep huff across from him. Too big to be a rabbit, or coyote or even a javelina. Majid scrambled to his feet, his glasses dropping unnoticed to the ground. Standing less than twenty feet away was the unmistakable silhouette of a camel. It towered over seven feet tall and the firelight played over its red hair giving the strange impression that it was on fire. Even in the moonlight, he could see the thick scars and indentations on its chest and sides. And even if he didn't believe it was a ghost, the Red Ghost, the unnatural glow in its eyes gave away that it was more than just a flesh and blood being.

"I've been looking for you," Majid said softly.

The camel burbled and stared at him. The wind ruffled the curly hairs on the top of its hump and it chewed placidly, its gaze never leaving his.

Majid took a step closer and reached out a hand.

The camel reared back and opened its mouth showing large yellow teeth.

"It'll be all right. I won't hurt you. I'm here to set you free."

Could he even touch a ghost camel? Was there anything to touch or would his hand pass right through—Majid's hand came up against solid flesh. It's neck soft and warm. He rubbed his fingers over the fine hairs and tugged affectionately at the coarse ones. Everything was a rich deep red. He leaned his forehead against the camel's neck and inhaled deeply. He knew that smell from his childhood.

The camel gave out a deep throated grunt and swung its head around to look at him.

"You've been waiting a long time." He patted it, the reassuring slap of palm against skin. Majid ran his hand down its neck to its side, his fingers tracing the deep gashes where the straps had once held a skeleton rider.

He walked all the way around the camel, crooning at it in Arabic. His words were soft and slow and gentle but his thoughts raced. How could this be? Was it real? Did it matter? He continued to pat the creature. It leaned into his affections. The camel was here but its rider was not. Had he already gone on to his reward? Majid clicked his tongue in disapproval. The man had left the camel behind.

The light in the East grew as daybreak loomed. The camel's form wavered in the rising heat waves and early light, seeming less solid.

Majid swallowed and spoke. "Kush."

The word was quiet, raspy. He hadn't used that command since he was a small boy. He'd been seven years old. That was a lifetime ago, 9000 miles ago, a wife, children, even grandchildren ago. But how glorious it had been when he had raced across the sands, rocking wildly on the back of a camel as crowds cheered and the beasts bugled and boys shouted and slapped their camels with sticks.

"Kush." He said it again.

And just like that, the great red demon of Arizona lurched forward, going to its knees and then back as its hind legs settled under it. There was no halter, nor saddle, but Majid didn't need one. He kicked off his boots and eagerly peeled off his socks. He tossed them aside like so much other debris. Swinging one leg over the camel's back, he settled into position. His fingers wove lovingly into the thick hair on its hump and his toes curled comfortably into the camel's neck.

"Yalla." He said, and clicked his tongue.

The camel let out a low rumble and stood, back legs first. Majid's weight flew forward and for a moment he thought he would pitch forward over the animal's head. Then his weight was thrown back forcefully as the camel rose to its feet at the front.

"Yalla!" Majid said firmly and the camel began to move.

Its long gangly legs stretched out over the terrain. Faster and faster. The camel extended its neck as it began to run in earnest. Majid hung on, the early morning air filling his lungs as they raced toward the sunrise. It had been so many years. For both of them. Majid rode across the Arizona scrub, the red ghost between his knees, an exultant shout escaping his lips.

MAJID GENTLY SANK to the floor of his beloved desert as his breath shuddered to a halt and his heart ceased to beat.

And that is what they did. And what they did not.

Contributors

Day Al-Mohamed is an author, filmmaker, and disability policy expert with over 15 years of experience. Currently a Senior Policy Advisor with the Federal government, she is a proven leader in organizational transformation, legislation and regulation development/analysis, and innovative program design. A sought-after presenter and moderator, Ms. Al-Mohamed has written two novels: *Baba Ali and the Clockwork Djinn*, and *The Labyrinth's Archivist*. In addition, she writes short stories, comics, films, and critical essays. She is a regular host on Idobi Radio's Geek Girl Riot with an audience of 80,000+ listeners and a Founding Member of FWD-Doc (Documentary Filmmakers with Disabilities). However, she is most proud of being invited to teach a workshop on storytelling at the White House in February 2016. Ms. Al-Mohamed lives in Washington DC with her wife, N.R. Brown and her guide dog, Gamma. Visit her online at DayAlMohamed.com and on Twitter @ DayAlMohamed

Laura Arciniega is from Southern California, where she lives with her family. Her work has appeared in *Maudlin House, FIVE:2:ONE Magazine, Gargoyle Magazine, Relief Journal,* and elsewhere. You can find her online at lauraaliciaarciniega.wordpress.com.

Phoebe Barton is a queer trans science fiction writer. Her short fiction has appeared in venues such as *Analog* and *Lightspeed*, and she wrote the Nebula Award-finalist interactive game *The Luminous Underground* for Choice of Games. She is a 2019 graduate of the Clarion West Writers Workshop, and after spending two years in New Westminster, she lives with a robot near the shore of Lake Ontario. Find her on Twitter at @aphoebebarton or online at phoebebartonsf.com.

Kate Bernheimer has been called "one of the living masters of the fairy tale" (*Tin House*). She is the author of a novel trilogy and the story collections *Horse, Flower, Bird* and *How a Mother Weaned Her Girl from Fairy Tales*, and the editor of four anthologies, including the World Fantasy Award winning and bestselling *My Mother She Killed Me, My Father He Ate Me: Forty New Fairy Tales* and xo *Orpheus: 50 New Myths*. She is a Professor of English at the University of Arizona in Tucson, where she teaches fairy tales and creative writing.

Jos Burns's fiction has appeared in the micro-press anthology *Colossus: Home* and in the *WordSwell Crazy Child Scribbler*. She butters her bread with Geographic Information Systems and remote sensing expertise, when she's not dabbling in entomology. She lives in the San Francisco Bay Area with two daughters, two cats, and a piebald curiosity.

Katie Carmer is an educator and musician who lives in Phoenix, Arizona, with her husband and daughter. A Michigan native who now calls the desert home, she most often finds herself writing about memory, nature, and family history.

Matt Carney is a Latinx writer and musician living in San Francisco. He earned his MA and MFA from San Francisco State University. His fiction and poetry have appeared in *A cappella Zoo, Inkwell, Red Light Lit, Writing Without Walls, sPARKLE & bLINK, Entropy, Anti-Heroin Chic, Tilted House* and in readings at seedy bars across California. His short story "On Becoming" was a finalist in the 2017 *Omnidawn* Fabulist Fiction Contest. He is the co-creator and producer of Club Chicxulub, a fabulist science fiction performance series. Find his synthrock art project N! on Bandcamp and Spotify. linktr.ee/mattscottcarney

Andrew E. Colarusso, as of May 2022, has logged upwards of 1825 hours in *Animal Crossing: New Horizons.* The dream address is DA-9042-8632-0080 for those interested in visiting the island. He is also the co-author of the collaborative prose collection *Souvenirs* (Baobab Press 2022).

Jaydn DeWald is the author of *The Rosebud Variations* (Broken Sleep Books, 2022), *Sheets of Sound* (BSB, 2021), and several limited-edition chapbooks, most recently *A Love Supreme: fragments & ephemera*, winner of the 2019 *Quarterly West* Chapbook Contest. A California native, DeWald now lives in Athens, Georgia, and is Assistant Professor of English and Director of Creative Writing at Piedmont University.

Dominique Dickey is a writer, editor, and cultural consultant working in RPGs and fiction. In addition to creating *TRIAL*, a narrative courtroom tabletop role-playing game about race in the criminal justice system, and co-creating *Tomorrow* on Revelation III, a tabletop role-playing game about surviving and building community on a hyper -capitalist space station, Dominique has written for *Thirsty Sword Lesbians, Sea of Legends*, and *Dungeons & Dragons*. Their fiction has also appeared in *Anathema Magazine* and *Fantasy Magazine*. You can find them on Twitter at @DomSDickey or at dominiquedickey.com

Lisa Dillman lives in Decatur, Georgia, where she translates Spanish-language fiction and teaches at Emory University. Her recent translations include National Book Award finalist *The Bitch* by Pilar Quintana and *A Silent Fury* by Yuri Herrera.

Enotea is a writer and a musician living and working in Berlin.

Tessa Fontaine grew up among California's redwood trees, and is the author of *The Electric Woman: A Memoir in Death-Defying Acts,* a New York Times Editors' Choice, finalist for the Utah Book Award, and best book of 2018 from Southern Living, Amazon Editors', the *New York Post*, and elsewhere. Other writing can be found in *Outside, The New York Times Book Review, Glamour, The Believer,* and *Creative Nonfiction*. Tessa founded Salt Lake City's Writers in the Schools program, has taught in prisons and jails around the country and was a professor of creative writing at Warren Wilson College. Her debut novel is forthcoming from FSG in early 2024.

Alyson Hagy is the author of eight works of fiction, including *Hardware River* (Poseidon Press, 1991), *Keeneland* (Simon & Schuster, 2000), *Graveyard of the Atlantic* (Graywolf Press, 2000), *Snow, Ashes* (Graywolf Press, 2007), *Ghosts of Wyoming* (Graywolf Press, 2010), *Boleto* (Graywolf Press, 2012), and *Scribe* (Graywolf Press, 2018). She has been awarded fellowships from the National Endowment for the Arts and the Christopher Isherwood Foundation. Her work has won a Pushcart Prize, the Nelson Algren Prize, the High Plains Book Award, the Devil's Kitchen Award, the Syndicated Fiction Award, and been included in *Best American Short Stories. Recent fiction has appeared in Drunken Boat, The Idaho Review, Kenyon Review, INCH,* and *Michigan Quarterly Review.*

BORN IN Actopan, Mexico, in 1970, **Yuri Herrera** studied Politics in Mexico, Creative Writing in El Paso and took his PhD in literature at Berkeley. His first novel to appear in English, *Signs Preceding the End of the World*, was published to great critical acclaim in 2015 and included in many Best-of-Year lists, including *The Guardian*'s Best Fiction and NBC News's Ten Great Latino Books, going on to win the 2016 Best Translated Book Award. He is currently teaching at the Tulane University, in New Orleans, and his collection *Ten Planets* will publish with Graywolf Press in 2023.

Vanessa Hua is an award-winning columnist for the *San Francisco Chronicle* and the author of the national bestsellers *Forbidden City* and *A River of Stars*, as well as *Deceit and Other Possibilities*, winner of the Asian/Pacific American Award for Literature and NYT Editors Pick. A National Endowment for the Arts Literature Fellow, she has also received a Rona Jaffe Foundation Writers' Award, and a Steinbeck Fellowship in Creative Writing, as well as honors from the Society of Professional Journalists and the Asian American Journalists Association. She has filed stories from China, Burma, South Korea, Panama, and Ecuador, and her work has appeared in publications including the *New York Times, Washington Post*, and *The Atlantic*. She has taught, most recently, at the Warren Wilson MFA Program for Writers and the Sewanee Writers' Conference. The daughter of Chinese immigrants, she lives in the San Francisco Bay Area with her family.

Jac Jemc is the author of *The Grip of It, False Bingo, My Only Wife,* and *A Different Bed Every Time*. Her novel, *Empty Theatre*, will be released from MCD x FSG books in February 2023. She teaches creative writing at the University of California San Diego.

Karen An-hwei Lee is the author of the novel *The Maze of Transparencies* (Ellipsis Press) plus nine volumes of poetry, translation, and fiction. Her work has been honored by *Best Spiritual Writing* and the National Endowment of the Arts. She currently serves at Wheaton College.

Ken Liu is an American author of speculative fiction. A winner of the Nebula, Hugo, and World Fantasy awards, he wrote *The Dandelion Dynasty*, a silkpunk epic fantasy series (*The Grace of Kings* + sequels), as well as *The Paper Menagerie and Other Stories* and *The Hidden Girl and Other Stories*. He also penned the Star Wars novel, *The Legends of Luke Skywalker.* Prior to becoming a full-time writer, Liu worked as a software engineer, corporate lawyer, and litigation consultant. Liu frequently speaks at conferences and universities on a variety of topics, including futurism, cryptocurrency, history of technology, bookmaking, narrative futures, and the mathematics of origami. (http://kenliu.name)

Tara Lynn Masih is a National Jewish Book Award Finalist and winner of a Julia Ward Howe Award for her debut novel, *My Real Name Is Hanna*. Her anthologies include *The Rose Metal Press Field Guide to Writing Flash Fiction* and *The Chalk Circle: Intercultural Prizewinning Essays*. *How We Disappear: Novella & Stories* is her second collection from Press 53. She founded *The Best Small Fictions* series in 2015. Additional awards for her work include the Lou P. Bunce Creative Writing Award, *The Ledge Magazine*'s Fiction Award, a finalist fiction grant from the Massachusetts Cultural Council, *Wigleaf* Top 50 recognition, and Pushcart Prize nominations for both fiction and creative nonfiction. www.taramasih.com

Isle McElroy's debut novel, *The Atmospherians*, was named a *New York Times* Editors' Choice. Their second novel, *People Collide*, will be published in 2023. Other writing appears in *The New York Times, NYT Magazine, The Guardian, The Cut, Vulture, GQ, Vogue, The Atlantic, Tin House*, and elsewhere. Isle was named one of The Strand's 30 Writers to Watch. They have received fellowships from The Bread Loaf Writers' Conference, The Tin House Summer Workshop, The Sewanee Writers Conference, The Inprint Foundation, The Elizabeth George Foundation, and The National Parks Service.

Kathleen McNamara's fiction and essays have appeared in *The North American Review, The Columbia Journal, Witness, Redivider, Nimrod, The Carolina Quarterly, Reed* and other journals. She teaches at Arizona State University, and has been supported by the Arizona Commission on the Arts and the Virginia G. Piper Center for Creative Writing. She lives in central Arizona with her husband and their two sons.

Caitlin Palmer is a writer primarily of the Midwest, though she's called many places home, including five years in Idaho. She has work published at *Essay Daily, DIAGRAM, Hobart, Ghost Proposal,* and others. She was the Hemingway Fellow at the University of Idaho, and a mentorship recipient at the Tin House Writers Workshop. She is represented by Janklow & Nesbit Associates for a novel about sand-mining in Missouri.

Benjamin Percy is the author of six novels, the most recent among them *The Unfamiliar Garden* (Mariner Books/William Morrow, 2022). He is also the author of *The Ninth Metal* (Mariner Books, 2021), *The Dead Lands* (Grand Central/Hachette, 2015), *Red Moon* (Grand Central/Hachette, 2013) and *The Wilding* (Graywolf Press, 2010), as well as three books of short stories, *Suicide Woods* (Graywolf Press, 2019), *Refresh, Refresh* (Graywolf Press, 2007) and T*he Language of Elk* (Grand Central/Hachette, 2012; Carnegie Mellon University Press, 2006). His craft book—*Thrill Me: Essays on Fiction*—was published by Graywolf

Press in 2016 and is now widely taught in creative writing classrooms. He broke in to comics in 2014, with a two-issue Batman story arc for Detective Comics. He is known for his celebrated runs on Nightwing, Green Arrow, Teen Titans, and James Bond. He currently writes Wolverine, X-Force, and Ghost Rider for Marvel Comics.

BORN AND raised in Reno, Nevada, **Willy Vlautin** is the author of six novels and is the founder of the bands Richmond Fontaine and The Delines. Vlautin has been the recipient of three Oregon Book Awards, The Nevada Silver Pen Award, and was inducted into the Nevada Writers Hall of Fame and the Oregon Music Hall of Fame. He was a finalist for the PEN/Faulkner Award and was shortlisted for the Impac Award (International Dublin Literary Award). Two of his novels, *The Motel Life* and *Lean on Pete*, have been adapted as films. His novels have been translated into eleven languages. Vlautin teaches at Pacific University's MFA in Writing program. Vlautin lives near Portland, Oregon, with his wife, dog, cats, and horses.

Permissions

"Ghosts in the Desert" Copyright © 2023 by Day Al-Mohamed.

"Thank You, Little Queens" Copyright © 2023 by Laura Arciniega.

"A Billion Miles from What Was Home" Copyright © 2023 by Phoebe Barton.

"Canada, Maybe Even California, or Other States (Wyoming? Montana?)" Copyright © 2023 by Kate Bernheimer.

"The Wind's Last Breath" Copyright © 2023 by Jos Burns.

"The Last Genuine Cowboy" Copyright © 2023 by Katie Carmer.

"In Fresno, One Last Bath in Dust" Copyright © 2023 by Matt Carney.

"The Drone Pilot" first appeared in *The Sovereign* (Dalkey Archive Press 2017). Copyright © 2017 by Andrew Colarusso. Reprinted with the permission of the author.

"Variation on a Myth" Copyright © 2023 by Jaydn DeWald.

"Variation on a Legend" Copyright © 2023 by Jaydn DeWald.

"There Are Ghosts Here" first appeared in *Anathema* (Issue 7, December 2018). Copyright © 2018 by Dominique Dickey. Reprinted with the permission of the author.

"Once Called California" first appeared as a broadside designed by Rose Marie Johansen and Camilla Louisa Nicholls to accompany an album of the same name. Copyright © 2020 by Christian Tranberg. Reprinted with permission of the author.

"Crepuscular" Copyright © 2023 by Tessa Fontaine.

The body of *This Side of the Divide* is set in Vendetta OT, designed by John Downer for Emigre Fonts. Vendetta unites roman type design with contemporary concerns for the optimal display of letterforms on computer screens.

The headers are set in Summa, developed for Delve Fonts by Don Sterrenburg. The classic roman spirit and bracketed, cupped serifs together with the narrow width and elevated x-height of Summa give it a lofty, elegant appearance and an economic use of space.

CPSIA information can be obtained
at www.ICGtesting.com
Printed in the USA
JSHW020948060223
37299JS00002B/2

9 781936 097463